EVENTIDE

EVENTIDE

The Days of Redemption Series, Book Three

SHELLEY SHEPARD GRAY

AVON

INSPIRE

An Imprint of HarperCollinsPublishers

P.S.™ is a trademark of HarperCollins Publishers.

ISBN 978-1-62490-786-9

*To Lynne. Thank you for your friendship,
your pep talks, your kindness, for everything!*

It speaks of peace that comes after strife,
Of the rest He sends to the hearts He tried,
Of the calm that follows the stormiest life—
God's eventide.

~From Eventide, by John McCrae

He shows mercy from generation to generation to all who fear him.

~Luke 1:50 (NLT)

prologue

Ten Years Ago

She could see.

Elsie Keim closed her eyes, then looked through the brand-new lenses again.

Dr. Palmer, standing over her right shoulder, met her gaze in the mirror and grinned. "What do you think, Elsie?"

"I think it's *wunderbaar*," she whispered.

"I hope that means you're pleased?"

Gently fingering the brown plastic frames that now outlined her eyes, she thought she looked very smart. She hoped she did, anyway. A couple of kids in her school had been calling her "*dumm Elsie*" for months now. She'd been too embarrassed to tell them that the problem wasn't that she couldn't read; it was that she couldn't see the words on the board.

Turning away from her reflection, she smiled brightly at Dr. Palmer. "I'm mighty pleased, *doktah*. *Danke* for the glasses."

"It's my job, Elsie, and I am happy for you. Now, don't forget to take things slow. The world might look a little different now that you can see so much better." Shaking a finger playfully, he warned, "Don't forget what I said about the headaches."

"I won't."

Dr. Palmer had explained that her body might need a couple of days to get used to the changes in her vision, and not to be afraid to take some pain reliever if the headaches got too painful.

He handed her a business card. "I'll give your parents a card, but I want you to always have my number, too." He paused. "You did say you could walk down to your phone shanty, yes?"

She nodded.

"Then please listen closely. These are *your* eyes, and when it comes to that, you're the smartest person around. If your vision begins to blur, or your headaches get worse . . . or anything else happens out of the ordinary, call me."

She folded her hand around his card. She didn't want to be without his phone number ever. So far, Dr. Palmer was the only person with whom she'd been able to discuss her poor eyesight with complete honesty.

"So, are you ready to go show your new glasses to your family?"

"I am." She knew she looked anxious and overly eager, but she couldn't help it. Finally, she was going to be able to explain to them that she was just fine. Now she would be able to be a big help around the house, just like her brother and twin sister. She wouldn't be the sister who couldn't do anything anymore.

Dr. Palmer patted her shoulder. "Let's go show you off, then."

She chuckled as she followed him out of the examining room, down the hall, past the nurses and the lab. Finally, he opened a door and waved her forward.

She walked out to the waiting room, sure she was flashing the biggest smile of her life.

But instead of looking happy, her mother burst into tears. "Oh Elsie, look at you!"

Startled, she turned to her father for an explanation. But Daed wasn't looking her way, he was comforting her *mamm*. And Roman was staring like he'd never seen her before. Even her grandparents looked sad, like they were on their way to a funeral.

Little by little, her confidence drained away. Things weren't better.

She felt Dr. Palmer tense beside her.

"Doktah?" she whispered. "They're not happy."

"It's okay, Elsie," he whispered right back. "They just don't understand. But they will. No matter what happens, you are going to be just fine, I promise you that. Give them a chance to come around."

Taking his words to heart, she walked to her twin's side. "Viola, what do you think of my new glasses?" she asked, doing her best to keep her voice bright. "Do ya like them? I couldn't decide between gold rims and these brown ones."

Viola bit her lip, then nodded. "You look fine."

Elsie lifted her chin up. "Vi, I can *see* now. I can see everything."

But Viola didn't seem to understand what a happy day this was. She grabbed Elsie's hand. "Elsie, I'm so sorry. I feel terrible," she muttered as tears filled her eyes. "I don't know why you had to be the one to go blind and not me."

When Dr. Palmer left, leaving her alone with her family, she looked around the room. Their expressions were sad, dismayed, and dismal.

She knew, because she could see each one of them almost perfectly.

And now, for the first time in her life, she wished she had already gone blind. It was becoming very clear that sometimes, it was far better to be left in the dark.

chapter one

There were three machines attached to her mother. Each one made a different noise, and in the silence of the intensive care room, they clattered and wheezed and rang in a type of discordant melody.

Elsie was almost used to it now.

Six days earlier, her mother had collapsed when she'd gone to pick up her father from the bus station. When her father had seen how ill she was, he quickly hired an *Englischer* to take them to Union Hospital in Dover. The doctors at the hospital discovered she had a severe case of pneumonia, a terribly high fever, and several other complications.

Well, that was what Elsie had heard.

Now, her mother seemed to be drifting in and out of consciousness with sluggish ease, much to the physicians' dismay. It seemed most people responded to the medication and were better after a day or so. That wasn't the case of Marie Keim, however. No matter how much any of them begged or prayed, she didn't seem in any hurry to return to them. Even when she opened her eyes, she rarely seemed aware of her surroundings. So they'd all had to make do with holding her hand and hoping for a miracle.

Elsie was okay with doing that, though she'd privately given up on waiting for miracles years ago. Now that she was twenty-two, she had quite a bit of experience with the

Lord's will. If He wanted something to happen, no amount of prayer or wishing could change His plans.

"Ach, Mamm," she said. "When are you going to get better? We need your help at home. Things are a real mess, and they don't look to get straightened out anytime soon."

Though she didn't really expect an answer, Elsie stared at her mother, hoping against hope that she would suddenly open her eyes and tell her what to do.

But, of course, the only sound she heard was the steady beeping of the machines.

"How's she doing today, Elsie?" Dr. Bolin said from the doorway. He was a pulmonary specialist, and he headed up the team of doctors who checked on her mother. Dr. Bolin's hospital rounds always seemed to coincide with Elsie's visits.

She was glad of that. She liked the man, who was about her parents' age and from Alabama. He had a chatty, kind way about him, and she trusted him. Far more than the rest of the family seemed to.

Perhaps it was because she was used to doctors poking at her head and staring into her eyes, or asking her to lie down in fancy MRI machines.

Looking back at her mother, Elsie said, "I'm afraid things seem about the same, Doktah Bolin. Every once in a while, she opens her eyes, but closes them fast again." She pointed to the little computer that all the doctors and nurses used now. "What do you think?"

Pulling up a metal chair, he sat down next to her. "I'm sorry, Elsie. I thought she would have recovered by now."

"Me, too," she said softly. "Mamm is always *gut*. She's the one who takes care of the rest of us. It feels strange to go home and not see her bustling around the kitchen."

"I bet." He stared solemnly at the machines, paying close attention to one of the screens that showed little lines rising and falling. "How are you doing?"

"Me? I'm fine."

"Your sister told me that you've been in the hospital before for tests."

"Only for my eyes. And usually, I go over to Sugarbush Eye and Laser Centre, in Ashland." Lifting her chin, she peered at him through thick lenses. "I've got a bad case of keratoconus. Slowly but surely, I'm losing my vision."

As she heard her voice, sounding so prickly and combative, she inwardly winced. She'd always had a chip on her shoulder about her disease, ever since she'd gotten glasses and felt she was cured, only to see that her family saw it as the greatest failure of all.

But instead of being taken aback, she was almost sure she saw the doctor's lips curve upward. "Your sister also told me that you had more spunk than your demure nature suggested."

"Don't tell anyone, but that might be true," she said with a smile.

He chuckled. "Well, if you need something, be sure and let me know, Elsie. Either for your mother, or for your eyes. I happen to know a couple of good specialists."

"*Danke*, but I have Dr. Palmer. The Sugarbush Centre is part of the Cleveland Clinic, you know." Inwardly, she winced. She sounded full of herself.

"You are in good hands, then. Even I have heard of Dr. Palmer. He has a formidable reputation." Standing up, he patted her shoulder. "I'll be back this evening, Elsie." Playfully, he wagged a finger at her. "But you had better not be here."

She smiled. "I won't. My time is almost up. There's so many of us, we have to take turns visiting."

When he left, Elsie leaned back again and watched her mother sleep. She hoped that before long, Mamm would soon be wide awake and bossing them all around.

Closing her eyes, she prayed that would be the case. And as the machines beeped and rang around her, she gave herself over to their mechanical rhythm and prayed some more.

"Elsie?" her father said from the doorway. "The driver has arrived. Viola's going to take her turn now, so we need to head on home."

"All right." After kissing her mother's paperlike cheek, she followed her *daed* out to the waiting room, pausing only briefly to glance her twin's way.

Then, they walked outside into the bright sunlight, where the van was waiting.

The sudden change in light stung her eyes something awful. If she'd been alone, she would have stopped and pressed her palms to her eyes in a puny effort to shield her vision.

But her father was there, and he already had so many worries, she was afraid if she added one more burden, he might not be able to handle it. So she squinted and walked across the small covered portico.

Pretended she felt no pain.

And tried not to show how upset she was that the light of day was making her long for the dark of night. It didn't seem fair that she was yearning for the darkness when soon that would be all she had.

It was going to be time to call Dr. Palmer again. He'd warned her of this . . . that one day things were going to get bad enough that they'd have to talk seriously about her future.

Of course, she hadn't counted on that day being so soon.

But she wasn't going to call, not quite yet. Once she knew the truth there would be no going back.

Instead, she decided to let her mind drift to Roman's new friend Landon. So far, she'd seen him almost every day this week. And though they hadn't talked much, she'd felt his eyes rest on her a time or two.

Just as she'd found herself gazing his way when she was sure he wasn't looking.

As their van sped east along on the interstate, Peter Keim glanced at his daughter, saw she was staring straight ahead with a pained expression, and considered again how to best phrase his question.

Questioning Elsie always took a bit of forethought.

"You've been awful quiet this afternoon. Is anything the matter? I mean, besides the obvious."

With a turn of her head, she looked at him, just as if she'd suddenly realized he was sitting by her side. "Nothing is wrong." She winced. "I mean, I was just thinking about someone. I mean something."

"What? Who?"

"Nothing. I'm fine, Daed."

He'd noticed the look of pain on her face. "Are you sure? Are you more worried than usual about Mamm? Or are your eyes bothering you? It seemed like you were wincing a bit when we stepped outside."

"I am fine, Daed. Please don't worry."

Did she sound more tense than usual? More on edge?

Perhaps, like Viola, she was blaming him for their mother's collapse. After all, Marie wouldn't have ended up in the hospital if he'd been home. He would have made sure she would have gone to the doctor the moment her cough got bad.

The very fact that he'd even been away was his doing, too. He was the one who had an alcohol problem. It had gotten so bad that he'd been forced to go to a treatment program near Columbus to combat it.

Once he'd gotten there, his optimism had faltered just about the moment the depth of his addiction hit home. Because of the insular nature of the program, he hadn't been allowed to call home much, and when he had, Marie's voice had sounded flustered and rushed. He'd felt so guilty about leaving her that those feelings had overridden any feelings of satisfaction he'd been experiencing about his recovery.

Now, he was the one who was trying to hold everyone together while Marie was the one in need.

He soon realized that his absence had created a terrible crack in their family's foundation. It was going to take patience and effort to put things to right. But, just as his counselor had said time and again, all he had to do was take small steps. Even small steps counted as moving forward.

He cleared his throat, determined to try again. "You know, we've still got almost another hour of sitting in the van. Then, when we get home, we're liable to be surrounded by the family. We ought to use this time to chat, just the two of us."

"You want to chat? Now?" Her voice seemed a little clipped. A little un-Elsie-like.

He was embarrassed. The counselor had warned him that his new resolve to talk about things instead of bury them was going to be new for his family.

"Are you upset with me?" Of course, the moment he asked that, he wished he could take the question back. Elsie had to be upset with him. He'd betrayed the family's trust by secretly drinking for months. When he'd been unable to stop on his own, he'd left them at the worst possible time.

Small steps. "Elsie, if you are upset, I understand," he said, his words sounding foreign even to his ears. "We can talk about that, if you'd like."

Her mouth tightened. *"Nee.* Don't worry."

"I can't help but worry about you, Elsie. It's a parent's job to worry, you know. And I still can do that just fine."

But instead of making her smile like he'd intended, she blushed. Just as if he'd suddenly embarrassed her. "Daed, I am a grown woman. Why do you insist on talking to me as if I were a child?"

Shocked by her accusation, he floundered. "I . . . I was only attempting—"

"I never hear you speak like this to Viola or Roman. I don't need your extra concern."

Stung, he ached to explain himself, to tell her how worried they all were about her eyesight. Perhaps God would soon give him the perfect words to say.

But now? There was nothing to do but sit back in silence and watch the countryside pass them by.

chapter two

"Roman, there's no need to bring me inside your *haus*," Landon Troyer protested. "I don't need anything to drink. I'll be fine until I get to my own home."

But his neighbor Roman Keim merely kept walking toward his house, his muddy boots kicking up chunks of dirt in their wake.

"Nonsense," he called out over his shoulder. "The least I can do is give you a glass of water. You've been helping me plow for two straight days."

Landon didn't like feeling like he'd done anything special. All he'd done was help out a neighbor. "You would have done the same for me, Roman."

"Maybe I would have . . . but your help was a godsend." After taking a few more steps, Roman stopped and turned to face him. "I have no idea what we would have done if you hadn't been here to help me prep the fields. There's no way I would have gotten that alfalfa in on time if it weren't for you."

All this praise was embarrassing. "It was nothing." Besides, after he'd first seen Roman's sister Elsie, he'd had an ulterior motive to visit. He'd wanted to see her again. So far, he'd gotten lucky. Their paths had crossed several times, and once, he'd even talked to her briefly.

That had been all the incentive he'd needed to visit again.

There was something about Elsie that struck his fancy, and he was eager to discover what it was.

Roman, on the other hand, thought he'd only been helping out because he was so selfless.

"Come now. You only moved in two weeks ago, and you've been spending at least half your time on our land."

"Not quite half."

"Plus, it's been raining and miserable out." He grimaced as he gazed at his muddy boots. "I was only out there for five hours, and I'm practically covered head to toe with muck."

Landon was covered with dirt and mud and who knew what else as well.

Which was yet another reason to stay out of the Keim's picture-perfect house. If, by chance, Elsie was inside, he had no desire for her to see him in his current state.

Nothing set a woman off like the smell of fresh manure.

"I've been glad to help your family in any way I could. That's what neighbors are for, ain't so?"

"*Jah.*" Roman nodded. "And, neighbors give each other glasses of water, too. So, you're going to come in and let me at least do this. Right?" He lowered his voice. "Besides, I want you to meet Amanda."

Just saying his wife's name put a smile on Roman's face. Landon knew Roman was a newlywed. It was obvious he was reveling in his new station in life, and anxious to show his wife off.

And Landon supposed if he was ever in that situation, he would feel the same way. "I'd like to meet her, too."

"Now you're seeing things my way." Roman grinned.

Stopping at the stoop, Landon followed Roman's lead and pulled off his muddy boots. "So, you think Amanda is in here?"

"Pretty sure. The women are usually working on supper about this time of day."

After placing his boots neatly against the wall, he said, "I still can't believe we married so quickly, and with my *mamm* in the hospital, too." Roman paused with his hand at the door. "But Amanda said life was for living, you know? She wanted us to be together during this tough time, and I wanted it, too. Plus, she's already had a big wedding," he added, his words slipping off his tongue at lightning speed. "She said she didn't need all that fuss again."

Landon recalled that Roman's wife was a widow, and with a young daughter as well. After leading Landon into the mudroom, Roman continued, his voice almost a whisper. "The bishop gave us a quiet ceremony soon after we arrived in town. My family wasn't too pleased that we married without them, but they got over it. Amanda's that special."

As Roman washed his hands, Landon shrugged off his black jacket and hung it on a peg. He, for one, couldn't imagine doing something so spontaneous. Marrying a woman on the spur of the moment sounded as foreign to him as suddenly wanting to drive a car.

Though, he realized with a bit of chagrin, he could imagine being intrigued by a woman after only the briefest of conversations.

But there was no reason for Roman to know that. "You're a lucky man," he said instead. "Truly blessed."

"I am, indeed." He dried his hands as Landon washed off his grime. Then they walked into the kitchen, which was filled with feminine laughter.

Then it stopped, as one by one, the three women inside caught sight of them.

One woman had to be in her sixties. She had fine brown

eyes that were sharp, and seemed to take in every bit of him from top to bottom. On either side of her were two women who looked to be about Roman's age. One was all shades of gold, from her lightly tanned face and arms, to her blond hair and bright blue eyes. She was shredding carrots.

The other was Elsie. And once again, she was gazing at him through a pair of thick lenses in a most direct way.

He wondered what she thought about him. Wondered what she'd say if she discovered that he'd been hoping to see her every time he'd visited her farm.

Feeling a bit flustered, he looked away, but not before noticing that she looked as pretty as ever. Today she wore a violet dress with a crisp black apron over it. Her hair lay smooth and neat under her white kapp.

In front of her on the table was a beige stoneware bowl half filled with snapped green beans.

As the seconds passed, Landon stood awkwardly in the doorway. He rarely felt tongue-tied, and he rarely stood still. He was a man usually characterized by action.

But at the moment? He had his hands clasped in front of him like a schoolboy and was trying not to meet Elsie's direct gaze. If he did, he knew he would probably start blushing or some such nonsense.

The elderly woman broke the silence. "Who are you?" she asked.

Roman stepped forward, just as if he didn't notice a bit of the tension in the room. "Mommi, this is Landon Troyer. He's our new neighbor. Do you remember me saying that someone moved to the land on our east?"

"I remember."

Roman grinned, obviously used to his grandmother's tart way of speaking. "Landon, this is my grandmother Lovina

Keim." Next, he pointed to his sister. "And I believe you've met Elsie before."

He nodded in her direction. "It's good to see you again, Elsie."

Her eyes widened, then she nodded, too. "Hello, Landon."

Roman, completely oblivious to Landon's mood, gestured at the lovely golden-haired woman. "And this here is Amanda, my wife."

Before he could say a word in response, Mrs. Keim spoke. "You bought the Gingriches' farm?"

"I did."

"Why did they sell it?"

"I'm not sure. But I bought it because the price was right," he replied. "It's a good piece of land, for sure."

"Hmmph. Where do you hail from?"

"Near Medina." He drew in a breath, hoping to ask a question or two. Maybe even say something more to Elsie . . . but Lovina fired off another question.

"What brings you here? Was it only the land?"

Landon fought to keep back his smile. He couldn't remember the last time he'd been questioned in such a manner. "The land is good, but I came out because of my brother Daniel. He moved to Berlin a couple of years ago and started a flooring business. I wanted to work with him."

There was much more to his story, of course. After hearing about Daniel's success, Landon knew joining his business made good sense. And though Daniel had offered a spare bedroom in his house, Landon didn't want to start out in a new town like that.

He'd wanted a place of his own.

So, he'd bided his time, and spent the last two years working as much as he could. He'd saved almost every penny and had asked his brother to keep an eye out for farms for sale. Just recently, it had all come together.

And then there was Tricia, of course, the woman who'd nearly broken his heart when she told him that she couldn't wait for his time lines . . . and had actually found another man who didn't have such grand plans so far away from her family.

Her rejection had pushed him to move forward even faster.

"Are you married?" Mrs. Keim blurted.

"Nee."

"Ever?"

"Never, ever." He smiled, enjoying the rapid questioning. He raised his chin, ready to hear her next jab.

But Roman held up a hand instead. "Mommi, stop. I brought Landon inside to get a drink, not to be interrogated."

"I'm hardly interrogating him. Just being neighborly."

"Mommi, neighbors don't badger. Not good ones, at least."

"Hmmph."

"Landon, you mustn't mind my grandmother," Elsie interjected smoothly. "She's like this with everyone. And, just so you know, you certainly don't ever have to answer her questions. Why, sometimes I pretend I don't hear her."

Lovina looked Elsie's way. "I hear you, however."

"Thank you for the advice." Landon chuckled softly.

"Anytime. I'm happy to help."

Forgetting that he was covered with mud and manure, he crossed his arms in front of his chest. "Maybe next time I see you, we can talk some more."

"Perhaps," she said demurely.

Looking from Elsie to Landon, Amanda smiled. "Landon, would you care to sit down and join us? We'd like to get to know you better."

"I would enjoy that. *Verra* much. But I'm pretty muddy. Perhaps another time?" He kept his words polite, general. Tried to look anywhere instead of only at Elsie. It wouldn't do to continue to mildly flirt with her. Roman seemed like the sort who wouldn't appreciate that much at all.

"You know? Here I invited you over, but never even gave you something to drink." Roman walked to the refrigerator and got out a pitcher of water. After filling two glasses, he handed one to Landon. "Here."

Feeling a bit conspicuous, Landon sipped as quickly as he dared while the women watched.

Too tempted to stare at Roman's sister again, he set his glass back on the counter with a bit too much force. *"Danke."*

Mrs. Keim clucked her tongue. "Is everything all right?"

"It is fine. I simply need to get going." Glancing at the women, he nodded. "See you soon."

"Goodbye, Landon," Elsie said with a sunny smile.

Roman looked at his sister for a moment, then turned toward the door. "Let me walk you out, Landon. I hadn't realized it was so late."

"No need to walk me anywhere. I can find my way out without a problem," he said lightly.

After all, Landon reflected as he grabbed his coat and slipped back on his boots, he had certainly found a way to return.

When the kitchen door closed behind the men, Lovina tried her best to look irritated. She wasn't supposed to be amused by a young man's impudence . . . or the small flash of interest she'd spied in both Landon's and Elsie's eyes.

There was something about that man that she liked. She'd

been impressed with the way he hadn't been cowed by all the women inspecting him like he was a new product out for their enjoyment. She'd been particularly impressed by the way he'd held his ground about his private life. As a person who'd kept her share of secrets, she knew keeping a steady hold on one's privacy wasn't an especially easy thing to do.

"Hmmph. What did you girls think of Landon Troyer?" she asked.

"Prickly," Amanda said with a grin. "He's not one to put up with much nonsense, is he?"

"Not from me, at least," she admitted.

Amanda laughed easily. "As a new member of the Keim family, I have to admit to being mighty impressed by his refusal to tell you anything else about himself. I certainly wasn't that relaxed when we first met."

"Pshaw. You had no reason to ever be wary of me. After all, your Regina had me wrapped around her pinky from the first moment we met."

Amanda grinned. "I think she felt the same way about you and Aaron. I didn't expect Regina to become so close to you so fast . . . but I'm glad she did."

"Me, too. That little girl of yours has brightened our lives considerably."

The Lord had certainly been working through Amanda and Roman, Lovina decided. When Roman had decided to join his aunt and uncle and cousins on their annual trip to Pinecraft, Florida, he'd only wanted to enjoy some time away from all the troubles they'd been experiencing here. But soon after he arrived there, he'd met Amanda and her daughter, Regina, and a romance had blossomed.

They'd had a few trying moments, but in the end, they'd decided to marry quickly and live in Berlin with the family.

Now, none of them could imagine their lives without Roman's kind wife and adorable four-year-old.

Turning to Elsie, Lovina noticed that she was being unusually quiet. In fact, she seemed to be lost in thought. She was sitting down again, but she was no longer snapping the ends off the beans; her fingers lay flat on the table.

Well, this was interesting. Her usually unflappable granddaughter seemed to be unable to look anywhere but at the back door where Landon had just exited. "Elsie, you've met Landon a time or two. What do you think of him?"

"He seems nice."

"*Jah* . . . but it seemed like there might be something between you. Is there?"

Elsie grabbed a handful of beans. "We've only spoken a few times. There isn't anything special about that."

Amanda leaned forward. "I noticed that he only had eyes for you."

Elsie's dark brown eyes looked like saucers behind her thick lenses. "He did?" A look of pleasure flashed across her face before she visibly tamped it down. "I mean, I doubt that."

"He also seemed eager to chat with you."

"That was only because Mommi was asking so many questions."

Lovina chuckled, realizing that Amanda might be on the right track. "I think Amanda is right."

"Why wouldn't he be interested? You're a lovely woman." Amanda's voice turned teasing. "And you're of marriageable age."

Elsie suddenly smiled. "You know what? You're right."

Elsie looked hopeful. Eager and excited.

Lovina now wished she'd never needled that Landon Troyer so much about being unmarried. She knew her granddaughter was feeling the sting of being the only single sibling. Although she was only twenty-two, her twin sister, Viola, was already engaged to Edward, a missionary. And now Roman was married, and he was just a little more than a year older.

And though she wasn't opposed to her granddaughter flirting a bit, Lovina also didn't want her to get her hopes up. After all, Elsie might be the same age as her twin, but she had a far different future ahead of her. "Landon Troyer must be a mighty kind and charitable man, helping us in our time of need."

A burst of anger, followed by a new awareness, entered Elsie's gaze. After a moment, she nodded. "*Jah*, Mommi," she murmured. "You are right, of course. He was simply being kind when he came inside and talked to us."

Feeling relieved, Lovina nodded. "Exactly."

Pushing up her glasses, Elsie pulled the bowl of beans closer; then she continued trimming them.

"Elsie, something still could happen," Amanda murmured. "Don't give up on romance yet," she teased.

"Oh, I haven't. At least, not yet."

Silence descended on them then, making Lovina wonder yet again what was really going on in her granddaughter's head. Until now, she'd been sure she knew Elsie the best.

Now, it was obvious she knew none of them well at all.

chapter three

As the din of male conversation floated around him, Landon was once again glad that he was finally in Berlin, working at his brother's side.

Having a goal that had been so hard to achieve had been daunting. But he'd persevered, and now he was enjoying the fruits of his labor. He had a job he enjoyed, was making some friends, and every night he could go home to a patch of land that was all his.

Feeling like everything was finally coming together, he stared at the partially completed floor they'd spent the last four hours installing. Satisfaction rolled through him.

Their hard work and attention to detail was paying off. It was a fine-looking floor—the seams were straight and even; the boards were smooth and buttery looking.

"It looks *gut*," Daniel stated as he straightened his back and pulled off one of his worn leather gloves. "Almost perfect. The Russells are going to be right pleased with our work, I'm sure of it." Turning to the other two men on their team, Zip and Craig, he said. "I think we can call it a day."

After the four of them spent the next few minutes putting their tools neatly into the lockbox, Craig stretched. "Okay if me and Zip get on out of here? It is Friday."

Daniel nodded. "Yep. You've earned your weekend. See you on Monday morning."

"Will do."

After gathering up the rest of their supplies, Zip and Craig left through the garage. Seconds later, the roar of their powerful truck's engine echoed down the street.

"Hey, have you ever asked why Zip is called 'Zip'?" Landon asked as they, too, headed for the door.

"I never thought to ask."

"Why not?"

Daniel shrugged. "Didn't think it mattered. A man shouldn't have to go around answering for his name. It is what it is, don't you think?"

Landon mentally rolled his eyes. His older brother always did step around anything he thought was touchy. "It's just a name, not a closely guarded secret. You know what? I'll ask him myself. And then I'm going to keep that information to myself until you're so curious you want to pry it out of me." He smiled slowly. "That's going to be great."

"Don't hold your breath for that day." Picking up his lunch pail, Daniel asked, "Hey, want to come over tonight? Edith and I are going to cook out on the barbecue."

Daniel's wife, Edith, was a mighty fine cook. But there was something else that Landon was looking forward to seeing and it had nothing to do with food. "*Danke*, but *nee*."

"Sure? We'd be happy to have you join us. You know how the boys love when you come over."

Daniel and Edith's twins, Bo and Ben, were three and extremely cute. But even the thought of watching their antics couldn't detract him from his plan.

"I'm going to go over to the Keims'. I promised my neighbor that I'd stop by to see if he needed any more help."

"You're going over there yet again?" Daniel scowled.

"Don't sound like that. I'm being neighborly. That's all."

"I'm starting to think it's far more than that. They're taking advantage of you, Landon." Throwing a hand in the air, he added, "Why, I bet every night they give thanks that you moved in next door. You're spending more time over at their farm than at your own place. And you've barely moved in."

"Listen, the wife is in the hospital with some kind of pneumonia. That's a difficult thing, for sure. I feel blessed that I have two good arms and two good legs. Helping them out so they can visit her at the hospital is a small thing."

Daniel sobered. "I didn't know she was in the hospital. I hear ya. I would be beside myself if my Edith was that sick."

"I know you would. You're a blessed man, brother. Edith is a wonderful-*gut frau*."

"She's the best," he said softly.

With effort, Landon shoved aside the twinge of envy he felt whenever his brother talked about Edith. He didn't begrudge Daniel's happiness, but he did wonder how the Lord had seen fit to match Daniel so early in life . . . and him so late.

Shrugging off those feelings, he walked toward the door and pulled out his key ring from a pocket. "So, see you on Monday?" With no church that weekend, they usually took some time apart. There was no reason for them to be living in each other's back pocket seven days a week.

"I guess so, since you don't want to stop by for supper."

Just before turning away, Daniel said, "Hey, Landon?"

"*Jah?*"

"Be careful now, will ya? You don't want to get too sidetracked by your neighbor's needs. Not when you have plenty of your own problems to solve. And we have a business to run."

"I won't get sidetracked."

They went their separate ways then, Daniel walking back toward Market Street. Landon, on the other hand, grabbed his bike resting on the side of the house and got ready to pedal his way to his new, very small farm with its broken-down barn and dilapidated house.

And his new neighbors.

As he pushed off and started pedaling down the almost-empty street, Landon smiled slightly. Well, perhaps he had a secret, too. His reasons for visiting the Keims' farm weren't completely unselfish.

There was a very pretty brown-haired lady there who he'd like to get to know a bit better. And if luck was on his side?

Roman would ask him if he'd like another glass of water . . . and Elsie Keim would just happen to be back in that kitchen and in a chatty mood.

He's out there again," Viola exclaimed as she bounded into their bedroom just an hour before dinner.

Elsie blearily opened her eyes, which had been bothering her all day. When her head had started to pound, too, she'd escaped to their bedroom for a few minutes' rest.

But, by the sound of things, she'd slept far longer. As she struggled to get her bearings, she sat up and scooted off the bed. "Who is out where?"

"Landon Troyer is out in our barn."

"Landon?" Though a spark of interest flared in her, she did her best to act nonchalant. "Is he helping Roman with chores again?"

"I don't think so; it's a little late in the day for that."

Elsie rubbed her eyes again. "Hmm. I wonder why he stopped by."

"It looks like he merely came over to visit with Roman."

"I guess they've become *gut* friends."

"Perhaps." Glancing out the window, Viola softly chuckled. "Elsie, it was so funny. When our new neighbor first saw me, he did a double take."

"I wonder why."

"One reason, of course. He thought I was you." Turning back to Elsie, she still looked amused. "I had to explain to him that, though we might look a whole lot alike, we aren't identical twins."

Despite that fact, Viola and Elsie shared the same coloring, height, and build. When they were little, only the smallest differences could be found: Viola freckled easily; Elsie did not. Elsie had inherited her mother's long, slim hands, while Viola had shorter fingers and wider palms.

As the years continued, their differences became more pronounced. Viola was outgoing and possessed a bossy nature. She was restless and had always been a favorite for impromptu kickball or volleyball games. Elsie had been quieter, more apt to be found in the kitchen helping their grandmother than playing with the other children in their neighborhood.

Then, of course, came her diagnosis and glasses. Afterward, no one confused her and Viola.

Now, however, Elsie was surprised even a brief acquaintance like Landon Troyer could mistake her for her vibrant sister. After all, her thick glasses were hard to overlook.

After studying her for a long moment, Viola sat on her twin bed across from Elsie. "So, you fell asleep. Even though it's almost suppertime."

"I don't know what happened," she fibbed. "I guess the day just caught up to me. The house was so noisy last night, I couldn't get to sleep."

"It was noisy last night," Viola allowed after a pause. "It's been fun having Onkle Aden, Aunt Rachel, and cousin Beth here. When you add in Beth's *kinner*, it's mighty crowded."

"I'm just glad they've been spending time with Onkle Sam and Aunt Lorene, too. I'm *verra* glad everyone is here to see Mamm and Daed, but all this company can be overwhelming."

Actually, Elsie was finding it harder and harder to keep her bearings with so much noise and comings and goings in the house, which made her realize just how much she'd been relying on her other senses to get through each day.

Her sister's voice turned soft. "Are you having a tough time, Elsie?"

"*Jah.*" Elsie wouldn't have admitted that to anyone else. "My . . . my eyes have been bothering me a bit more than usual."

"You should call your *doktah*."

"There's no need. Dr. Palmer told me years ago that stress can sometimes make my vision weak. I bet things will get better when Mamm comes home." Having the family here was a blessing. But that didn't mean they didn't bring more work and more stress.

Viola nodded. "We need for Mamm to get better."

After getting to her feet, Elsie was dismayed to see that her dress was wrinkled and that some of the pins had come loose. With a sigh, she unpinned the majority of them and prepared to painstakingly pin the dress back together.

After a moment of watching her struggle, Viola crossed the room and helped her. Usually Elsie brushed off her twin's offers of help but today she felt too sluggish to refuse.

"I think you need to go back to the eye doctor as soon as you can, Elsie. More might be wrong than just stress."

"I know." She couldn't hide her problems from her twin easily, and for the most part, didn't even like trying. "I'll call when Mamm gets better."

"You know Mamm would want you to call Dr. Palmer and hire a driver to take you to Ashland." She snapped her fingers. "I know, you could ask the driver to take you to Ashland from the hospital in Dover after you see Mamm tomorrow."

Elsie shrugged. It was going to be hard enough to go to the doctor with the immediate family asking her question after question about it. The last thing she wanted was for all her aunts and uncles to get involved, too.

It was her mother who needed everyone's prayers and concern, not her.

"I'll go when the time is right. That isn't now. And besides, tomorrow is Saturday. The doctor's office is closed on Saturdays," she said as she carefully brushed her hair, then pinned it back.

"Elsie, please—"

When her kapp was on, Elsie walked to the door, hoping to dash into the bathroom. "Thank you for worrying about me, Vi."

"You do understand that my worry is because I love you, right? I'm not nagging for any other reason."

That sparked a burst of laughter. Her sister loved to nag! "I'll try to remember that."

She was still chuckling about Viola's explanation a few minutes later when she made her way downstairs. Her twin was as bossy as a mother goose with a barn full of goslings. Viola couldn't help managing things.

"You seem especially happy," Roman commented. "Anything new?"

She looked at him in surprise. She'd been sure he was still in the barn with Landon. "Oh, it's nothing, just something Viola said." Curious about their neighbor, she said, "Viola said we had company?"

"You mean beyond all the family here?"

"Yes. Do we have a guest?" she asked almost nonchalantly, just as Landon walked in from the mudroom.

"Only me," Landon said.

Feeling her cheeks heat, she thanked the Lord she hadn't had time to finish her questions. She would have been so embarrassed if Landon had heard her ask about him. "Hello, again," she said.

"Good to see you." After a beat, he added, "I met your twin earlier."

"Yes, ah, Viola mentioned that she met you."

"For a moment I thought she was you, but now I realize you two look very different."

Fingering her glasses self-consciously, she nodded. "Yes, I suppose we do."

Immediately, Landon looked embarrassed. "I wasn't talking about your glasses. I was talking about—"

"Roman?" Regina called out. "Roman?"

"That's my daughter," Roman interrupted, already turning toward the hallway. "I better go see what she needs." Glancing at Elsie, he seemed to be asking her to stay with his friend. "Sorry about this, I'll be right back."

"Don't worry about me," Landon said. "I'm fine right here."

When they were alone, Landon gestured to the table.

Elsie realized that he wasn't going to sit down without her

sitting first. She also was starting to realize that he wanted to sit with her.

Yes, he definitely wanted to be with her.

Carefully, she pulled out a chair and took a seat.

Immediately, he sat down, too.

Though her vision was flawed, she noticed that his gaze was as direct as ever, and that she was still drawn to his rugged good looks, with his dark hair and matching eyes. But there was something else about him that had captured her fancy.

He seemed to have a bottled-up power inside him. An energy, almost a glow. Charisma. She couldn't help but be drawn to that.

He leaned forward on his elbows that were resting on the table. "So . . . can you keep a secret?"

He looked so focused, so intent, she felt a quiver of tension roll through her body. "Of course."

"I didn't come over to see Roman. I stopped by because I was hoping to see you again."

As his words sank in, Elsie was glad she was sitting down. Perhaps, after all this time, she really had been wrong.

Perhaps the Lord actually did listen . . . and could actually make her dreams come true.

chapter four

I stopped by because I was hoping to see you again.

Elsie gulped as Landon's words sank in. And as they did, she came to a startling conclusion: Though she'd always wanted a man to pay attention to her, had always hoped a man would one day look at her like she was special . . . she was utterly unprepared to deal with it.

As Landon continued to gaze at her, a bit of humor tingeing the interest that she'd spied in his eyes, she awkwardly sputtered. "Is that right?" she asked.

Completely unnecessarily.

Of course, she was already wishing it was possible to take those words right back and exchange them with something far more charming. And if she couldn't manage charming? Well, coherent would be good!

His lips curved. Looking almost sheepish, he added, "Oh, I wanted to help Roman out with the farm however I could. But ever since we first said hello, I knew I wanted to get to know you."

"I'm not quite sure how to respond to that."

His brows rose. "Uh-oh. Did I say too much?"

"*Nee,*" she blurted. No, the problem wasn't his saying too much. It was her saying too little!

Come on, Elsie, that little voice of reason coaxed in her

head. *Make sense. Quick-like.* "Um, what I meant to say was that I had no idea you felt that way about me."

Suddenly, simply sitting across from him felt impossible. "I need to take some towels and sheets off the line. Do you mind if we talk while I do that?"

"Not at all. I can even help you, if you'd like," he said as they walked toward the back door.

After she slipped on a thick black cardigan over her dress, she pointed to a basket. "Would you like to carry the laundry basket?"

"I'd love to carry it." He picked it up with one hand and a grin.

As they walked outside, she raised her face to the sun. The temperature wasn't especially warm, only in the high sixties. But there was a warm breeze threading through the air, and it made her more aware than ever that spring had definitely arrived. "I'm so glad it didn't rain today. I had to get some of the wash done."

"Do you do all the laundry?"

She nodded. "Most of it."

"That seems kind of a lot for one person."

"I don't mind the chore, especially since my mother is in the hospital." She'd also taken over the chore because it was one of the few things she didn't need perfect vision to do.

"I hope she gets better soon."

"Me, too." Reaching up, she unfastened a couple of pins and tossed them in the basket. Then she carefully folded a towel and handed it to Landon. He took the towel and set in the basket.

She wasn't sure what else to say, so she repeated the process several more times, tossing clothespins, folding towels, and handing them to Landon.

He didn't seem to need to converse much, either. In fact, he seemed to be fairly content just to be outside with her.

After four towels were neatly set in the basket, he spoke. "Elsie, you remind me a lot of my sister Mary."

She hoped that was a good thing. "How so?"

"Mary is kind of a surprising person. She's a tiny thing, doesn't look like she'd amount to much . . . but she's pretty tough. Even though I don't know you all that well yet, I'm starting to get the feeling that you're the same way."

She was glad she was busy folding a sheet because otherwise she'd be forced to look at him, and that would be a disaster. "I'll take that as a compliment."

"I hope you will. I meant for it to be. Elsie, you aren't seeing anyone are you?"

Holding the now neatly folded sheet, she turned to him. "No, I'm not. Are you?"

"*Nee.*" He looked like he wanted to add more, but then his gaze drifted behind her. "If I come back tomorrow, on Saturday, will you be home?"

"I'll be here in the afternoon. I'm going to visit my mother in the morning."

"If I did come by, and you were home . . . would you talk with me some more?"

His asking was clumsy. Stilted. Almost like an insecure teenager.

But maybe because of that, she found it endearing. It certainly made her want to see him again. "If I'm home when you come over, I'll look forward to talking with you."

He smiled as he picked up her basket of laundry, then handed it over to Roman who'd just joined them.

"What's this?" Roman asked.

"Your laundry. Carry it in for your sister," Landon said.

Then, with a slight tip of his hat in Elsie's direction, he walked off.

A line formed between Roman's brows as he watched Landon walk away. "What was that about?"

"Nothing at all." She shrugged. "I guess he had to leave suddenly."

"I guess so." Looking at the basket in his hands, he said, "I suppose you want me to carry it inside for you?"

She hid a grin. "Well, since you're holding it and all? I do."

On Saturday afternoon, after a short visit to the hospital followed by a quick lunch at a fast food restaurant, Elsie set about putting the house to rights. With the extra company in the house, along with everyone's crazy schedules, the whole house was in constant disarray.

She'd taken over the majority of the day-to-day upkeep. Since she couldn't do much cooking or sewing, she was glad of the chores and to be of use.

She just wished they wouldn't be so constant.

She'd just finished dusting and sweeping the front room when Landon arrived.

Unlike the other times, today he'd come to the front door.

He was also looking remarkably clean, which made her smile.

"What's so funny?" he asked after she led him inside.

"Oh, nothing. It's just that I was beginning to wonder if I was ever going to see you in clean clothes." When he looked embarrassed, she held up a hand. "I meant that in the best of ways, Landon. I can't help but admire a hard worker."

His expression warmed. "I'm thankful to find you home . . . and alone. I'm starting to get the feeling that your family enjoys looking out for you. . . . Your brother especially."

"That is true. Roman and I are pretty close. Actually, I'm close to all of my family. . . ." She fumbled, trying to figure out how to explain enough without having to explain her disability and how her family always babied her because of it.

"I mean that in the best way, Elsie," he said, echoing her words. "Anyway, I'm mighty glad you were home today. I didn't know how much longer I could just happen to stop by without a good reason. Roman's already told me he's run out of chores for me to do." He grinned at his joke.

She tried to smile right back, but failed. It was becoming more and more obvious that she had few skills when it came to speaking with the opposite sex.

As he waited for her to reply, she felt his gaze settle on her face. Wishing she could see his expression a little bit better, Elsie began to really wish she and Viola were a whole lot more alike.

Funny, she'd never envied Viola's good vision. But now she did envy her ability to chat with men. Over the years, Viola had had her share of beaus. Nothing too serious, but she'd been friends with enough boys in their church district to know how to respond to something like this.

As for herself? Well, she was feeling hopelessly out of her element.

Landon Troyer appeared to have no trouble. He seemed to be without the slightest trace of nervousness. Instead, it was as if he told girls he liked them all the time.

But now, she'd forgotten what he'd said. Perhaps it was best to move things along? Before they knew it, her family would be bustling in to get supper on the table. She got to her feet. "So, um, was there something special that you wanted to talk about today?"

"*Jah.*" He stood up. too. Then smiled again, obviously enjoying her nervousness.

"What was it?"

"Well, I came over to see if I could persuade you to go on a buggy ride with me."

"You did?"

"Uh-huh." He rocked back on his heels. He looked at her directly. "What do you think about that?"

What did she think? She'd never been asked on a buggy ride before. She had no idea how to respond. Was she supposed to act excited, or aloof, like she got requests like this all the time?

"Well . . . " she said, hoping to find a way to put into words everything she was feeling.

Landon Troyer had come over to ask her out. *On a date.* Elsie was so stunned, she was surprised her mouth wasn't hanging open. He was interested in her, thick glasses and all.

She didn't know what her brother would say about this. Sometimes he became too protective. So did Viola. And her parents. And her uncles and aunts and grandparents. Everyone around her seemed determined to focus on her dark future instead of her present.

And, she realized with a twinge of dismay, she'd even fallen into that trap a time or two.

For the first time since he'd entered the house, Landon seemed hesitant. "Elsie, does that appeal to you? If not, we can certainly do something else. It's warm enough to go for a walk." He paused. "Or we could go out for *kaffi* or something. I mean, it was just an idea."

"I'd like that, Landon," she blurted. "I mean, *jah*, I would like to go on a buggy ride with you. *Verra* much."

His ghost of a smile turned into a full-fledged grin. "When?"

There were many reasons to put this off. They had a household of family visiting. Her mother was in the hospital. It would be best to wait. But she was tired of waiting. Waiting for her time, waiting for the right time. "Whenever you want."

"How about later tonight?"

"Truly? Tonight?" That sounded very soon. She had no idea what to wear. Or what she was going to say. Plus, it was already almost time for supper.

"I'm afraid if we push it into the future, I'm going to have to track you down again, which is no easy task."

She couldn't help it; she laughed. "You wouldn't have to do that."

"Hope not," he murmured. A little more loudly, he added, "So, may I pick you up tonight for that buggy ride?"

That sounded almost like a challenge, and it was exactly what she needed to remind herself that it was past time to take some chances. If she wanted to live her own life, she had to start somewhere. "*Jah.*"

He stepped toward the door. "I'll be here at eight o'clock, if that's all right?"

"Eight o'clock is perfect. *Danke*," she said politely, and with far more finesse than she'd imagined just as Roman came out of the kitchen, Regina, Amanda, and their dog, Goldie, on his heels.

As her brother glanced from her to Landon and back again, his steps faltered. "Landon, I thought I heard your voice. When did you get here?"

"Only a few minutes ago. I merely stopped by to talk to Elsie."

Roman's eyes narrowed. "Elsie?"

"Yes, me, *bruder*," she said dryly.

"What's happening at eight?"

"Landon is going to take me on a buggy ride," Elsie answered before Landon was forced to explain himself.

Roman's expression was almost comical. "Landon, you're wantin' to take Elsie out?"

Landon looked at Roman strangely. "That's what she just said."

Roman looked even more perturbed, almost as if he had the right to have some say in whether Landon should be asking . . . or if Elsie should be going.

That was all the impetus she needed to get rid of the silly giddiness that had been plaguing her. "Landon, I'll see you later," she said firmly. Then she turned to her brother and gave him a look that said he better not say a word.

"I'll be here." Just as he turned the handle, he looked her way again. "I'm glad you said yes, Elsie."

After they heard the back door open and close, Elsie sighed. For some reason, handsome, attractive Landon Troyer really wanted to get to know her. He'd gone to a lot of trouble to ask her out, too.

Her, when it was obvious that he could probably have his choice of many women in the area.

At last, she didn't feel so different, so awkward, so ugly with her thick glasses and scary future.

Maybe now really was her time.

Then she realized that the other occupants in the room didn't seem to share her excitement.

chapter five

"What is wrong?" Elsie asked nervously. Though Regina was playing with Goldie, rolling a tennis ball across the newly swept floor while the dog chased it, Roman and Amanda were staring at her in various stages of disbelief and concern. Almost as if she were a strange *Englischer* who had wandered uninvited onto their property.

After a moment's pause, Roman started toward the door. "I think I'd better go talk to Landon."

Stepping to her left, she grabbed his arm. "Don't you dare."

He stopped, but jerked his arm out of her grip. "Elsie, what is wrong with you? What could you possibly be thinking?"

"That I am going on a date." At long last.

"Don't be cute. Did you tell Landon about your failing eyesight?"

"I wear glasses, Roman," she said sarcastically. "It's pretty obvious that I can't see too well."

He grunted. "You know what I mean. Did you tell him that you're going blind, Elsie? Did you tell him that?"

Though her eventual blindness was no secret in this family, hearing him discuss her disease like she was contagious was mortifying.

She didn't want to have this conversation, and especially not in front of Amanda and Regina. *"Nee."* She kept her chin up, but inside, she felt her earlier excitement quickly deflating.

"You should have. He needs to know before anything can happen between the two of you."

"Landon asked me on a buggy ride, Roman, not to spend the rest of my life with him."

"But your eyes—"

"He didn't ask me to sew his clothes, either," she countered sharply. "You might think differently, but I don't happen to think that I need perfect vision to spend time with him. It's just a buggy ride. That's all."

"But I saw the way he was looking at you."

"And what did you see?" she countered. But despite her sharp retort, her stomach clenched. Had Landon looked at her in a special way, like he was truly interested in her? Or merely as a friend?

But instead of giving her some insight, Roman continued to be critical. "See, this is exactly what I'm talking about. If you could see his expression clearly, you would know how he looked. Which is exactly the problem!"

What had gotten into her brother? Normally the one member of the family who liked to avoid drama, here he was, instigating it. She turned her back on him, walking into the kitchen. Someone needed to get started on dinner. And as usual, it was up to her. Despite the fact they all seemed to think she was incompetent, she was the one running this house right now. "Roman, I'm not going to talk about this with you." She sighed as she headed toward the sink to wash her hands. "Even if Landon does need to know about my poor vision, it's not your place to tell him."

"I agree." Amanda finally spoke up. "Roman, you need to step back and stay out of your sister's business."

He shook his head. "Amanda, you don't understand."

"Oh, I believe I understand enough, Roman."

As the tension rose, Viola joined the fray as she bustled into the kitchen, followed by their grandparents along with Beth and her children, Cale and Lindy. "What's going on? What business is Roman poking into now?" she asked. "We were just outside. First we saw Landon Troyer leave, and then we heard your voices all the way from the back stoop."

Elsie was so used to being on the fringes of family dramas that she had a whole new appreciation of just how awful it felt to be the center of so much unwanted attention. As the family filtered in, all eyes on her, looking anxious to get involved in the discussion, she knew she would have given just about anything to disappear. Immediately.

Luckily, Regina scampered over to Lindy's side, then the three youngsters darted off to the living room, Goldie at their heels. Beth followed, probably recognizing that the kids needed to be out of the kitchen for a while.

But everyone else stood quietly, looking from Elsie to Amanda to Roman.

But Amanda merely folded her arms across her chest. "This is Elsie's business, not mine."

"It was nothing," Elsie said quickly. "I mean, it was nothing important." She turned to her grandmother. "Mommi, we should probably get supper ready, don't you think? It's past time to get started."

Her grandmother nodded, but her steady gaze remained on Elsie. "We'll get to it, dear. In a minute."

As the seconds passed like hours, Elsie made a shooing motion with her hands. "Um, Dawdi, maybe you could take everyone else out of here. I think this room is getting awfully crowded."

"I will. Soon."

"Come now," Viola prodded. "Roman looks like he's about to burst at the seams, and I don't remember the last time I saw you look so worried. Did you call the eye doctor? Did he give you any idea about why your vision has suddenly gotten worse?"

Roman folded his arms over his chest. "Viola, what are you talking about?"

"She fell asleep yesterday afternoon," Viola explained. "She said her eyes were tired."

"They were?" he asked, as if she'd just announced that she'd started bleeding uncontrollably. "You didn't mention that, Elsie."

"Oh, for heaven's sake, Roman. Stop. I am not a child and you are certainly not my father."

"Maybe we should get Daed involved."

"We do not need Daed."

As if on cue, their father peeked in. "You do not need me for what?"

"Nothing," Elsie said.

Ignoring her, their father looked at Roman. "Is everything all right?"

"Everything is fine," Elsie said through clenched teeth. If one didn't mind living in the midst of far too many nosy people.

"Elsie is going out with Landon tonight," Roman announced, frustration staining every word.

Cupping a hand around his ear, her father said, "Say again?"

"Landon is taking Elsie out," Roman repeated.

"Landon is the new neighbor," Mommi supplied.

"He's taking her for a buggy ride," Roman added with a scowl. "Just the two of them."

The tension in the room increased. Elsie felt a headache coming on. Here she was, imagining that her dreams were really coming true, and now her family was going to throw water over everything.

"Are you sure you should do that, Elsie?" her father asked. "Perhaps you should give him a call and say you changed you mind."

"Or maybe I should go talk to him, like I was about to before you grabbed my arm," Roman said.

"I don't want to change my mind." Looking around at her assembled family, each vying for the chance to offer an opinion, Elsie backed toward the door. "I am not doing anything wrong."

Viola blurted, "But you've never been out courting—"

"I know," she said bitterly. "Believe me, I know. You all treat me as if I'm sixteen years old. Or maybe even younger!"

"You're acting like a foolish teen," Roman said.

"If I am, so are you. But I am a grown woman with a good brain. I'm not doing anything untoward."

"Daed, Landon doesn't know about her blindness," Roman pointed out, speaking over her, as if she weren't even there.

"He doesn't need to know."

"Of course he needs to know," Mommi murmured.

"Yes. I mean, what are you going to do when Landon finds out that you won't be able to see one day?" Viola asked, tapping her foot. "Don't you think he'll be upset that you kept that from him?"

She hated this. She hated how everyone thought that she didn't deserve to think about love and relationships. "Who is going to tell him?" she asked. "Mommi? Amanda? Dawdi?"

When the three looked down at their feet, she angrily turned to the other three surrounding her. "What about you,

Roman? Is that what you were so anxious to do? To rush out and tell him that he shouldn't be interested in me, ever? That I'm not worth it?"

"I didn't say that."

"What about you, Viola? Or you, Daed? Do you two feel like you need to be the ones to make sure I always stay home and never venture out because I'm not perfect?"

As she'd expected, this time both Viola and her father turned away, obviously embarrassed.

Feeling vindicated, her voice became heated. "Listen, I know none of us is perfect. But at least all of you have had chances to do things without everyone getting involved. I think I deserve that right, too. You must stop treating me as if my future has already been decided."

"We're merely trying to protect you, daughter," her father said. "At the very least, wait until your mother is out of the hospital before you go out with this Landon. Then she could advise you."

"There's nothing to advise. I'm going on a buggy ride. That's it."

"But there's—"

She was going to have to make them see her point of view if it was the last thing she ever did! "You're not trying to protect me," she countered. "I think you are trying to protect yourselves. As long as I stay at home, surrounded by all of you, I'll never change."

"But Elsie, you might get hurt," Daad whispered.

"But don't you see? I want to live my life. And if I get hurt, it will be my business." She was so frustrated, tears welled in her eyes. What she didn't feel brave enough to share was that she'd already been hurt. For years, she'd felt as if she wasn't quite a part of the family. They'd overlooked her attempts to help, fearing that she might mess things up or get hurt.

They'd overlooked her need to do "regular" things, not remembering that even blind—or almost blind—girls sometimes just wanted to be girls. She ached to make mistakes and appear foolish. She wanted to have things to laugh at or be embarrassed about.

She wanted to be normal.

While she'd come to terms with the knowledge that she wasn't going to be able to see one day, for now, she could experience life like everyone else, except with glasses. "I need some fresh air. I'm going to go outside for a moment. And then I'm going to come in and help with supper."

"Elsie . . . " Viola's voice was plaintive. But Elsie didn't let her finish.

"Viola, I thought you, at the very least, would have understood. I couldn't be more disappointed." And with that, she grabbed her bonnet and cloak, then walked outside and finally let free the emotions that had been brimming to the surface.

As they watched Elsie storm across the field, Lovina shook her head. She should have said something more. She knew better.

As the silence continued and the tension rose, her other granddaughter, in her typical impatient fashion, turned and stared at the rest of them.

Well, at least she could speak up now.

"Viola, how many times has Elsie stood up for you, even when she didn't agree with you?"

Viola shifted uncomfortably. "Always."

"And when was the last time she ever sided against you in front of the rest of us?"

"I never remember her doing that," Viola admitted after a moment. Looking miserable, she said, "She didn't even try to talk me out of going to Belize."

"Well, I hate to admit it, but I'm afraid Elsie might have a point about our hovering." Lovina looked at each of them in turn.

Making her tone a little harder, she continued. "Elsie is a capable woman and it's time we recognized that, even if it makes us uncomfortable."

With a small smile, Amanda curved a hand around Roman's arm. "I couldn't agree more."

"*Jah*. And it is only a buggy ride," Peter said with a wry shake of his head. "We're making mountains out of molehills."

"But I think Elsie's vision loss is much worse than she lets on," Viola blurted.

"What makes you say that?" Lovina asked.

"Just little things. She needs more help pinning her dress. Sometimes I don't think she sees everyone in the room. Her steps seem to be more tentative."

"Has anyone else noticed these things, too?" Peter asked.

Roman shrugged. "Maybe."

"We need your mother here. She would know what to do." Peter walked over to the window and gazed out.

Not having his wife here, especially on the heels of his alcohol treatment, was weighing on her son. Lovina could see that.

Looking resolved, Viola started toward the door. "I'm going to go find Elsie and talk to her. Try to explain what I was thinking."

When Roman and his father nodded, Amanda spoke up. "I think you should leave her alone, Viola."

"I second that," Lovina said quickly.

Viola turned to her in surprise. "Why?"

"You will soon be in Belize," Lovina chided softly. "If you truly want to help Elsie, you should be her sister, not her caretaker."

Roman frowned. "Mommi, Viola's only trying to help."

With a glance at her husband, Lovina let a smile play on her lips. "Viola is only trying to help her own peace of mind. As you are. It's time we let Elsie make some of her own decisions."

"But she could get hurt."

"Then she's in good company, yes?" Lovina said, looking around the room. "We've all had our share of triumphs and disappointments. But we've lived them. No one has stopped us. And yet . . . we survived, *jah?* Roman, we all could have stepped in and said you didn't know Amanda long enough to marry her, right? But we trusted you. We allowed you to move forward in your life, knowing that you could make your own decisions. Doesn't Elsie deserve that as well?"

Viola stared at her grandmother with something close to wonder in her eyes. "When did you get so smart, Mommi?"

"It's only happened lately, and here I am in my sixties," she teased.

But as they each slowly got back to their chores, Lovina thought that they should all be as smart as Elsie. Lovina realized that getting hurt was sometimes inevitable. But she knew for sure that doing nothing was a far worse choice.

If only she had been that wise forty years ago.

chapter six

Landon was twenty-six years old. He'd had his share of girl-
friends and had gone on his share of buggy rides. But now, as
he guided his gelding up the Keims' long driveway, he didn't
remember ever being as pleased about the opportunity to
spend time with a woman.

As Mike clip-clopped along the gravel drive, Landon noticed the first buds on the pear trees that lined the road and
thanked his good fortune one more time. So many good
things had happened in his life lately. He was finally near his
brother, he was in business with him, and now had his very
own farm. He was so glad he'd made the decision two years
ago to work hard and save every penny to buy his own piece
of land and join his brother's business.

Living at home and working dozens of hours at a local
hardware store had really paid off. Staying true to his goals
and plans had been the right thing to do.

The Lord was surely rewarding him by giving him the gift
of Elsie Keim right next door. She seemed to be just the
type of woman he'd dreamed about spending a lifetime with
when he'd been putting in all those hours. She was pretty
and sweet and had a little spark in her that he was anxious to
discover more about.

Just as he slowed Mike over the hill, he caught sight of
Elsie standing on the edge of the front walkway. She had on

a different dress than the one she'd worn earlier. This one was a deep pink, so dark it was bordering on red. He loved the bright color on her, loved how it seemed to represent so much about her . . . perfectly Amish . . . but also perfectly her own person.

No matter how quiet she might seem, Elsie was no shy flower. No, she had a spunk about her that demanded to be noticed.

As soon as he reined Mike to a halt and set the brake on the buggy, he strode to her side.

"Elsie, you didn't have to wait outside. I would have been happy to come to your door to get you."

Her cheeks brightened a bit, and something told him that it had nothing to do with the cool breeze in the evening air. "Actually, being out here was my choice. I was ready for a bit of space."

"Is that right?"

She nodded. "Our house is mighty full today."

He laughed as he got out and helped her into his buggy. "I have noticed that there seem to be folks all around your place."

"Lots and lots of folks," she said wearily. "Of course, we're all together to see my *mamm*, but when we're not at my mother's side at the hospital, things can be a bit overwhelming. And loud."

He handed her an old quilt that his grandmother had given him when he'd graduated eighth grade. "I hope you won't be too cold. The days are warm but the nights are still a little cool."

She unfolded it a bit and tucked it around her lap. "This should be fine." She smiled softly. "It's a pretty quilt, Landon."

"My grandmother made it," he said, as he settled in next

to her, immediately noticing the nice sensation of feeling her slim body against his. "So, are you ready?"

"Very ready."

After he released the brake and clicked the reins, Mike started forward with a quick jerk.

Beside him, Elsie laughed. "He's a bit frisky, huh?"

"I guess so," he said with a grin. "I've been riding my bicycle around town a lot, so Mike hasn't been getting out too much. He's a pretty young guy. No doubt, he's ready to let off a little steam."

"I know the feeling."

Landon looked at her curiously, wondering what had sparked that statement. But when she didn't add a word, he decided to let it go. Seconds later they were sailing down the driveway. "Do you mind if we go up the back roads?" he asked when they got to the highway. "I didn't have anywhere special in mind to take you."

"Anywhere is fine with me."

Eager to please her, he said, "Is there somewhere you especially like to go on buggy rides?"

"You mean when I've gone out before?"

"Well . . . yeah," he said awkwardly. He wasn't particularly crazy about talking about her other dates, but she seemed a little tense.

"I don't care where we go."

"Um, okay."

Making a sudden decision, he carefully guided Mike through a right turn, then let him slow a bit. They were on a narrow-laned road that looked like it had little use. Then he peeked at her. "Elsie? Is everything okay?"

"I was just trying to find a way to tell you that I've never been courted before."

He was glad he was twenty-six and not eighteen. Years ago, he would have blurted something stupid, like asking her why not. Had she not liked any of the other guys? Or had they not liked her?

Luckily he'd lived long enough to realize that sometimes things simply happened for a reason . . . or for no reason. He had no problem dating a woman who hadn't already gone out with a lot of men. That only added to her attraction for him. It didn't detract from it.

Instinct told him to keep things light. "You don't have to worry about telling me anything, Elsie. All I want is to spend time with you."

She looked at him with a smile. "I can't tell you what it means to me to hear you say that."

"If you're that easy to please, we're going to get along fine."

She relaxed a bit next to him. "Tell me about your family, Landon. And your work."

"I'll be glad to. But I have to warn you that there's nothing very exciting about any of us. Stop me if I bore you."

She laughed softly. "I promise, I won't find a thing boring about a quiet family."

Once again, he found her comment to be almost cryptic, as if there was something that she wasn't quite ready to share. He liked the air of mystery surrounding her. So many women he knew talked so much he could hardly get a word in edgewise.

"Well, I have a brother, Daniel, who's married to Edith. They have two little twin boys, Bo and Ben, and they live here in town. I also have a younger sister named Mary. She's just twenty."

"And your parents?"

"I'm blessed to still have them both, and they live in

Medina. Living down the road from them are my grandparents, and I even have a great-grandmother who lives in their *dawdi haus*."

"And they are all okay with the fact that you and Daniel live in Berlin now?"

He shrugged. "I guess you could say we're a little bit of an anomaly in the Amish world. We like our space."

She smiled softly at that.

"I don't have much more to say, really. About two years ago, I decided that I wanted to work with my brother. Daniel was all for it, too. He even went so far as to offer his guest room for me to live in for a while. But I wanted my own space." He glanced her way, wondering if she could follow what he was trying to say. "I wanted something that was all mine, you know?"

She nodded. "You wanted your independence."

"*Jah.*" Quickly, he attempted to sum up the rest of his story. "So, even though it took a bit longer, I farmed our land and worked at a hardware store on nights and weekends. When I had enough money to feel like I could afford a little piece of land of my own, I moved. And that's my story."

"You were able to earn all that in two years?"

"Just the last chunk. I'm one of those planner type of people, Elsie. Once I set a goal, I hate to stray from it. I feel like I've practically spent my whole life waiting to live my life the way I envisioned it. Now it's finally happening—I have my own piece of land and I work with my brother."

With a slight smile, he added, "And now we've met each other. I have to say that I couldn't be happier with how things turned out."

Elsie smiled back at him, but then she bit her lip. Like she was worried.

"Did I say something wrong?"

"Not at all," she replied. Then she flashed a smile and he noticed the tiniest of dimples in her right cheek. "Tell me more, Landon. What do you like to do for fun?"

"Haven't we talked about me enough?"

"Definitely not."

This wasn't how he'd imagined talking with her would be. He'd hoped for more of a give-and-take, a true conversation. "But Elsie, I don't want to talk nonstop. I want to know more about you, too."

But instead of taking his hint, she shook her head. "There's nothing too interesting about me, Landon."

"But—"

"Please," she said. "I'll tell you more about me next time."

Well, that was something, he supposed. She wanted to see him again. He, for one, couldn't wait to spend more time with her. After a pause, he started talking again. He talked until they came to a dead end, and then after turning around, he talked some more.

And by the time they pulled into her driveway, he realized to his chagrin that she'd barely told him a thing about herself.

And that she seemed perfectly fine about that, too.

Sitting in their small living room, a fire chasing the chill away, Lovina found herself checking the clock every fifteen minutes.

Aaron noticed. "Watching the clock won't make her come home any faster, you know."

"Do you think she's having a good time?"

"Don't know."

"Do you think Elsie told that boy about her blindness?"

He chuckled. "Knowing Elsie? Nope. That granddaughter of ours is as sweet as they come . . . and twice as stubborn." After a pause, he added, "Just like someone else I know."

Raising her brows, she did her best to attempt to look shocked. "Who? Me?"

He nodded. With careful movements, he folded up his newspaper before glancing at her over the rims of his glasses. "When we first met, I thought you were a sweet girl."

"And later you discovered how stubborn I could be?"

"*Jah*. But then by that time it was too late. I was already in love with you."

She chuckled. "That doesn't sound too romantic, Aaron."

"Well, it was different back then. *We* were different back then, you know."

She knew he was referring to the first few months of their relationship, back in Pennsylvania. She had been young, barely a high school graduate, and had been getting over a difficult senior year and Jack's death.

Even thinking his name brought a slight melancholy sting to her heart. Jack had been a boy she'd had a crush on. Eventually, he'd returned her regard, and she'd even gone to a dance with him. She'd been anticipating the dance for weeks, sure it would change her life.

And it had, but not in any way that she'd imagined. Both she and Jack had made some very poor choices, which had resulted in the death of a friend and Jack's deciding to enlist in the army.

Just as she'd wrapped her arms about that, she'd learned that he'd been killed in action.

Aaron, on the other hand, had been mourning his wife and child, who had died in a buggy accident.

Looking back on it now, Lovina realized that they'd truly been two people who'd had little else to depend on besides each other and a desire to escape their present situations.

"Yes, we were very different people back then," she said quietly. "I didn't know how to be Amish. Or a wife."

"And I thought I knew everything."

Lovina bit the inside of her cheek to keep from smiling. Oh, but Aaron surely had thought he was infallible!

Worse, she'd thought he was always right, too. It was only later, when the shiny newness of her life had faded into a sense of normalcy, that she'd realized he'd been just as flawed as she was when it came to relationships.

"Lovina, we did all right. Ain't so?"

"After a time, yes we did."

For a moment, he stared at her, and that one silent look told her so much. "Have you thought any more about going back to Pennsylvania?" she asked.

He opened a drawer and pulled out a letter. "I'd like to go soon. I received another letter this week."

Only recently had she learned that Karl, Aaron's first wife's younger brother, blamed him for Laura Beth's death. For forty years, he'd been sending Aaron a photocopied newspaper clipping of her death announcement, and a note that said he'd never forget that her death was Aaron's fault.

Though she was still coming to terms with the fact that Aaron had hidden the truth from her for decades, and was actually the one driving the buggy that day, she was determined to move past their problems and grievances. "What did this one say?"

"The same as all the rest. But instead of burning it like I always do, I thought you might want to see it."

With an anxious heart, she took it from him. While he

watched, she opened the flap and pulled out the sheet of notebook paper. As she unfolded the letter, the clipping about the buggy accident fell out.

It was a small thing, no more than a few inches long and wide. Though it named Laura Beth and Ben, it mainly quoted various statistics about buggy accidents, especially ones in poor weather.

But what was chilling was the word written across the article in red pen. *LIAR*. The four letters practically screamed at her.

Warily, she glanced at Aaron. He stared back, his body motionless, his expression blank.

Only then did she read the rest of the enclosed letter. Written in careful print, there were only four lines. But though the letter was short, it was obvious that Karl still held Aaron in contempt. "Aaron, this is awful."

He took the letter from her, then walked to the fireplace and tossed it in the crackling flames.

Lovina watched him stand in front of the fire. He seemed determined to watch every inch of the paper burn to ashes. Almost as if he was afraid if he didn't watch it burn, it wouldn't really be removed from his life.

"I want to go back to Pennsylvania as soon as Marie gets home from the hospital, Lovina. I want to finally face Karl. I need to tell him in person that Laura Beth's death was an accident." Slowly, he turned. Faced her. "I need to tell him that I didn't kill my Ben. I don't know if their dying was God's will or if it was out of all of our hands. But I do know that it wasn't my fault."

She was glad to hear that he was still committed to facing his past. And though a part of her feared that Aaron had even more secrets about his past, and what had happened the night Laura Beth and Ben died, she knew he needed to go back and finally bring some closure to that part of his life.

Of course, she needed to face her past just as much. She'd gone from being an active, social English teenager to becoming an Amish wife and mother within a span of two years.

And because her family had never understood her desire to become Amish, she'd cut ties with them instead of trying harder to make them understand why she'd chosen the life she had.

Yes, the trip was bound to be difficult. But the alternative would be even harder. If they didn't make this trip, Lovina knew they'd never completely find peace.

"You are right, Aaron," she said quietly. "As soon as Marie gets home from the hospital, we should go."

"It is decided." Looking relieved, Aaron headed back to their bedroom. "We'll go and face our pasts. Together." He hesitated, then said quietly, "And perhaps we'll even be brave enough to face our eldest daughter, too."

Lovina heard their bedroom door click. She knew it was time to go to bed, but couldn't seem to make her body move. Instead, she stared into the fire and thought about their eldest daughter, Sara. Would she welcome them with open arms . . . or would she push them away, resenting the fact that they'd never once come to visit her in New York or when she later moved to Pennsylvania?

Now she realized that fear had played a big part in her actions. Wanting to ensure Sara would never face the pain that she had in her teens, Lovina had been firm. Judgmental. Strict. Perhaps, too strict.

Instead of offering her support and compassion, she'd offered rules and consequences.

It was no wonder her daughter had married early and moved far away.

Perhaps the real surprise was that any of her children had stayed nearby at all.

chapter seven

When Landon pulled away, Elsie remained at the stoop, letting the delicious warmth from his parting smile sink into her. The evening had been everything she'd ever hoped for—and so much more, too.

Only when the glow of his buggy's reflectors had faded, and the last echoes of his horse's hooves could no longer be heard did she enter the house.

Inside, the atmosphere couldn't have been more different.

Roman, Amanda, and Viola were sitting in the kitchen. Daed was there, too. Even Uncle Aden and Beth were there, sipping coffee.

It was a strange sensation.

Elsie was used to being the one waiting for information from Roman or Viola about their evenings out. When they were younger, she'd been beside herself with jealousy, sure her time was never going to come.

Now, for the first time, at the ripe age of twenty-two, she was the one who felt everyone's curious stare settling on her expectantly.

"Well?" Viola asked impatiently. "What happened?"

"I went for a ride with Landon."

Roman rolled his eyes. "We know that. Come on, tell us more. Where did you go? What else did you do?"

"Pull up a chair," Uncle Aden offered. "We want to hear everything."

Elsie was getting the feeling that these questions were only the tip of the iceberg. She, for one, was in no hurry to talk about her time with Landon.

It was too special. Certainly too personal to share with the whole family. "I'm going to go upstairs," she announced.

"Not so quick!" Viola exclaimed.

"Viola, not now."

"Come on," her twin cajoled, looking mildly hurt. "I'm not asking you anything you haven't asked me after a date."

Her sister was right. They'd been in this same situation many a time. But it felt different now that their places were switched.

Moreover, she didn't have the confidence that Viola had. She felt shy about her date, and not too eager to share how special she felt. She wanted to keep that to herself, at least for a little while longer. "Landon and I went for a drive. That's all."

"Come on, Elsie," her cousin Beth said merrily. "Just fill us in a little bit. We've been curious, you know. Did you have fun?"

Standing awkwardly in front of them, she nodded.

Roman suddenly looked concerned. "Landon didn't try anything, did he?"

"What?" Indignation, combined with a healthy amount of embarrassment, made her voice harsh. "Of course not. Roman, I can't believe you asked such a thing!"

"Why not? We don't know him all that well . . ."

"He's spent hours helping you in the fields and in the barn," she pointed out. "I suppose you only thought he was good enough to help you work?"

"That's not fair." Shifting uncomfortably, he added, "And one has nothing to do with the other."

"We're interested, not prying, Elsie," Beth said, her tone attempting to be reassuring. "Don't you want to talk to us?"

She didn't. At least, not right at that moment. She hated the thought of her family interfering with the first date she'd ever had. Hated the thought of everyone talking about her, all trying to manage her. As if she were helpless.

So the only thing to do was to turn in. It would give her the space she needed to savor the memories of her first date, ever.

"I think I'll say good night now." She turned and headed toward the staircase, refusing to allow anyone to stop her progress.

But as soon as she'd slipped on a nightgown and washed her face and brushed her teeth, Elsie discovered that Viola was waiting for her in their room.

"Couldn't stay away?"

"Of course not," Viola said. "Now that we're alone, you can tell me what really happened," she said with a conspiring smile.

"I was telling the truth before. There isn't much to share. Landon took me for a ride and then he dropped me home."

"And that's it?"

"*Jah*. That's it," Elsie lied.

Viola stared at her a moment longer, then shook her head. "Um . . . I know you, Elsie. You wouldn't be so secretive if you weren't hiding something."

Though she could feel her cheeks burn with embarrassment, she valiantly tried to cover it up. "That's ridiculous."

Moving from her bed to Elsie's, Viola's voice turned wheedling. "Come on, twin, tell me how Landon was. Romantic?

Chatty? Solemn? Do you think you're going to want to see him again?"

"I'm not going to talk about him." She didn't know how she felt, which was why she wanted to keep it all to herself.

"But I'm your sister."

"And you are my favorite sister, too. But I'm still not ready to tell you what I think. I want to keep the memories close to my heart for a bit."

Though Viola had always shared openly after all of her dates, Elsie was different from her twin. She kept things to herself more and wasn't someone to just chat about everything. Viola had to understand that. Plus, Elsie liked knowing that she had something special to think about that was hers alone.

You seem happy today," Daniel said to Landon when they took a break from sanding the floors. "Every time we've stopped for a break, you've been whistling to yourself. What's going on?"

Landon's face flushed. He didn't realize his mood was so obvious. "If I told you it was because we were making good progress, would you believe me?"

"Nope." After taking off the mask over his nose and mouth, Daniel wiped his forehead with a bandana. "You hate sanding as much as I do."

Landon reached for his bottled water and drank thirstily. "That's true. I always feel like I inhale half of the grit that fills the air. Even though we wear masks, I always go home with a mouthful."

Daniel held out his arm. "It's the dust that settles into my skin that gets me." After draining half his bottle of water in one gulp, he asked, "So, since it's definitely not sanding . . . what has you so happy?"

After debating another second or two, Landon spilled the beans. "I took Elsie Keim out for a buggy ride last weekend."

Daniel's eyes lit up. "You went calling last weekend? How come you didn't tell me what you were up to?"

"It's been kind of a sudden thing," he said. Though of course that wasn't true. Ever since he and Elsie started talking, he'd been hoping to take her out.

As he wiped his neck with a damp bandana again, he added, "There's something about her that makes me anxious. Like if I don't try to make something happen fast, I could lose her."

Stuffing his own bandana in a back pocket, Daniel whistled low. "Hmm."

There were a hundred meanings in that one sound. "What?"

"I've never seen you so smitten."

"There's something special about Elsie." After a pause, he decided to be completely truthful. "Actually, I think there might even be something special between us. When we talk, it feels different, ya know?"

"Oh, I know." He smirked. "Don't keep me in suspense, brother. How did it go?"

Landon debated for about a second before replying honestly. His feelings embarrassed him a bit. Never had he imagined that he'd ever feel so smitten with a woman he hardly knew.

But he trusted his brother more than anyone else in his life, so it stood to reason that Daniel could give him the best advice. "I feel like I can't wait to see her again." He shook his head in wonder. "When I dropped her off, it was all I could do not to ask her out again."

Daniel chuckled. "You're on your way, man. Ha, I had begun to think you were going to be an old man before you started courting."

"I'm hardly old."

"*Jah*, but you're determined to stick to your grand plan."

Landon knew what his brother meant. For most of his life, he'd always claimed that sticking to his goals and plans were far more important than fostering relationships. He'd even given Daniel a little bit of a hard time when he'd been courting Edith.

Now, though, he understood. He really liked Elsie, and she was so perfect for him and his life. He felt she would make a wonderful wife for some man. She seemed so competent and calm.

"I hope I don't mess this up."

"You won't." As they got ready to get back to work, Daniel said, "I'm sitting here, trying to remember the last woman you were so taken with."

"It was Tricia."

"Ah, yes." His gaze turned serious. "You're better off without her, for sure."

He didn't want to think badly of Tricia, but she really had put him through the ringer. He'd been devastated when he'd realized that Tricia had been lying to him about her dreams and goals. After opening his heart and sharing his plans with her, he'd discovered that she'd never had any intention of living anywhere but in Medina. And preferably right next to her parents.

The revelation had come as something of a shock. Tricia had been quite a wild teenager and had often been in trouble when they'd first met. After they'd started seeing each other, she'd been all for his plans, and had even hinted that she would love to live in Berlin one day.

But then, just as he was about to make the offer on his land, she'd revealed that she didn't want to ever move so far from her family. Worse, she'd asked him to forget about his dream of working alongside his brother and farm in Medina instead.

When he'd told her that he simply couldn't do that, she moved on with lightning speed to another man in their church district.

Just as if what they'd shared had meant nothing.

He'd been hurt and confused. And had been determined not to even think about women for years.

But then he'd spied Elsie and everything had changed in an instant.

"No matter what happens with Elsie, I'll be grateful to her for making you think of something besides work and your grand plans."

"I hear you," Landon said sheepishly. Even his parents had mentioned that his focus on his future had been exasperating. He'd spent too long ignoring the gifts of the present because he'd been so determined to have the future he was sure he needed.

Now, at long last, he could finally relax and enjoy the moment. Elsie was going to make all the waiting and hardship and doing without worth it.

The Lord had definitely been looking out for him when He'd put Elsie in his life. Carefully, Landon covered his mouth and nose with the mask again. "Break's over. The sooner we get back to work, the sooner the sanding will be over."

Daniel nodded, checked the generator, then turned the sander back on. "That, at least, is something we agree on."

Further talking was prevented by the drone of the machine and the diligent concentration that was required to complete this part of the job.

chapter eight

In the dim light of the hospital room, Peter once again found himself pouring his heart out to his sleeping wife.

"And so that is yet another reason why we really need you to get better, Marie," he murmured. "I'm at a loss for what to do about Elsie. Every time I try to talk to her about her eyes, she redirects the conversation. And Viola has even shared that she thinks Elsie is hiding the true extent of her vision problems."

He paused for breath, remembering the frustrating conversations he'd had with Elsie recently.

And he wasn't the only one concerned about the way she'd been ignoring their cautions and bits of advice. Honestly, it was like all of a sudden his agreeable, biddable daughter had been replaced with a new, far more stubborn woman.

Gently caressing the soft skin of Marie's hand, he sighed. "I'm tempted to make the doctor's appointment for her myself, but she's a grown woman. That don't seem right. I mean, her twin sister is planning her wedding and preparing to be a missionary's wife in a foreign country. Elsie needs to be the one making this decision. Ain't so?"

He waited a heartbeat, halfheartedly hoping she'd suddenly answer him. But of course she remained asleep.

"Ah, Marie," he said, caressing her hand again. "I do worry

about you. Please come back to us. You're my wife, my best friend. I want to take care of you, and I'm willing to do whatever it takes to help you get better." He lowered his voice. "Just meet me partway, Marie. If you do that, then I'll do the rest. I want you in my life. I want you back."

Pausing for breath, he scanned Marie's face again, preparing himself to see the same thing he saw yesterday and the day before, and the day before that: his lovely wife sleeping.

But now her eyes were open.

He was so surprised, he was sure his mouth was hanging open. With a shake of his head, he leaned closer. "Marie? Marie, *mein lieb*, are you awake?"

When she merely stared at him, her blue eyes looking vacant, panic set in. Had her terrible fever injured her mind?

"Marie, do you know where you are? Can you understand me?"

After a clumsy attempt to form words, she nodded.

"Oh, praise God!" After glancing through the windows but seeing no one to gesture to, he reached for the call button. "Marie, I am so, so glad to see your lovely blue eyes."

Just like that, her gaze softened, bringing the compassion and love into her expression that had always been his refuge.

"Elsie?" she said after a bit more of a struggle.

"*Jah*. I was speaking of Elsie. But not to worry. She's all right. I mean, she will be. It is you who we've all been worried about." Unable to stop himself, he bent down and pressed his lips to her brow. "Marie, I've been so worried. So worried."

"Peter," she rasped, then curved her lips slightly.

And that half smile felt like it illuminated the whole room.

At last, he rang for the nurse. "My Marie is awake," he

announced, his voice loud and joyful. After the nurses told him they'd be right in, he turned back to Marie. "They'll be right here, dear," he said. "How are you feeling? Are you in pain?"

A line formed between her brows. "You've been here, haven't you?"

Her voice sounded as if it was filled with wonder, as if she couldn't believe that he would be sitting by her side as much as possible.

"*Jah.* I have," he said, his voice thick with emotion. "For days and days I've been here. We've all been here—Roman and Viola and Elsie. Lorene and Aden. My parents."

"Aden is in Ohio?" She shifted, looking like she was struggling to sit up.

To stop her, Peter laid a comforting hand on her shoulder. "Easy, Marie. You've been mighty sick," he murmured. "But yes, Aden is here. Judith, too. As is their daughter Beth. Sam and Mary Beth have been coming up to the hospital as often as they can. Even Jacob and Martha have been calling regularly to check your progress. We've all been worried about you. Frankly, Marie, I—"

His next words were cut off by the rush of nurses and the doctor. As they crowded around Marie, he stepped to the side, allowing them to check her vitals, to do their jobs.

Standing against the wall, he was grateful for the few minutes of reprieve. Closing his eyes, he let tears of relief fall while he silently gave thanks and praise to the one who had healed her.

To the one who'd been so instrumental over the last few months. "*Danke,*" he whispered. It wasn't much to say, and certainly not poetic, but it was heartfelt. And because of that, Peter knew it was enough for now. The Lord knew he was grateful.

"Peter?" His parents were at the door, Roman and Lorene standing right behind them. Each looked more anxious than the next.

"Did I hear right?" his mother asked. "Is Marie awake? We just arrived to take our shift when we heard the commotion at the nurses' station."

He stepped into the hall. "I don't know too much yet. But she is awake, and she seems to understand what is going on around her, too. It's a miracle."

"Praise Got!" Aaron said.

Roman nodded, pure relief filling his eyes.

Wrapping an arm around his son, Peter hugged him close. "This is a wonderful day, Roman. A blessed day."

"Indeed it is, Daed." Feeling his son's strong arms clasp him tightly, Peter's heart lifted. Marie's recovery felt like a turning point. At last, he had hope for their future again. Hope that all of their problems were only slight glitches in the total span of their lives. That now that Marie was on her way to feeling better, everything was going to be all right.

He was out of his alcohol treatment program, Roman and Viola were in good relationships, and despite the shocking revelations over the last few months, tensions were easing with his parents.

And through it all, the Lord had been with them, keeping them company, guiding their actions.

After stepping away, Roman gestured to Marie's hospital door. It was closed. They could hear the nurses talking with Marie, but not clearly enough to discern what was being said. "Daed, when can we go see Mamm?"

"As soon as the doctors and nurses say we can."

But the wait was longer than expected. After a few minutes, one of the nurses left. A little bit later, Marie's doctor walked out with little more than a cursory glance at the five of them waiting in the hall.

Peter's parents took two seats nearby while Roman walked to the nurses' station to use their telephone to call home.

As the minutes passed and no other doctor or nurse exited the room, some of his optimism began to fade.

As Peter glanced at his father, he saw much of the same resignation on his face.

"It's out of our hands. The Lord is in charge," his father murmured, his voice steady and sure. Like it had always been during times of trouble. "He is holding Marie's hands now, and working through the doctor and nurses, too. We have to believe that."

"I do," Peter murmured before bending his head down to pray again.

Over and over he asked the Lord to help Marie, and to give them all the strength to care for her in the ways that she needed them to.

As he prayed, he was aware of Roman returning, murmuring to their father, then joining them in prayer.

Then, at last, Marie's door opened and Dr. Bolin poked his head out.

They sat up abruptly, Peter slowly getting to his feet. As he stared at the doctor, he realized he was holding his breath. Peter could feel the collective tension whipping around them as they waited for the doctor's words.

"I do believe Marie has turned the corner. With more rest,

I see no reason why she won't make a complete recovery." He smiled kindly. "Would you like to see her now?"

Feeling like he'd just gotten the wind knocked out of him, Peter continued to stare at the doctor. "Are you sure that she . . . that my Marie going to be okay?"

Dr. Bolin smiled softly. "I think so, Peter. I examined Marie and read her charts. It looks like we've finally made it through the worst of it. Marie is on her way to a recovery."

"*Danke,*" he said to the doctor.

"You're welcome, though I think my work was only part of it. The whole staff has been monitoring her closely, you all have been here at her side the whole time . . . and we've all witnessed your prayers." He smiled kindly. "Together, it all helped."

After shaking the doctor's hand, Peter led the way to Marie's doorway. Inside, Marie was sitting up, dressed in a fresh hospital gown, and watching them hover with something that looked like amusement in her eyes.

One of the nurses chuckled as she saw how dumbstruck they all were. "It's okay," she said.

Hesitantly, he stepped forward, the others at his heels. "Marie," he said softly. "Look at you." It was hard to believe that just a few hours ago she'd been asleep for days.

"You look much improved, daughter," Lovina said.

"I wish I could say the same about all of you," Marie replied. "Peter, you're so pale, you look like you've seen a ghost," she said around a tired smile.

Peter *felt* like he was seeing a ghost.

But then Roman pushed his way forward, sat on the edge of Marie's bed, and reached for her hand. "Welcome back, Mamm," he said with a smile. "We missed you!"

The rest of them couldn't help but chuckle. Only Roman could sound so relaxed after such a trying string of days.

Marie reached out her arms for a hug. "I missed you too, *boo*," she whispered into his neck. "I've missed you, too."

As Peter stood flanked by his parents, he realized that his prayers really had been answered.

And then he let the tears flow unashamedly down his cheeks.

chapter nine

It was Monday afternoon. The whole house was in an uproar after hearing the wonderful-*gut* news about Marie's recovery.

While Viola and Beth went with Aden to the hospital, Elsie made the choice to stay with Amanda and make some cookies and casseroles. If Elsie knew her mother, the moment she started feeling better, she would want to start managing the household again. The only way to encourage her to rest was to have everything in order before she came home.

"What do you want to make first?" Amanda said. "Oatmeal cookies or chicken-and-stuffing casserole?"

"Let's make the cookies," Elsie decided. "The kids can have a few while we are working on the other dishes."

"Sounds like a plan." Amanda turned on the oven, then left to check on Regina, Lindy, and Caleb.

Elsie busied herself with getting out the ingredients for the cookies. She hardly needed the recipe; she'd made them so many times. But after she got out the mixing bowl and combined the brown sugar and the butter, her eyes began to betray her.

No matter how hard she tried, she couldn't read a single word on the recipe card. Her head started to pound behind her eyes as she squinted, trying to discover whether the recipe called for one tablespoon or one teaspoon of cinnamon, baking soda, and salt.

To her dismay, it seemed as if her vision had decided to take a sharp downward turn over the last week. Tears of frustration pricked her eyes as she realized that she wasn't going to be able to hide how bad things had gotten for much longer.

And just as frightening as the degeneration was the knowledge that her family would use it as an excuse to shelter her all the more.

That was the last thing they all needed, especially with her mother likely to come home from the hospital in the next day or two. Elsie didn't want all the attention centered on her instead of her mother.

She'd been concentrating so hard on trying to decipher the recipe's squiggly words and on her frustration, she didn't hear Amanda enter the kitchen until she was standing at her side.

Amanda laid a gentle hand on her shoulder. "Elsie, what's wrong?"

"I . . . I'm having trouble reading the recipe," she admitted.

After a pause, Amanda picked up the card. "What did you have trouble reading?" she asked, her voice even and matter-of-fact.

"I, uh, can't read the measurements for the seasonings," she said reluctantly. "I can't see the exact measurements."

"It says here we need one teaspoon of cinnamon, one teaspoon of baking soda, and a pinch of salt. Does that help?"

"*Jah*." Swallowing her pride, she said, "Could you read the rest of the recipe out loud to me?"

"Of course." Slowly, she recited the amount of flour and oatmeal needed, as well as the note her mother had made about vanilla.

When everything was in the bowl, she picked up a metal spoon. "*Danke*, Amanda. I've got it now."

"You're welcome." She turned away and started cutting up vegetables. But even with her poor eyesight, Elsie knew Amanda was struggling with holding her tongue.

Elsie felt Amanda's gaze as she stirred, then dropped spoonfuls of cookie dough onto the baking sheet. As one minute bled into two, Elsie braced herself for the inevitable lecture.

But Amanda stayed silent, the sound of her chopping more vegetables into neat, uniform pieces their only company.

Only when the cookies were almost ready to come out of the oven did Amanda speak.

"Elsie, what are you going to do?"

Elsie could have played dumb but she knew exactly what Amanda was referring to. She sighed. "I'm going to go to the *doktah* soon."

"When, exactly?"

"When things settle down around here," she replied, wincing. Even to her ears the excuse sounded feeble. She opened the oven door and busied herself with taking out the tray of cookies.

"You need to make an appointment, Elsie. You should have already made an appointment. We both know that."

"I said I will."

"Elsie . . ."

"There's no hurry. My sight has only recently taken a turn for the worse." Then, of course, there was the little matter of her being afraid to see the doctor and hearing what his prognosis was. Sometimes not knowing the truth was easier than confronting it head-on.

Amanda continued to work on the casserole, not looking Elsie's way. But her attention did not waver. "You're playing with fire, Elsie. It's wrong to ignore your problems, and you know it."

Elsie expected this kind of bossing from her sister, Viola, but Amanda was new to their family, and had seemed more reserved. This insistence was surprising. "I thought you would be more understanding."

Her voice gentled. "Elsie, my first husband died of cancer. Since then, I've had a little girl to raise by myself. I couldn't have gotten through any of it if I had been an ostrich. You can't ignore your body. It's a mistake to ignore a problem, and a bigger mistake to not get help when you need it. " With a grimace, she added, "Believe me, I tried."

"You don't understand. You've seen my family already. If my vision is worse, my family is going to treat me like a child, even more than they already do." Worse, like a prisoner, not letting her do anything without supervision.

Amanda turned from her preparations and looked at Elsie. "Listen to me. If you are pretending to see better than you can, something terrible could happen. What are you going to do if you hurt yourself or someone else?"

"I won't. At least, I hope I won't," she added under her breath as she picked up a spatula and started carefully transferring the cookies to the countertop to cool.

"But what if you do?"

Amanda's voice was so solemn, Elsie forced herself to stop and really look at her. That's when she noticed how very worried she was. Not just about Elsie, but about Regina, too.

A lump formed in Elsie's throat as the reality of her denial hit her hard. What would she do if she accidentally hurt Regina?

"All right. All right. I promise I will call the doctor." Sometime soon.

To her surprise, Amanda walked her to the phone. "How about you call right now?"

"Amanda—"

"Call now or I'm going to tell Roman. And we both know what he'll be like."

"That's not fair." Roman would bully her, practically drag her to the doctor, appointment or not.

"Don't you understand that there is nothing 'fair' about what happens to a person? People get sick and hurt. Accidents happen. God doesn't give everyone only what is fair. Instead, He gives us what He thinks we can handle."

Elsie wanted to protest again. But under her sister-in-law's watchful expression, she realized that she no longer had a choice about what to do. And worse, she realized that Amanda was right and she'd been wrong. There was something worse than knowing the truth about her blindness—hurting someone she loved through her stubbornness and fear.

Feeling resigned, she picked up the phone. Taped to the inside of one of the kitchen cabinets was Dr. Palmer's card. "Amanda, could you dial the number?" She couldn't bear to admit that she couldn't discern any of the numbers.

But then she realized she was fooling herself more than her sister-in-law. Amanda probably knew she couldn't read the numbers at all.

"Of course." She punched in the numbers, then handed the phone to her.

It only rang twice. "Doctor Palmer's offices," a pleasant voice said upon answering. "May I help you?"

"Yes. This is Elsie Keim. I'm . . . I'm afraid my vision has gotten worse. I need to come in."

After a pause, the receptionist said, "Well, Elsie, I'm sorry to hear that. Is it an emergency? Do you need to come in this week?"

"It's not an emergency. But I should probably come in soon," she said, not daring to look at Amanda.

"Please hold."

As she held the line, Elsie felt her stomach start to churn.

Finally, the receptionist returned. "Elsie, I just spoke with Dr. Palmer. He wants to see you, but he's booked fairly solid. Is there any way you could call us early next week? Sometime on Monday? By then, he should know when he can squeeze you in."

Glad for the tiny reprieve, Elsie took it and held on tight. "*Jah*. I mean, yes, I can do that. *Danke*."

When she hung up, she explained the situation to Amanda. "So, I should be seeing the doctor sometime next week," she said at last.

"I wish you had an appointment, but I guess he's a busy man. Well, listen, I'll go with you if you don't want to ask anyone else," Amanda said.

"You're not going to let me sneak to this appointment, are you?"

"I'm sorry, but I won't. This is too important. *You* are too important, Elsie."

It looked like the decision had been made. In a week, the news that she'd been dreading forever would become fact.

chapter ten

The floors of the kitchen they were sanding now felt as smooth as a newborn lamb's fleece.

Satisfied with the job they'd done, Daniel and Landon decided to end their day a little early. Tomorrow morning, they'd have Zip and Craig meet them at the house, and the four of them would apply layer after layer of stain, rubbing the color in with soft rags until Daniel was satisfied with the depth of color.

Landon headed home and hit the shower, washing the dust and grime off his tired body. He was just about to make a thick turkey and ham sandwich when Roman knocked on the door.

"Roman?"

"Hi. I was hoping you'd be home."

"You caught me on a good day. I'm usually still at work." He opened the door wider. "So, have you decided to offer your services to me this afternoon as payback for all of my hard labor?"

"I do owe you, that's for sure."

"I'll take you up on it one day soon. There ain't much that needs to be done at the moment." He paused and grinned. "But you can mow the grass if you've got a mind to do it."

Roman's lips curved in what could only be described as a reluctant smile. "I'll pass on that, but thanks." Still hovering in the doorway, he said, "I need to talk to you about something."

"Come on in, then." Landon led the way to his sparse kitchen. "Want a sandwich?"

"No, thanks, but you go ahead."

Landon was so hungry, he didn't need any further encouragement. But as he was chewing that first bite, he started to realize that Roman hadn't come over to talk about work. "What did you want to speak to me about?"

"Elsie."

"What about her?"

"I know you took her out."

Landon wondered why he brought that up. " You were there when I asked her."

His mouth suddenly felt dry. Grabbing his glass, he took a gulp of water. "I took her on a buggy ride, Roman. That's it." He hoped his friend knew his intentions were nothing but honorable. Being a big brother himself, he could imagine the protectiveness Roman might be feeling.

"I know. But my sister and I got the feeling that you might be seeing each other again soon."

"We might. Is that a problem?"

"Maybe." Looking increasingly uneasy, Roman took a chair. "We need to talk about you courting Elsie."

"I'm a grown man, Roman, and she's no child." Suddenly, a terrible thought entered his mind. "Is something wrong? Did Elsie say I upset her?" He couldn't imagine what she would have found fault with, but he'd learned that sometimes a woman's perception didn't always match what a man's was.

"It's nothing like that." Looking aggrieved, Roman added, "Matter of fact, she said she had a *gut* time with you."

"And why is that a problem?"

"You need to know something about my sister."

"What do you mean?" Landon didn't care for the way the conversation was going. He and his brother were close, and they'd both looked after their baby sister, Mary, too. But never had they ever interfered in each other's romances.

Or in his case, his *almost* romance. After all, all he'd shared with Elsie was a few conversations and one buggy ride.

Roman glanced at Landon's face, then at his sandwich, then settled on his folded hands. "It's like this. My sister Elsie has an eye disease."

Landon stopped chewing. Pushing his sandwich to one side, he gave Roman his full attention.

"She was diagnosed at age twelve."

"Diagnosed? I know she wears glasses . . . "

"It's more than that." After taking a breath, Roman exhaled softly. "Ever since she was a little girl, her eyesight has been steadily getting worse. Fact is, she'll one day be almost blind. Even now, her vision is very poor."

"What?" He chuckled, though what Roman was saying wasn't funny. "Roman, I watched her unpin clothes from the clothesline. I've walked by her side. She can see just fine."

"Not as well as you think." He cleared his throat. "We're starting to find out that Elsie can't see as well as she pretends to. And one day, probably sooner than she'd like to admit, she won't be able to see at all."

As Landon sat there, stunned, Roman continued. "I like you, Landon. I think you're a good neighbor, and I believe we could be close friends. But I also care for my sister *verra* much. I don't want to see her get hurt."

"And you think I might hurt her?"

"Maybe, if you don't want to marry a woman who can't see," he said bluntly. "Landon, I didn't come over here to make trouble. But I thought you needed to know this about her . . . just in case she didn't tell you about her vision problems herself."

"Obviously she didn't tell me. No one did," Landon said testily. He was starting to resent this situation. Both the fact the he hadn't even noticed her problem and the fact that no one had even hinted about her trouble. He'd worked hours by Roman's side and not once had he mentioned it.

"I didn't think she had." Roman shrugged. "I don't want Elsie getting her hopes up about a relationship, you see. On the off chance that your, ah, feelings for her might have changed."

"Because I wouldn't want to court a lady who is going blind." Landon knew his voice was flat.

"She's going to need to be cared for, Landon," Roman stated as he got to his feet. "I don't mind looking after her, and neither does anyone in my family. Elsie is a wonderful sister and a good person. She may be able to make some man a wonderful-*gut frau* one day. But she needs the right man."

Looking even more uncomfortable, he continued with his hat in his hand, "I'm not saying that's not you. . . . But sometimes, when a man looks for a wife? He wants a woman to be his helpmate. Anyway, I wanted you to know . . . to know the truth."

"And what did Elsie think about you coming over to tell me this?"

"She doesn't know. And she's going to be upset with me when she finds out."

"You aren't worried about that?"

"*Nee.* If hurting her now will save her from pain down the road, I knew I had to take that chance." Roman chewed on his lip, clearly contemplating whether to say any more.

"Landon, you've been a good friend. I figured you might not want to court a woman who is going blind, and I felt I owed it to you to tell you the truth. I also wanted you to take some care when you were with her. You can't simply assume . . ."

"That she could see," he finished quietly.

"*Jah.*" After shaking Landon's hand, he strode out of the house, leaving Landon grappling with the news. Slowly, he walked back to his kitchen table and reached for his plate again.

He wondered if he should have picked up signs. But everything he'd seen of Elsie revealed a determined, capable woman. He'd seen her in the kitchen, helping to cook, and she walked inside without needing any help when he dropped her off. She might not be able to see perfectly, but she definitely hadn't seemed helpless.

Roman had to be exaggerating. Most likely, he was simply being overprotective.

But as he worked his way through his sandwich, he began to reconsider.

From what he'd learned of Roman Keim, the man wasn't one to overstate things. He was honest to the point of bluntness. So telling a tall tale about his sister didn't make sense. Plus, why would he want to prevent her happiness?

As he washed his plate and dried it, Landon began to think about what he really wanted in a wife.

For the last few years, he'd done everything he could to realize his goals. Being able to achieve them in a relatively short amount of time had been a great source of pride. Now that he was working with Daniel, he wanted to be successful. When he married, he had expected that his wife would be much like Daniel's Edith. She would take care of things at home and be in charge of raising their children. That way he would be able to devote the time he needed to his job.

But what would it mean if he had a wife who couldn't see? How could a woman care for a baby if she couldn't see him? How could she do anything without help?

Once more, how would he feel about that? He was a fairly independent man. Did he want to have a wife whom he might have to care for like a child? Even a woman as sweet and attractive as Elsie?

He honestly didn't know.

Well, rather, he knew, but he didn't want to face his worst fears. He didn't want to believe that he was the type of man who wouldn't be interested in a woman who had a disability like that.

He was going to have to face the facts. . . . He wanted a wife one day. A real one in every sense of the word.

Not a blind one.

It didn't make him proud, but he couldn't deny how he felt.

Leaning against the wall, he rested his head back and closed his eyes. It was a difficult day, to realize one wasn't the person one hoped to be.

At least, not yet.

chapter eleven

As the evening sun's rays filtered through the window blinds, creating broad stripes on the foot of Marie's hospital bed, Peter scooted his chair closer to his wife.

"I can hardly believe we're sitting alone. At long last."

She smiled tiredly. "I have had a lot of visitors, for sure."

After their first, sweet greeting, the doctors and nurses had shooed everyone out and examined her. About an hour later, they moved her to a different room on a different floor.

Then, explaining how exhausted Marie was, they sent everyone home. He, too, had gone home reluctantly—only his own exhaustion had prevented him from staying.

Now, here they were, together again, and the world seemed a bit brighter.

Pulling his gaze away from Marie, he looked around the room. This one was a bit bigger and had a more homey feeling. It was on the second floor of the hospital, and located at the end of the hall. Now, instead of being across from a nurses' station, they were across from an empty room. It was a far quieter environment.

Before his visit, Marie had been allowed to take a shower and even slip on one of her white cotton nightgowns Viola had brought from home. After she'd showered, a nurse had kindly brushed out her hair, then pinned it neatly at the nape of her neck.

Marie was pale but otherwise looked much like her regular self. No cords or tubes were attached to her now. The nurse said she could get all of Marie's vitals by hourly visits instead of electric monitors.

"I am mighty glad not to have so much commotion around me," Marie commented.

"Do you remember much about when you were so sick?"

"I remember feeling exhausted and dizzy." Raising her eyes to his, she added, "And I remember many people sitting with me. Especially you."

"I hated to leave your side." Even now, after his month's absence, he still gazed at her eagerly, anxious to reacquaint himself with her. They had so much to catch up on. So much to discuss when the time was right.

But for now, he wanted to keep things easy. There would be plenty of time to talk about things when she was home. At the moment, he wanted to concentrate on the present.

"I was so worried about you, Marie."

She reached for his hand. "But I am better now."

"The *doktah* said if you are fever-free tomorrow, you can go home on Wednesday or Thursday."

"That will be wonderful-*gut*. I can't wait to be back in my own bed." She shifted a bit, rearranging the sheets and blanket across her chest. "Tell me about the *kinner*, Peter."

Afraid all of the news might worry her, he patted her hand. "There's time for all that later."

"Tell me," she coaxed. "Please? I want to think about something besides myself."

He leaned back, stretched his legs. Debated the best way to tell her about all the goings-on. Then decided some things just had to be told without much preparation. "First off, Roman married Amanda."

Her eyes widened. "What? Are you joking?" She struggled to sit up.

With one hand, he eased her back down. "Relax, dear. Don't get yourself worked up."

"I'm not—"

"You are."

Grumbling a bit, she eased back into the softness of her pillow. "I'm relaxed. Now talk. Are you serious?"

He grinned. "I like to tease you, wife, but I wouldn't tease you about this." Taking a moment to weigh his words, he scratched his beard. "As soon as they heard you were in the hospital, they jumped on the first bus from Florida, Regina and Goldie in tow."

"Goldie?"

"She's their dog. You'll meet her when you get home."

"Why did they marry so fast?"

"Amanda and Roman wanted to be here with you, and they didn't want to wait for a wedding. Roman talked to Bishop Coblenz, the bishop agreed, and married them on the spot. None of us attended. . . . They just walked into the house and announced they were husband and wife."

"We should have a party or reception or something." Her fingers drummed the mattress. "Maybe we could host a dinner in two weeks?" A pair of lines formed between her brows. "Or, is that too late?"

"I'm sure they will enjoy a party at any time."

"Maybe sooner than later . . . Maybe Lorene could help get things organized. What do you think?"

"I think your mind is already spinning." Unable to help himself, he leaned over and smoothed the crease in her brow. "Relax, dear."

"But there's so much to think about."

She didn't know the half of it! With a foolish grin he couldn't seem to temper, he playfully curved a hand around her shoulder. Pretending to hold her in place. "Settle down, Marie. We must watch your blood pressure and your lungs."

"My blood is fine. My lungs are, too—"

"Your lungs are hardly fine. And who knows what is going on with your pulse. You look like you're ready to leap out of the bed!" He hardened his voice a bit, just to let her know that he was serious. "Calm down or I won't give you another bit of information. You need to get better, not have a relapse."

"Fine." She coughed a bit, took a small sip of water with his help, then sighed. "I just can't believe they got married without me. Without any of us."

"This was their decision, Marie," he said patiently. "Remember, Amanda's already had a big wedding. And Roman? Well, he never was one for big events. They are both happy and living at home."

A bit of hope flashed in her eyes. "They're living at home? Is that what they've decided to do, live with us?"

"To be honest, I haven't even thought to ask them. We've been otherwise occupied, you know. And Amanda's been a big help around the house."

When she reached for her cup of water again, he leaned over and helped her sip through the straw. Her nurse had warned that Marie might tire easily. He gazed at Marie's face, searching for signs that she needed to rest.

She was starting to look drained. Already, her eyelids looked a bit heavy. "You should sleep now. We'll talk more when you wake up."

"Not yet. First . . . How is Viola? How was her trip to Belize? I didn't get to ask her much when she brought me my gown."

"From what I can tell, she said Belize was mighty different than Berlin. And I got the feeling that she didn't make the best first impression."

"That seems hard to imagine. Our Viola is always so put together and kind to others. I had hoped that everything would go smoothly." Marie frowned. "Is she going to go back? Maybe she'll want to live with us while Ed is away. Some married missionaries live apart, I think she mentioned."

That was so like his lovely, tenderhearted wife. She wanted the children nearby always—even when they weren't children anymore. "Well, Edward is scheduled to come home in three months. They plan to get married then . . . and then both go to Belize."

"August will be a *gut* time for a wedding," she said drowsily.

Unable to stop touching her, he picked up her hand and squeezed it gently. "You know what they say—*any* time is a *gut* time for a wedding."

She smiled at that, then shifted a bit. Yawned.

"Are you ready for a break, Marie? I don't want to tire you out."

"I am getting sleepy," she admitted. "But we still have one child to go. How is Elsie?"

For once, Elsie was the one he was most worried about. For a moment, he thought about not telling Marie about Elsie's latest development, but he decided no good would come from keeping any more secrets. "She went on a buggy ride with our new neighbor Landon Troyer, the other evening."

"That's nice. I bet she enjoyed that."

"No, you don't understand. It was a date."

Her eyes widened. "Oh my goodness. She's being courted? By a man?"

He chuckled at her phrasing. "I'm afraid so."

"She shouldn't be courting. Should she?"

"It's out of our hands. She's a grown woman."

"But her eyesight—"

"Is a concern. I agree. We told her she should talk to Landon and tell him about her eyes."

"Did she?"

"She won't talk to us, but I don't think so."

"My goodness. I need to get out of this hospital. I need to see Amanda. And meet Goldie . . ." Her voice was a bit slurred.

"You do need to get home. We need you *verra* much. But that is why you need to rest, dear. Why don't you close your eyes for a bit?"

"But we haven't even talked about you. Or your parents . . . Or Lorene . . " She yawned, cutting off her other words.

"We will discuss all of that later. That's the best thing about our life now, Marie. We have all the time in the world to talk and plan."

After another yawn, she opened her eyes halfway. "You really are back, aren't you? And . . . And you won't leave me again?"

He was back, both mentally and physically. As he watched Marie fall into a peaceful slumber, he was never so glad to have made that difficult call to seek help.

"I am back," he whispered, his voice hoarse with emotion. "Now, dear Marie, don't fret. I promise, I don't plan to ever leave you again."

chapter twelve

The house was in an uproar. Marie was due to come home the next morning, and everyone had a different idea about what to do to prepare for her return. After watching far too many of her offspring discuss, plan, argue, and stew, Lovina knew it was time to get involved.

Her many children and grandchildren would probably never admit it, but sometimes they still needed her to be in charge.

As the voices rose to an uncomfortable pitch, Lovina held up a hand. "That, children, is enough."

And, just like when she was far younger and had a houseful of *kinner*, the room fell silent.

She grinned. It was nice to know that she could still create order out of chaos.

Her second oldest son, Sam, stared at her like she'd lost her mind. "Mamm, did you just call us children? I'm forty-seven, you know."

She fought back a sigh. That boy never could hold his tongue. "Samuel, are you talking back to me?"

"*Nee*, Mamm."

Viola started to snicker, but Lovina put her fiercest glare on her face. Just as she'd hoped, Viola's expression turned contrite.

Now that the troublemakers had been tamed, the group stopped talking and waited for her to speak.

Pleased, she exhaled and began doing what she did best—ordering everyone around. "Elsie has been holding this household together long enough. I agree that we all need to do our part, but this is ridiculous." Pointing to Amanda, Viola, and their cousin Beth, she said, "You girls are in charge of your parents' room. With your mother being so sick, everything needs to be spic-and-span and fresh. After that, clean up the front room and the bathroom, too. *Jah?*"

"Yes, Mommi," Beth said obediently.

Satisfied, she turned to her daughter and daughters-in-law. "Lorene, Rachel, and Mary Beth, you are in charge of the kitchen. Plan three days of menus, and divide up the work. When the girls finish their cleaning, they can help you."

She paused for breath, and for good measure, cast a hard look on them. The women might be in their forties and mothers of adults, too, but sometimes they needed to be reminded of who was in charge. "Does that sound reasonable?"

"*Jah*, Mamm," Lorene said.

"*Gut.*" Now she turned to the men. "Peter, show the men what needs to be done outside, then go back to your wife."

"Are you sure, Mamm? Would you rather take a turn at the hospital?"

Though the idea of sitting with Marie was tempting, she knew her company wasn't what her daughter-in-law needed. "I've sat in my fair share of hospitals over the years, son. Besides, I am clearly needed here. This *haus* is on the verge of falling apart."

"We haven't been doing that bad of a job," Lorene muttered.

"Hmmph." Lovina folded her arms over her chest and did her best to look mighty put upon, practically daring them all to refute that.

Though she spied a couple of sardonic looks sneakily sent to each other, no one dared argue with that statement.

Until two of her boys grinned. "You haven't lost your touch, Mamm," Aden said around a smile.

Samuel chuckled. "You still can have me shaking in my boots."

She almost smiled. Instead, she raised her chin a bit, then eyed them the way she used to when they'd left their wooden blocks all over the floor. "*Gut*," she said crisply. Then she clapped her hands. "Well, off you all go. Time stands still for no one."

One by one, each went to his or her designated area, until only Regina remained by her side.

"Mommi Lovina?" she said while giving her apron a good tug.

Bending down, Lovina allowed her stern expression to soften as she met her sweet adopted great-granddaughter's face. "Yes, dear?"

"Are you mighty angry at all of us?"

Falling to one knee, she shook her head. "My goodness. I'm not angry at all. I was just pretending to be tough."

Hope blossomed in her eyes. "Truly?"

"*Jah*." Reaching out, she gave little Regina a quick hug. "I knew if I didn't act stern they'd do something foolish and come up with their own plan. They may be old, but they're not so old that I can't tell them what to do."

She giggled. "You even told my *mamm* what to do. And you called everyone *kinner*!"

"She might be your mother, but she's a child to me. They all are." Solemnly winking as she straightened, Lovina added, "But she listens *gut*, don't she?"

Regina nodded, then giggled again as she tugged on Lovina's apron again. "Mommi?"

"Yes, dear?"

"Can I help, too? Or am I too little?"

"You are never too little to be of use." Holding out her hand, she said, "Come with me. Regina. I have a mighty important job in mind for you."

Regina slipped her little hand in hers. "What?"

"I want you to come with me to the *dawdi haus.*"

Her eyes widened. "What's there?"

"Dawdi Aaron and a new puzzle."

"You want me to work on a puzzle with Dawdi?"

"Oh, yes. He can't put it together by himself. He's old, you know."

Practically skipping by her side, Regina said, "I like being with Dawdi Aaron."

"He likes being with you, too. I bet we could even make you both some hot chocolate."

"I love hot chocolate." Chuckling, Lovina opened the door and led the way to her little *haus* in the back of the bustling one. As Regina grabbed her hand, she murmured, "I love you, Mommi Lovina."

Stopping, Lovina knelt down and gave Regina another hug. "I love you, too." As she felt her great-granddaughter's slim arms wrap around her neck, Lovina's heart filled with love . . . and regret.

What she and Aaron weren't telling anyone was that while everyone was getting busy for Marie to come home, she and Aaron were packing to leave.

As much as it pained her to be leaving her family, it had to be done.

They planned to leave on the next bus to Lancaster County, which was in two days' time.

She knew it wasn't the greatest timing with Marie just out of the hospital. But some things couldn't be put off any longer. After all, they'd been ignored far too long already.

Another day, another job. After they'd overseen the staining of the Market Street house, Landon and Daniel passed the sealing on to Zip and Craig.

Now they were in an old home from the turn of the century that a fancy *Englischer* had purchased a few months ago. The plumbers and electricians had done their parts, and now Landon and Daniel were hired to patch walls and refinish the floors.

Although they refinished floors all the time, patching and repairing walls was a far trickier job. Especially for Landon. He had to rely on Daniel to give him step-by-step instructions, which, after ten hours of sweating and being corrected, were pushing his patience to the limit.

"*Nee*, Landon. You're applying the plaster too thick," Daniel said over his shoulder. He stopped and scowled at him. "I tell ya, I should've had you work with Craig and asked for Zip to work with me. At least he can follow directions. You are doing everything wrong."

"If you gave me better directions, I could follow them easier," Landon snapped.

"If you listened, you might be able to follow them better," Daniel countered, not putting up with Landon's testiness for one moment.

Landon felt his temper burn and threaten to erupt. Unfortunately, knowing his brother was right didn't make things any easier.

He needed to get his mind back to what he was doing, and off the problems that were spinning in his head.

After counting to five, he sighed. "You're right. I haven't been listening like I should've. I'm sorry."

Immediately, Daniel's scowl smoothed. "What is wrong? You've been acting like an angry bear all morning, and for some reason, I don't think patching and plastering walls has made you so upset."

It wasn't that at all. "It's personal."

"So?" Daniel scoffed. "Since when don't we talk to each other about things that are personal? You're my brother."

Daniel was his older, wiser brother. And usually Landon would have unloaded his problems on him and asked his opinion. But right now he wasn't so sure he wanted to hear his brother's advice. Even more important, he didn't want to risk creating a rift between them if he ignored what advice his brother provided.

Attempting to brush aside his worries, he shrugged. "Don't worry about it. It's just something I have to work out on my own."

Putting down the crowbar he'd been holding, Daniel nodded. "*Jah*, you could probably work out this personal problem on your own. That is true. But . . . if you don't mind me saying so? It ain't going so well for you."

That statement was so true, Landon couldn't help but grin. "You may have a point."

"I know I do. So? What's going on? I can only imagine that it has to do with Elsie," he said. "Only a woman can make a man feel like he's tied up in knots."

"It actually does concern Elsie." He should have known that his brother would be able to read his mind.

"What's wrong? I thought you had a nice time with her?"

With reluctance, he answered. "I did. I mean, I thought I did."

"Why are you making it so complicated? If you had fun, you did."

"Something happened afterward."

"What happened? Did she decide she didn't like you?" he joked.

"*Nee*. It's, uh, something else. Something important."

"You're driving me crazy. What happened?"

"Her brother told me something about her that she hadn't shared with me."

"Well, what did he say?"

Daniel's exasperation mirrored Landon's own frustration with himself. "Roman said Elsie's vision is fading. Or becoming blurry or something."

"You've told me she wears glasses."

"Yes, but it's more than that," Landon said. "He said in a few years she'll be completely blind."

All traces of levity left Daniel's voice. "Landon, that's terrible news."

"I agree." Noticing how dejected his brother looked, Landon shook his head with a sad smile. "You're wearing almost the same expression I imagine I was wearing when Roman first told me."

"Is he sure about this?"

Landon nodded. Now that he was sharing his load, he could breathe easier. "Elsie has thick glasses, but Roman said they don't help as much as most people think. I guess she's been losing her vision slowly for years and has learned to make adjustments for it. He thinks she'll be completely blind one day soon. I feel *verra* bad for her."

Daniel whistled low. "I sure am sorry, Landon."

"This is Elsie's disease, not my problem." But even as he said the words, he knew that wasn't true. He was starting to really care about her. And even if nothing became of the two of them, he certainly didn't want Elsie to face a future like the one Roman described.

"Thank goodness Roman told you the truth about her. You know, before it was too late."

Though he'd just been thinking that very thing, a small twinge of uneasiness crept into him. "Before it was too late?"

"Sure. I mean, before you did something stupid and really started to like her. Or worse, fell in love. Now you can start considering other women in town."

"She's going blind, not becoming dangerous," he snapped.

Daniel looked at him strangely. "Why are you getting angry? I'm only supporting you. I mean, you wouldn't want to marry a woman with so many problems, would you?"

"Daniel, I did really like her."

"But you're going to have to forget about her, though— right? I mean, you're not going to see her anymore now, are you?"

He hadn't planned to see her again. In fact, the morning after Roman's visit, when he'd woken up, he'd been determined to stay as far away from Elsie Keim as possible.

But now, hearing his brother talk about her like this? When he hadn't even met her? Well, it did something to his insides that he couldn't deny.

He felt like leaping to her defense.

"I might see her again," he said. "She really is a sweet woman. Pretty, too." Then he added something that had been nagging him since he'd decided not to court her any-more. "To be honest, I would feel pretty horrible if I never saw her again because of something that's not her fault."

Daniel looked incredulous. "Landon, you can't be serious. All you're going to do is hurt her feelings if you lead her on. That's almost cruel."

"Who said anything about leading her on?"

"Landon, think about it. You can't court a woman who can't help you, who can't manage a house or raise your chil-dren. You have a job where you're away from home for hours at a time, sometimes even days!"

Everything Daniel said was true. But another part of him ached to put aside reason. Ached to be the person in Elsie's life who didn't define her by her blindness

And the only way to figure out if he could be that person was to go see her again.

"I'm going to stop by her house tomorrow and talk to her."

"You're making a mistake. Leading her on when you don't have any intention of becoming serious is terribly mean."

It would be mean. Heartless, even. But he was starting to suspect that, despite what his brain was trying to tell him, his heart had decided that he might already be serious about Elsie.

"Maybe I am becoming serious."

"You hardly know her."

"What I do know of her, I really like."

After a long, judgmental look, Daniel picked up his crow-bar. "We got a lot of work to do. We better get busy."

"Sure. Fine." He probably shouldn't have even brought up Elsie's disability or his feelings about her. But talking about it out loud made him realize a few things.

A few pretty important things about himself.

Though the tension between him and Daniel had returned, Landon knew it would eventually blow over. They were brothers first.

And even if things did stay tense for a few days, he was okay with that. In fact, for the first time in days, he felt at peace. Now, at least, Landon was making plans for a future that he could be proud of, not be ashamed of.

And that was something he could live with.

chapter thirteen

When Elsie's *daed* escorted her *mamm* inside, the household erupted in celebration—even Goldie. Elsie found herself chuckling as Goldie bounded toward her mother with a series of happy barks.

Leaning down, her mother gently patted the dog between her ears before smiling at the family that surrounded her. Her blue eyes looked bright and her cheeks pink. To Elsie, she looked perfectly beautiful.

"I've never seen such a commotion about something so little," Mamm marveled.

"You being in the hospital wasna something 'little,' Marie," Lorene said. "All of us were worried about you."

"Mighty worried," her husband, John, added.

Still holding Daed's elbow, Mamm's expression softened. "Well, worry no longer. I'm home now."

"Thank goodness," Viola said. "And Mamm, just so you know, you aren't allowed to get sick again. We can't take it."

"I'll certainly do my best not to." Mamm walked toward the kitchen table and oohed and ahhed over the amount of food set out. "What a feast!" Leaning forward a bit, her eyes brightened. "Is that a coconut cream pie?"

"It certainly is," Beth said. "Amanda and I made it and whoopee pies this morning."

"It all looks *wunderbaar*. My goodness, you all have been

busy." She gestured to the spotless counters, the sparkling-clean windows, the polished furniture. "The *haus* looks beautiful." With a mock frown, she added, "I didn't know you all could clean so well."

"We had no choice," Sam said. "Mamm might be a great-grandmother, but she hasn't lost her touch for ordering us about."

Elsie chuckled as her grandmother attempted to look fierce but couldn't quite manage it.

"After a little bit of direction, you all did *gut*," she said. "I'm proud of you."

"Does that mean we can finally eat something?" Aden asked after a moment. "I'm starving."

Like locusts, the crowd of people grabbed paper plates and swarmed the table. There was much joshing and teasing as Elsie's uncles vied for position in line, as if they were small boys instead of grown men.

With everyone occupied, Elsie walked to her mother's side. "I am glad you're back home, Mamm. We were worried about you."

Gently hugging her, her mother said, "I'm glad to be home, too, my sweet Elsie. After all the hustle and bustle ends, you and me are going to have to catch up."

There was only one thing that her mother could be referring to, and that was Landon. "Of course," Elsie said awkwardly.

"Maybe we could speak later on this afternoon?"

Thankfully, her father interrupted before Elsie could reply. "Marie, let's feed you before everyone eats all the food." Her mother looked chagrined, but let herself be guided back to the table.

Not hungry, Elsie moved to the kitchen. It was so nice to

have her *mamm* home, and somehow it finally made it feel right to have all the family cluttering up the house. But as she gazed out the kitchen window, a sadness claimed her chest. While she hoped that her new friendship with Landon meant that the dreams of her heart might be coming true, she couldn't deny that her life might be far different from her mother's, her grandmother's, or even Viola's. If she never married or had children, she'd never have moments like this.

She'd never have a husband to fuss over her after an illness or on a special day.

She might never have a noisy house full of children and grandchildren eager—or not so eager—to do her bidding.

She might be doomed to staying in the background. As the *blind* daughter. The *needy* aunt. The *frail* great-aunt who required extra help.

Nothing sounded worse.

Unable to help herself, she stewed on that bleak future while she brewed tea and coffee. When the family moved to the hearth room, surrounding her mother, Elsie still wasn't ready to be a part of the crowd. Instead, she occupied herself with clearing the table, throwing out paper plates, and washing a few of the dishes.

Eventually, Beth, Viola, and Amanda joined her. She chatted with them a bit as they continued to wash and dry dishes. But though she enjoyed the girls' conversation, she kept finding herself listening for her mother's laugh. Then, she would know her mother was truly back.

Elsie smiled as she listened to her mother's melodic voice, followed by a low chuckle. It felt as familiar as an old, comfortable robe and as precious as the quilt her grandmother had made her when she was a little girl.

Some things were like that. Perfect just the way they were.

Then, all too soon, Elsie heard her father firmly announce that the party was over and it was time for her *mamm* to get some rest.

As if she sensed Elsie's feelings, Viola walked to her side and linked her hand through her arm. "It feels *gut* to have Mamm home, ain't so?"

"*Jah.*"

Stepping a little closer, Viola lowered her voice. "Elsie . . . are you all right? You look a little blue."

"I'm fine. There's simply a lot going on, you know?"

"I know," Viola said. Her words were agreeable, but everything about her body language said that she wasn't buying Elsie's weak excuse. Tilting her head to one side, she stared at Elsie intently. "Is that all that's wrong?" she prodded. "We can talk later, if you want."

"I don't need to talk about anything. I'm fine."

"All right, if you're sure?"

"I'm positive." No way was she going to share her depressing thoughts with her sister. Viola had so much to be happy about that Elsie feared she'd only make her twin feel guilty about how she was blessed with good eyesight and a future that looked bright. Viola was preparing to make her own way in the world as a missionary's wife in Belize. Her future couldn't be more different from Elsie's.

chapter fourteen

Less than an hour later, Aden, Rachel, Beth, and her children had left, anxious to get back home to Indiana. On their heels, Aunt Lorene and her husband, John, had also gone home, along with Sam, his wife, and their three children.

Amanda had taken Regina to her room for a nap, Roman was out in the barn with their *daed* to feed and groom the horses, and Viola had gone upstairs, a new letter from her Edward in her hands that the mailman had just delivered.

Things felt almost . . . normal.

When Marie woke from her nap and insisted that she didn't want to sit alone for another minute, Elsie and her grandparents pulled three chairs into the bedroom.

Marie had slipped on a fluffy blue robe and looked almost like her old self propped up on a pile of down pillows.

"Tell me about everything, you three," she said. "I couldn't keep up with all the talking and chattering when the whole family was here."

"What do you want to know?" Elsie asked. "Daed said that he filled you in on the latest news when you were at the hospital."

"Oh, he did. But you know how your father is. Why give me a paragraph when he could shorten a story into two sentences?"

Elsie chuckled. That was true. Her father never had been much of a storyteller. "That sounds like you, Dawdi."

Her grandfather's cheeks brightened. "Perhaps that's where Peter got it from?"

As Elsie had hoped, her grandmother took over the announcements, and steadily filled her mother in with all the latest news. Little by little, she found herself relaxing as her grandmother shared stories about Regina and the other great-grandchildren.

They talked a little about the idea of a wedding party for Roman and Amanda, but Elsie noticed Lovina didn't sound too enthusiastic about it.

"Mommi, I would have thought you would have enjoyed planning a party for Roman and Amanda," Elsie said.

For the first time, her grandparents looked uncomfortable.

Before her mother could speak, Elsie blurted. "What's wrong?"

"Well," Lovina answered. "There is something we need to tell you all."

"What is it?" her mother asked.

Dawdi cleared his throat. "Lovina and I wanted to wait to tell you until you'd had a chance to settle in."

"It sounds serious," Marie said.

After yet another slow, meaningful glance at her grandmother, Dawdi sighed, resolved that the time to share his news had come. "Lovina and I are heading to Pennsylvania tomorrow morning."

Her mother looked as startled as Elsie felt.

"I'm mighty surprised," Marie said. "How long have you been planning this?"

"Only a few days. We wanted to wait until you were better, but we're anxious to get back there."

Elsie frowned. "I thought you both had finally come to peace with your past?"

Looking uncomfortable, her grandmother faltered with her reply. "Dawdi and I decided it is high time that the two of us face some things that happened long ago. It's past time, if you want to know the truth," she added in a rush. "And we need to see Sara, too."

Her grandfather nodded. "We need to pay her a visit." Clearing this throat, he added, "We should have visited her long ago."

Her mother gazed at them for a long moment, then shrugged. "All right. I wish you safe travels."

Elsie gaped at her mother. That was it? *Safe travels?* That was all the questioning she had? She couldn't see well, but even she could tell that both of her grandparents looked like they were hiding yet more information.

Well, she, for one, was not satisfied with these vague answers. "Dawdi, how long are you going to be gone?"

"I'm not sure. At least a couple of days." He scratched his head. "Maybe even a week? Ten days? As long as we need to, I suppose. I'm sure the Lord will let us know when the time is right to stay . . . and to go."

"It feels so sudden."

"Well, we didn't tell anyone of our plans because we didn't want to leave when you were in the hospital," Dawdi said. "Once we heard you'd recovered, we didn't want to wait any longer."

Her grandmother frowned. "To be honest, now doesn't seem like the best time, either. You're not on your feet yet, Marie." Then she looked at Elsie's grandfather. "However, I fear we have no choice. We've paid for the tickets. Plus, if we don't go now . . ."

"We might postpone it yet again," Dawdi finished. "It is time to head north. I'm sorry, Marie."

"There's nothing to be apologizing for," her mother said. "Believe me, I understand. And yes, it is time."

"Mommi, who is going with you and Dawdi?"

"Why, no one," her grandmother said.

"But don't you need help?"

"Not at all. We aren't so old that we can't travel without assistance, Elsie."

"I didn't mean that. But don't you want some support? Maybe you will need someone with you to lean on."

Her grandfather looked at her pointedly. "Are you offering, Elsie?"

"Yes, if you would like me to come with you."

"Oh, Elsie. You would go, wouldn't you?" her grandmother murmured. "It's kind of you to offer, but you can't come, dear. Aaron and I have to do this on our own. We must."

There it was again, that vague sense that there was more to their story than they were sharing. "Why?"

Mommi's eyes narrowed. "It's not your place to question, Elsie."

"You're needed here, Elsie. As is everyone else," her grandfather said. "Besides, I don't think this is something for the family. It's only for your grandmother and me." He stood up. "Now that we've told you, Marie, I'm going to tell Peter and Roman. Then we're going to need to finish packing and get ready."

"Our bus leaves bright and early in the morning." Mommi stood up and shook out her skirts. "Thank you for understanding, Marie."

As her grandparents shuffled out of the room, Elsie reached for her mother's hand. "Mamm, I can't remember a time when this family has been coming and going so much."

"That's because there hasn't been a time. But I guess that's to be expected. Life brings challenges. Some wonderful-*gut*, like Roman and Amanda getting married. And others like my illness. You can't plan for it all."

Her mother's words gave her the courage to share her own news. She knew her family had probably clued her in but she knew her *mamm*. She'd want to hear it all from her directly. "Mamm, Landon Troyer took me out for a buggy ride last weekend."

"I heard a little about that. Did you have a *gut* time?"

"I did." She bit her lip. "I'm kind of surprised that I haven't heard from him since, though. I would have thought he'd stop by again."

"Perhaps he doesn't want to seem too eager."

"You think?"

"Maybe. Men are silly like that."

It struck Elsie that this was the first conversation she'd actually had about dating. "Mamm, you're the first person not to tell me that I shouldn't have gone."

"If I've learned anything over the last few months, it's that it's time to stop judging and guessing and advising. Sometimes the Lord just wants us to listen and offer support. He gives us two ears and just one mouth, you know. Now, has your time with Landon made you happy?"

"It did," she said quickly.

"If it made you happy, then you deserve to be happy. That's enough for me."

Elsie felt tears prick her eyes. She really needed someone to believe in her. She'd needed someone to be happy for her.

"I'm so glad you're back home, Mamm."

"No one is happier than me, dear." She smiled weakly, then closed her eyes. "But I am a little sleepy."

"I'll stay with you until you fall asleep."

"There's no need."

"I'm happy to sit with you."

"You always have been the best daughter," her mother said sleepily.

Elsie laughed. That phrase had been something their mother had said time and again over the years to her and Viola.

Maybe things really were getting back to normal.

As Peter watched his father's slightly stooped form exit the barn, he picked up the old broom and gave it a hard swipe across the dusty ground. "Just when I think everything's back to normal, something else happens. Now your grandparents are off to Pennsylvania tomorrow morning."

Roman shrugged his shoulders. His son always did seem to keep his wits about him, no matter what happened. It allowed him to stay out of the drama that seemed to always plague Peter's complicated family.

"I'm going to worry about them something awful. If they would have waited a bit, Sam or I could have gone with them."

"So you could help them . . . or find out what they're going to do?"

Peter chuckled as he placed the broom against the wall. "Both, I suppose. Ever since we discovered your grandmother was once English I've felt like I don't really know my parents at all. Now I want to do everything I've never dared to do before. I want to ask them prying questions and learn everything I can." He gave the ground a couple more hard swipes with the broom.

"I guess we'll have to hope they feel like telling us their news when they get home."

"I'll be disappointed if they use this trip as another excuse to keep secrets."

"I think we're beyond that, Daed, don't you think?"

"I hope so." Though it wasn't all that hot out, Peter realized he'd broken out in a sweat. He wiped his brow. "I must have gotten out of shape in that treatment center. I'm feeling winded already."

Roman nodded, but then his eyes narrowed as he gazed over Peter's shoulder. "Hold on. I cannot believe he had the nerve to show up here."

Peter turned around and looked out the open barn door. "Who are you talking about?"

"Landon."

"Ah. So he has returned." With a faint smile, he murmured, "Hmm. I wonder who he came to see . . . you or Elsie?"

"It better be me," Roman said. "I went over and talked to him a couple of days ago."

"What about?"

"About Elsie. I told him that she was going blind." He shook his head in obvious frustration. "I thought he understood that I didn't want him to see Elsie anymore."

Though Peter had been concerned about Elsie seeing the young man next door, he was focused on trying to convince Elsie to change her mind—not talking to Landon.

"You shouldn't have done that, son."

"Why? Elsie needs someone looking out for her."

"But you weren't doing that. You were getting into her business. There's a difference."

Roman shrugged off his warning hand. "Daed, remember it was Elsie who got on the phone and called Amanda and invited her and Regina out here. It's a little too late for you to worry about us getting involved in each other's lives. It's obviously what we do."

"That was different, Roman," he warned. "That was to help your relationship, not put on the brakes."

Still watching Landon, Roman's voice rose a bit. "Look at that, he isn't even walking over this way. He's going directly to the front door, just like he's been invited or something. I better go see what he wants."

"Roman, if you're not careful, you're going to get them both upset with you."

"They might be upset now, but they'll each thank me one day. I'm doing the right thing, Daed."

As Roman marched out the door, Peter picked up the broom, but after a halfhearted swipe, he set it against the wall. He was far more interested in Roman's trek to the house, where he was undoubtedly getting ready to stick his nose into things that weren't his business.

Imagining the words that were about to be exchanged, he whistled low. He had a feeling things were about to get ugly, indeed.

What had happened to his even-keeled son who always kept to himself?

chapter fifteen

He'd come back.

"Landon, I'm so happy to see you," Elsie said as she laid his coat over the back of a kitchen chair.

Then, realizing she sounded a bit too exuberant, she attempted to temper her enthusiasm. "Of course, it's a bit of a surprise to see you so early. I thought you worked late every night."

"Not every night. Since we stopped early, I decided to take a chance and see if you were home. I'm glad you are," he added as he followed her through the house. "I hope it isn't a bad time?"

"Not at all." She thought his voice sounded a bit strained, but she brushed it off, blaming her nerves instead of his manner.

She was nervous. But excited, too. As they walked, she was thankful that most of the family had already left and that her brother and father were in the barn.

She didn't want a single thing to happen to disrupt the moment. She had a caller!

When they sat down next to each other on the overstuffed sofa in the living room, she couldn't help but recall the day Edward had come over to see Viola, his dog, Gretta, in tow. They'd all teased Viola of course.

But Elsie vividly recalled feeling more than a little jealous.

That day, she'd believed what Roman and Viola had always thought to be true: that she would never have a caller of her own.

"Have you been busy with work?" she asked politely.

He shrugged. "Busy enough."

"Um, how is your *haus*? I mean, is everything going well with your new home?"

"It is fine." He folded his hands together and let them hang while he braced his arms on his knees. "Actually, Elsie, I came over here for a specific reason."

"Oh?"

"Yeah." He straightened. "Something happened since we went for a buggy ride."

He's met someone else. He's realized that he really didn't like me after all. Forcing herself to keep her expression neutral, she nodded. "I see. What happened?"

"Your brother came to see me."

With those six words, all thoughts of romance fled, replaced quickly with a burning feeling of betrayal. "Roman went to see you . . . about me?"

"*Jah.*" He inhaled, then exhaled in a rush. "He told me about your disease, Elsie."

"I . . . I see." She was struggling with her anger, her hurt, all the feelings churning inside her, when she heard the kitchen door open and footsteps on the wooden floor striding their way.

Scrambling to her feet, she faced the doorway, not a doubt in her head about who had suddenly decided to join them.

Next to her, Landon stood as well.

The moment Roman strode into sight, he scowled at the two of them. "Landon, what are you doing here?"

"I believe it's fairly evident," Landon retorted. His tone

was cool and angry, and his stance looked aggressive, definitely not cowed by her brother's anger.

It was a side of him she'd never seen before.

Roman acted like she wasn't there. "Landon, I told you not to court Elsie."

"I know what you said."

Folding his arms over his chest, Roman tapped a foot. "Then why are you here?"

Incredulous at her brother's actions and tone, she couldn't help but interrupt. "Roman, how could you do such a thing?" Already she could feel tears welling in her eyes, hear her voice quiver with frustration. Oh, but that was not the way she wanted to handle this!

Her brother ignored her, but Landon immediately glanced her way. He must not have liked what he saw, because he pursed his lips before turning back to Roman. "I don't answer to you," he said quietly.

Feeling the tension rise in the room, Elsie knew she needed to do something and fast. "You need to leave us alone," she said, giving her brother a firm stare.

Even with her poor eyesight, she could see that she'd caught him off guard.

"Elsie, I know you're upset. We'll talk about this later."

"We surely will not! I don't want to talk to you about this. Or anything at all, for that matter."

"But—"

As Roman continued to stand in front of her, ready to issue more orders, Elsie felt one of the tears she'd been trying so hard to keep at bay fall down her cheek.

She was so embarrassed, so humiliated. Why, Landon probably couldn't wait to run out of their house and never look back!

And since there was no going back, she let her temper fly, the temper she hadn't even realized she had. "Roman, now!"

Beside her, Landon reached out and patted her back. "It's okay, Elsie," he whispered. "I promise."

Still glaring at her interfering brother, she shook her head. "*Nee.* It is definitely *not* okay."

To her dismay, Roman still stood there. As she eyed him, she tried to think of a way to convince him to leave without making the situation even worse.

Was there any way to salvage the conversation?

"Roman?" Amanda said from the entrance of the dining room. "What are you doing?"

"Nothing you need to worry about."

After glancing at Elsie and Landon, she clicked her tongue. "I think otherwise." Walking to her husband's side, she wrapped one slim hand around his elbow and tugged. "I truly am sorry, Elsie," she murmured before directing all her attention to her husband. "Roman, you need to come with me upstairs."

When he hesitated, she hardened her voice. "Right away."

At last, he turned and walked out. When they were out of sight, Elsie felt more tears threatening to spill onto her cheeks.

This had to be one of the worst moments of her life. Even harder to bear than the day she'd gotten glasses and been so excited to show her family, only to realize they saw them not as the gift they were, but as a symbol of her handicap.

Wearily, she sat down and waited for Landon to turn and leave.

Instead, he sat down beside her, this time a little closer.

"You're staying?" she asked in surprise.

"I am . . . unless you want me to leave, too?"

"You don't want to get out of here?" She would. She would have run out the door as fast as her feet could carry her!

"I came over to talk to you," he said gently. "That's what I intend to do. If your brother will let us do that," he added with a roll of his eyes.

"I am so sorry about my *bruder*."

"You never have to apologize for him. I have a brother, too," he said with a low chuckle. "I love Daniel, but even he can get carried away with his own agenda sometimes."

"Is he older, too?"

"He is, but not by much. Although, it hardly matters now. We're both adults."

"I'm glad I'm not the only one blessed with such a brother."

"I think older brothers are all the same everywhere. Though I hate to admit it, I know I've been a bit heavy-handed with my own sister, Mary." Turning more serious, he said, "Elsie, I do have questions about your disease. Are you willing to talk about it?"

"*Jah*." She was resigned.

"Talk to me, then. What is wrong with your eyes?"

"I have a disease called keratoconus. It means that my eyes are slowly failing me. Most folks that have this don't have troubles until their thirties or forties. But a small percentage somehow contract the disease at a young age. That's what happened to me. I was diagnosed when I was twelve."

"So . . . are you really going blind?"

"More or less." She ached to give him hope, to give them *both* hope. But sometimes there was nothing to say in the face of the hard truth.

She felt him scan her face, almost as if he were looking for flaws. "Can you see much now?"

"I can see, but a lot of what I see is hazy. I can't always see details." She bit her tongue as he nodded his understanding. Here she was, trying to be honest, but she was still glossing over the worst.

She couldn't see *any* details now. She couldn't read. Couldn't always judge people's expressions. Hardly ever saw stray toys on the floor. Doing something as simple as putting a key in a lock was almost impossible.

He breathed in deeply. "Is there, uh, anything else you need to tell me?"

"Only . . . only that it's just my eyes that have failed me, Landon. The rest of me is perfectly fine. And I'm more than two bad eyes," she said quickly. "I'm smart and I'm a hard worker."

He chuckled softly. "You sound as if you're applying for a job."

She winced, thinking he was right. "I sometimes feel as if no one sees me for who I am. They only see their fears about my future."

"Your family cares about you."

"I know. However, I'm not helpless. I can do things, especially if it's in a place where I'm comfortable. But the fact is . . . one day I won't be able to see much at all."

"What are you going to do then?"

"I suppose I'll figure out how to live with being technically blind," she said, almost surprising herself. "I don't want to sit and be coddled." Straightening her shoulders a bit, she added, "I'm not the first person to have this disease, Landon. I sure won't be the last. I need to learn to live with this disease, not simply be a victim of it."

She felt his gaze settle on her. She might have been imagining it, but it felt comforting and warm. Almost like a fond caress. Not the revulsion or pity that she'd half expected.

"Elsie, why didn't you tell me about your eyesight earlier? I let you walk to the door all by yourself. I could have escorted you."

"I didn't need your help walking to the door, Landon."

"Still, you should have told me. I had no idea."

There was no way she could easily explain how it felt to be around someone who saw her as completely normal. Knowing she wouldn't do justice to her feelings at the moment, she settled for an easy explanation. "We talked when you came over. You helped me with the laundry. We went on a buggy ride, Landon. That's it. I didn't know if you'd want to go on a second one."

She shrugged her shoulders. "Maybe you don't have anything about yourself that you're sometimes hesitant to share, but I wanted to wait to tell you, at least until I thought we might have something more."

"That makes a lot of sense."

"Does it?" She still couldn't believe that he'd sided with her against Roman, and that he hadn't bade her a quick good-bye after she'd told him the worst about herself.

"Elsie, I'm going to be real honest here. Ever since I first saw you, I knew I wanted to get to know you. Every time we've talked, I've enjoyed your company. Our time together the other night only made those feelings stronger for me."

"What are you saying?"

"I'm saying, if you'd like to go out with me again, if you'd like to spend more time together, I would like that. *Verra* much."

His words were honest—almost blunt. But what she noticed the most was that he wasn't adding limits or constraints to his request. "That's it?" she asked.

He smiled so broadly, even she could see his full mouth of white teeth. "Yeah. There's just one thing that I ask."

"What is that?"

"Please be honest with me. I can deal with anything if it's the truth." He clenched his hands together. "I once courted a woman who I liked a lot. I thought she was the one for me, you know?" When she nodded, he continued. "Anyway, it turned out that Tricia lied to me about quite a few things."

"That's horrible."

"I thought so. Anyway, because of that, I have to warn you that I'm kind of a stickler for the truth. Please don't lie to me, even if it's something small."

She thought about that and figured she could definitely agree with his stipulations. Feeling brave, she said, "If you can handle the truth about my vision, then I would like to get to know you better."

To her disbelief, he held out his hand. Whether to shake it, or to clasp it, she didn't know.

As she looked at his hand, reaching out to her, palm up, she felt flushed and flustered and tentative.

But she still placed her hand in his.

Then, to her surprise, he covered her hand with his other one and pressed their hands together. Warmth flowed through. It felt good to have her hand clasped in both of his. She felt almost protected.

And, even though she'd practically told him that she didn't need his protection, it felt safe to know she wasn't alone.

Before she knew it, he let go and stood up. "Elsie, would you care to go walking in Berlin tomorrow afternoon? We could stop and get a slice of pie or a cup of coffee."

"I'd like that."

He smiled. "*Gut.* I'm going to go now. You stay here, I'll walk myself out."

"Goodbye, Landon," she said softly.

He flashed her another smile, then left the room. Leaning back against the cushions of the couch, she heard his footsteps enter the kitchen, heard the rustle of him slipping on his coat, heard the back door open and close.

Only then did she stand up and walk up the stairs to her bedroom, where she shut the door firmly behind her. She finally had all the time she needed to do what mattered to her the most.

She silently gave a little cheer and raised her arms above her head. It had finally happened.

Landon Troyer liked her. He liked *her*.

It was a wonderful, wonderful day. The best ever.

chapter sixteen

It was late, probably too late to be sipping chamomile tea at the kitchen table and talking. But here they were, doing it anyway.

"It's been years since we've sat up late and talked, Aaron," Lovina mused. "It almost makes me nostalgic for the past."

Her husband smiled faintly. "I was thinking the same thing. Remember when our Sara used to get so sick with croup?"

"We spent hours sipping tea and walking the halls of that house with her in our arms." Lovina took another fortifying sip of tea, hoping to cover up the pain. It had been years since she'd seen their eldest daughter. Years ago, they moved to Pennsylvania. To her amazement, Sara and Jay had decided to settle in Bird-in-Hand. Their home lay just a few miles from the bank where she and Aaron had met. The one place Lovina and Aaron had never wanted to see again. As the years passed, Sara had given birth to three children in five years, making it next to impossible for her family to travel back to Ohio.

Repeatedly, Sara had asked Lovina to travel north to visit. But of course she never had.

Until now.

"Do you have Sara's phone number packed in our bags?" she asked tentatively. "I should call her when we're in Lancaster County."

Aaron shook his head. "I thought you had your address book in your purse. You'd better go put it inside there now."

Quietly, she slipped her worn address book and calendar in her purse.

"Then we should get some sleep."

"In a moment." Though she knew she was only procrastinating, she murmured, "What do you think about Elsie and her man?"

He chuckled. "To be honest, the first thing I thought was that Got is always right."

That was exactly the last thing she'd expected him to say. "What do you mean?"

"That for all our lives, the whole family has tried to do what we think is best for our Elsie. We've gone to the *doktohs*, talked about plans, protected her. Talked until we were blue in the face about *what we should do about Elsie*."

"We prayed, too," Lovina pointed out.

"Oh, yes, we prayed. And it seems as if our prayers were answered. Elsie is ready and willing to manage her own life . . . with the Lord's help. I think it's time we all took a step backward and let the inevitable happen. Our Lord won't let sweet Elsie down."

Lovina felt her heart soften as she gazed at her husband's calm expression. For too long Aaron had been content to make statements and then walk away without having to explain himself.

She was finding that she liked hearing his reasons for doing things.

"I hope you're right."

To her surprise, Aaron picked up her empty teacup, rinsed it in the sink, then set it on the rack to dry. "I hope so, too," he said lightly. "Come, Lovina. We'd best get some sleep. Morning waits for no man . . . or woman."

She was still chuckling about that bit of wisdom when sleep claimed her.

As discussed, Landon and Elsie talked on the phone, and since he was working in Berlin, they'd decided to meet in town instead of him coming to her house first. She'd gotten a ride with her sister.

His two hours with her had been pleasant. More than pleasant. As they walked along the streets of Berlin, they talked about everything and nothing. And when they went to a local bakery and both chose thick slices of chocolate cream pie, they'd laughed.

All too soon, she left with her aunt.

And he drove his buggy to the Berlin Public Library.

He needed to get some answers, and to his way of thinking, there was only one way to do that: read.

After leaving the Keims' home, he'd spent most of the night rehashing the conversation with Elsie in his mind. Ironically, learning more about Elsie's condition had increased his interest in her instead of diminishing it. She was brave and seemed to approach her disability with grace instead of scorn.

Her understanding that she'd been afflicted with something she couldn't change but would learn to deal with had awed him.

It also made him want to learn more about keratoconus. The word was hard to say and even harder to spell.

But more important, it represented a mystery to him. He needed answers.

But he didn't want to be the person in Elsie's life who peppered her with questions or made ignorant statements. Instead, he was determined to be one of the people in her life who supported her. Not by diminishing her abilities, but by acknowledging them—and then moving forward.

If he'd learned anything yesterday, it was that Elsie craved her independence as much as anyone else. Maybe more so, because she was forced to be dependent for some things. She also had a family who was used to doing things for her.

With that in mind, he'd spent more than an hour carefully writing down questions about eye diseases. Though he realized this first visit was the first of many he would take to the library for answers, he felt proud of himself for taking the first step.

As he entered the building on Elm Street, he walked right over to the librarian at the circulation desk.

"I need some information about eye diseases," he said bluntly.

The gray-haired lady's eyes lit up like she'd just been issued a challenge. "I can help you with that. Do you want books, or to use the computer?"

"I'm not sure how to use the computer."

"I can help you with that."

"That would be better than a book?"

"Maybe to start with," she said easily as she walked over to one of the computer terminals lining the back wall. "The information will be more current and, depending on what you need, it's sometimes easier to understand."

"That's what I need then," he said, hoping he sounded far more confident and self-assured than he felt.

As he followed the lady through the maze of books, he

kept his eyes averted from the other patrons in the build-ing. There was the usual mix of Amish, Mennonite, and English here, like in just about every store or public area of Berlin.

But he did notice that he was in the definite minority when it came to age. Mostly he saw people far older or younger than him.

But perhaps that made sense. After all, he usually was working in the middle of the day.

After he took a seat, he listened carefully as the librar-ian clicked on her mouse to different screens. Next thing he knew, he was unfolding his list of questions, borrowing one of the library's pencils, and trying to understand all about macular degeneration.

Slowly, Elsie's problems became more apparent and easier to understand.

He also began to realize that Elsie had been kind to him while giving him her explanations about her disease. Most folks he read about in the case studies talked of fear and a little bit of pain, too.

They also talked about how emotionally difficult it was to lose their independence.

More often than not, Landon felt himself staring at the screen, lost in thought. Now that he knew a little more, he had more questions to ask Elsie instead of less.

Carefully, he wrote down his new questions, hoping the Lord would give him the tools to ask Elsie without being too intrusive.

Just as he was clicking on the mouse and clearing the screens, the librarian approached him.

"Did you find the information you needed?" she asked kindly.

"Some. I bet I'll be back with more questions soon, though." He rubbed a hand down his cheeks. "I hope I'll be able to get back on that computer site."

"If I'm not here, someone else can help you." She smiled encouragingly. "That's what we're here for, you know."

"*Danke.*"

She paused. "Do you happen to have a friend who has this disorder?"

"Yes."

"I'm not sure what your church district would think, but we have a lot of books on tape."

"What does that mean?"

She walked him over to a large area with row after row of plastic cases. "Some of our patrons who don't see too well rely on listening to books instead of reading them." She paused. "Is your friend a man or a woman?"

"A woman."

"We have a lot of fiction titles that she might enjoy. You might mention that to her."

As he looked at the rows of audio books, he made a quick decision. "Could I check two of them out, to show her?"

"Of course. Do you have a library card?"

"No."

"But you live in Berlin?"

"I do."

"Then it will be no problem. Want me to pick out two popular titles?"

After he agreed, she picked out two cases with women on the covers, one who looked to be an Amish girl, the other a woman in an old-fashioned gown. Then he followed the lady to the counter, presented his identification card, and in no time was walking back to his buggy.

He drove toward the work site with a sense of satisfaction. He just hoped that when he saw Elsie that evening she would think he had done something nice, and that he wouldn't make her feel worse about things.

chapter seventeen

Elsie's grip on the phone cord was so tight, she was surprised the curly cord wasn't tearing in half. So far, her call to the doctor's office was taking far longer than she'd anticipated.

The receptionist kept getting interrupted by people in the office, and then she kept making mistakes with the doctor's schedule. It seemed no one could decide just how long Elsie's visit was going to take.

Through it all, Elsie tapped her fingers on the counter and looked at the open doorway furtively, praying for the family to give her some privacy and space.

But that was what happened when a person had to make a private phone call in the middle of the busiest room in the house. Then and there, she vowed to herself to have the house phone installed somewhere far more private than the kitchen whenever she had her own home.

At the moment, though, she had to make do with praying that the phone call would finish soon. It was bad enough that Amanda was standing again by her side. She couldn't bear for anyone else to overhear her conversation.

The receptionist's voice came on the line, but it was a different one than the one she'd started with. "Elsie, this is Jennifer. I'm sorry but Alice had to help someone here in the office. Could you tell me why you called?"

With barely controlled patience, she said, "I need to come

in and get my eyes checked. Alice said I needed to call back this week."

After a faint rustle of papers and clicks on the computer, Jennifer asked, "I'm sorry. I can't find those notes right here. Can you tell me specifically what is wrong?"

Feeling half resigned and half frightened to death, Elsie answered. "I think my vision's gotten worse." She lowered her voice. "A lot worse."

"Headaches?"

"Yes."

"Increased blurriness?"

"*Jah*." Elsie felt her pulse race. It was hard to be honest about the extent of her difficulties.

"Anything else?"

Elsie didn't know if she had the right words to describe what was happening. It was as if her eyes had finally decided that they'd had enough of struggling to see. "I'm just having trouble seeing," she said finally. "More than usual."

Now that she was being forced to explain her symptoms, Elsie felt her anxiety growing. Why had she waited to call?

"Hold on one more time please," Jennifer said, her tone now a bit more serious.

As she held the phone again, Elsie watched the doorway. Then felt her stomach fall to the floor as little Regina walked in.

"Hi, Elsie!" Regina said.

Elsie waved, but put a finger to her lips, making a universal "shh" sign.

"Do you want me to take her out?" Amanda whispered.

"*Jah*. That is, if you don't mind."

"Come on, Gina," Amanda said. "Let's go check on the horse for a few minutes before we have our snack."

Elsie breathed a sigh of relief when they left, just as Jennifer got back on the line. "Elsie, we just juggled some meetings around. Dr. Palmer can see you tomorrow at eleven. Will you be able to find transportation that quickly?" They were all used to her needing to find an English driver for appointments.

Elsie wasn't sure how she would arrange it that quickly, but she didn't want to back down now. If she did, she wasn't sure when she would have the nerve to pick up the phone and call again. "I will be there."

"We'll see you then, Elsie."

When she hung up, Elsie realized that she'd become so anxious her hands had turned damp. She knew she was going to have to tell her parents about the doctor's visit. They were going to have to help her pay for the driver.

Mentally preparing her speech, she headed out of the kitchen, and to her parents' room. She might as well just get it over with.

She lightly knocked on her mother's door before entering.

Her mother was dressed, and sitting on top of her neatly made bed. She was reading a novel and had a vibrant teal and purple crocheted throw loosely thrown over her lap.

For a split second, Elsie forgot her problems and simply gazed at her mother in happiness. It really was such a blessing that her *mamm* was recovering so well.

She looked up with a pleased smile. "Hello, dear. Have you come to check up on me?"

"*Jah*. But also to let you know that I have a doctor's appointment tomorrow."

She set her book to one side. "With Dr. Palmer?"

Throat feeling thick, Elsie nodded.

Her mother frowned. "Gosh, I must have really lost track

of time while I was sick. I thought your next checkup wasn't for a few weeks."

Seeing the chance to be evasive, Elsie grabbed hold of it quickly. With a studied shrug, she said, "It snuck up on me too. But I guess we have had a lot of other things to occupy us."

"You're right," her mother said with a laugh. "Yes, I would say that we have had quite a number of other things on our minds besides eye checkups. So, who is going with you tomorrow?"

"I thought I'd go by myself this time."

"All the way to Ashland? Definitely not." She bit her lip. "I bet I might be well enough to go tomorrow. . . ."

"*Nee*, Mamm. You are supposed to stay in bed, and that's where you need to stay. I'll see if Viola or even Aunt Lorene could go with me."

"I think Viola is working."

"Then I'll go call Aunt Lorene right now. She cut back on her hours at the cheese store now that she's married to John."

"Oh. *Gut!* Yes, do that, then call the driver service. I'll tell your *daed* to make sure we have enough cash for you to pay the driver."

Elsie thanked her *mamm* and then went back to the kitchen.

But this time, she didn't get so lucky. Amanda and Regina had returned and were joined by Roman. Goldie was sitting at her brother's feet, looking hopefully at the sandwich he was eating.

Inwardly, Elsie sighed. She still wasn't happy with her brother.

She ached to turn right around but she had to call for a

driver before they were all booked up. There was no escaping that.

"Excuse me, but I need to make a phone call."

"Another one?" Regina asked. "Who are ya callin' now, Elsie?"

"The English driver service. I need to go to the *doktah* tomorrow."

"What's wrong?" Roman asked.

"Nothing. I'm merely going to the eye *doktah* for a checkup." She was so tired of him trying to manage her, she added snidely, "Not that it's any of your concern."

"Of course it's my concern. You're my sister."

"Yes, but that doesn't mean you need to know all of my private business."

He looked at her strangely. "I thought we were talking about your eyes, Elsie. What's so private about that?"

What she was going through was much more complicated than simply her eyes.

Deciding to ignore the question since she had no intention of answering, she looked through a drawer for the driver service's phone number. Luckily, she found it easily, and the number was written large enough that she didn't have to ask Roman or Amanda to tell her the numbers.

Just as she began to punch in the numbers, Roman spoke again. "Who's going to go with you? Do you need me to go?"

His voice held genuine concern. She knew he cared about her, and she appreciated that. But she was tired of being treated like an invalid.

"I'll be fine," she replied, neatly ignoring his questions.

To her irritation, he took the phone out of her hand and put it back in its cradle, disconnecting the line. "Elsie, if you don't want me to go with you, that's fine. But someone needs to."

"Honestly, Roman . . . "

"Are you thinking of going alone?"

She stared at him, wondering what to say. She didn't want to lie, but she didn't want to debate it, either.

"I'm going with her," Amanda said quickly.

To Elsie's embarrassment, she stared at Amanda with as much surprise as Roman did.

"Right, Elsie?" Amanda prodded.

"Right. I mean, *jah*."

"What about Regina? What are you going to do with her while you're in Ashland?" Roman asked.

"I thought she could stay around here tomorrow. You said you'd be working in the barn, not out in the fields."

"I want to stay with you, Roman," Regina said.

Elsie exhaled, hoping her face wasn't flushed from all the subterfuge. "Now that this is all settled, may I call for a car and driver now? Or, do you want to take care of that, too?"

"You don't need to make this so hard, Elsie," he said before storming out of the kitchen.

"*Danke*," Elsie mouthed to Amanda before dialing the car service again. It looked like she was going to have some company after all. Which would be just fine, since it was Amanda. Amanda didn't pry. And she might even have some advice to give her about Landon.

Yes, things were working out just fine, she decided, just as the line connected and yet another receptionist asked her what she wanted.

They were on their way. As their charter bus from Elite continued north on the interstate, Lovina pulled out her knitting, glanced at her husband, and wondered if he was having

as difficult a time as she was. It wasn't because of their ac-
commodations. Their seats were comfortable and roomy, and
the bus was only about half full, allowing everyone plenty of
room to spread out and relax.

No, it was their destination that weighed heavy on their
minds. Hoping to infuse a bit of brightness into their conversation, she said, "In eight hours or so, we'll be in Intercourse.
I can hardly believe it."

"Me, neither." Aaron looked as if he'd like to add something more, but didn't.

Lovina supposed that was natural. She felt tongue-tied,
too. "Can you even think about anything but our families?"
she asked.

He shook his head. "All I can seem to think about is Laura
Beth's brother Karl. I keep imagining that seeing him in
person is going to be worse than I can even imagine. I don't
know what he'll think, seeing me after all this time." He ran
a hand around the base of his neck, obviously hoping to ease
a knot in his muscles.

"What could he possibly do? I mean, the accident was a
long time ago. Almost a whole lifetime! Besides, it wasn't
your fault, Aaron."

"It was my fault to a certain extent, Lovina." Turning to
her, his blue eyes looked more troubled than ever. "I'm beginning to wonder if maybe over time, I've chosen to forget
exactly what happened."

"What do you mean?"

"I mean that time can dull pain and blur the edges of re-
sponsibility," he said cryptically.

Lowering his voice, he leaned closer. "Lovina, what if over
the years I've somehow twisted things in my mind? What if
I made things seem less my fault than they actually were so

I could live with the consequences?" His voice turned anguished. "Maybe I really did kill my family."

Lovina felt a chill race through her bones. She'd never heard Aaron talk this way.

But she knew exactly what he meant. Years passing did take the edge off the worst memories. Perhaps a person's mind and heart and soul had a way of dealing with difficult things in order to not feel so bad about them. After all, a person could shoulder guilt only so long.

After that, it seemed a person ached to make things better, to move forward, if for no other reason than to be able to sleep at night.

Spinning in her mind, too, was the awareness that Aaron had kept so much of his burden from her for decades. He'd chosen to bear his burdens all alone, and it had affected both his mood and his relationship with her and with their children. Thinking about his headaches, the constant aches and pains in his muscles, she guessed it might have affected his health, too.

In an effort to make him feel better, she leaned close, so close that her lips were practically touching his ear, and whispered, "Come now, Aaron. You don't really think that, do you?"

Of course, she was prepared for only one answer.

Had expected to hear it right away.

But as she waited for his reply, as his silence stretched for what felt like hours, but must have been only thirty seconds at the most. . . .

She began to fear the worst.

At last he replied, his voice strained and harsh, but clear as day.

"I'm not sure."

Hands shaking, Lovina placed her knitting needles on her lap and faced the window. Well, she'd asked for the truth. Too bad she'd naïvely assumed that it would be easy to hear.

She closed her eyes and prayed for support as silence descended over them again like a thick, suffocating blanket.

chapter eighteen

It was becoming something of a routine, and Landon wasn't happy about it. After securing his horse's reins to the hitching post in front of the Keims' house, he stood with his arms crossed and watched Roman stride toward him.

"Roman, we're too old to be playing these games," he chided. "If you have a problem with me seeing your sister, you're going to have to take it up with her. I don't particularly enjoy going behind her back."

"I don't have a problem. I mean I don't anymore."

"Oh, really? What changed?"

His friend looked chagrined. "I've got a wife who reminded me that I don't know what's best for everyone."

Bemused, Landon raised a brow. "Is that a fact?"

"Well, there's a fair chance she might be right."

"All right. Well, I'm going to pay a call on Elsie now."

"Wait a moment, wouldja? I actually came out here to ask a favor of you."

"And what is that?"

"Elsie has an eye doctor appointment tomorrow. My wife, Amanda, is planning to go with her, but . . . I guess I thought if the two of you were really going to make a go at this, perhaps it might be better to have you accompany her."

The last of Roman's stubborn attitude drifted away. "I know we've all been treating her like she can't walk across the street by herself anymore." Rubbing a hand down his short beard, he said, "And I fear Elsie tends to conceal her problems so we won't worry. Maybe it's habit?" He shrugged. "Anyway, perhaps for someone to go with her who has fresh eyes and can hear what the doctor says with fresh perspective? Maybe that'd be best for everyone."

"Have you discussed this with her?"

"I'm only trying to make plans, Landon."

"Without Elsie, though. And I'm not going to be a part of that, Roman," Landon said firmly. He already knew he wanted a long relationship with Elsie. There was no way he was going to start "managing" her or sneaking around behind her back.

"So you're too busy with work? Or you don't want to get involved?"

"Neither," Landon said with barely controlled patience. "Neither. Listen, letting someone be independent means that you let them make their own choices."

"I don't need a lecture. I'm merely trying to help my sister."

"Then I suggest you let her do the decision making."

Roman looked like he fought back a retort, but then his countenance changed. Maybe Landon was finally getting through to him.

"If I go—and I haven't said I would—I want you to know that I'm doing it for Elsie, not because you came over here and pressured me."

"That's fine. Perfectly fine." Taking a breath, Roman added, "Look, I know you think the lot of us are a bit crazy, and we probably are. But don't let that work against my sister."

"I would never do that."

"We just want to make sure she's taken care of, you know?"

Landon heard the frustration in his friend's voice. And he

felt for him. Managing family members, especially siblings, was a tricky thing. After a certain age, they were almost impossible to boss around.

Remembering years ago, when Daniel had sprained his foot but refused to keep off it, Landon sympathized with Roman. It really was difficult to feel ineffectual around a person you cared about.

"We'll see if she's open to me going with her." Turning away, he pulled out an audio book. "Listen, since you're here, I have a question for you, too. It's a favor of a sort."

"What's that?"

Landon held out the audio book. "When I went to the library, one of the clerks told me about audio books. I thought maybe Elsie would like to listen to them."

"Listen, huh?"

"I'm hoping you can get permission from the bishop for Elsie to use a small CD player. She already told me that it was really hard for her to read. If she got permission from the bishop, she would be able to listen to some books."

"I never thought about that." Looking at the plastic case, he ran a hand along the cover. "You know—I'd forgotten, but when we were little she used to always have her nose in a book."

Landon was starting to wonder if Elsie hadn't been the only person in her family to be living in a bit of denial about the seriousness of her condition. "It's worth a try, don'tcha think?" he said lightly. "Elsie wants to be independent."

"I'll ask the bishop this week."

"*Danke*. And now, I better go on in. I don't want Elsie to think I'm showing up late." He turned away before Roman could hold on to him for another reminder about the doctor's appointment.

Two knocks later, Elsie's father opened the door.

"Landon, it's *gut* to see you."

"You as well."

"Elsie's waiting for you in the front room." He pointed to a well-lit, cozy-looking room. "You can go on in."

"*Danke.*" Relieved that her father wasn't attempting to ask him a dozen questions, Landon walked directly back. The moment he saw Elsie, all his aggravation about her brother's questions dissipated.

She stood up when he entered the room. "You made it."

"I did." Once again, he couldn't help but stare at her. Today she wore a plum-colored dress with a black apron. She had on black stockings and black clogs. As usual, her white kapp stood out in contrast to her honey-brown hair.

But more than any of that, he realized that she looked pretty to him. She had become important to him. And though he had no idea what the future would bring for both of them, he had a feeling he'd always have a soft spot for her.

All at once, he was tempted to tease her. Anything to make her smile.

She gestured to the coffee table in front of her. "I made us some fresh *kaffi* and a plate of cookies. Would you like some?"

"Of course." Unable to resist touching her, he reached out and lightly caressed her arm. "But I'll help myself. Okay?"

"Yes. And . . . And you can pour me some, too. That is, if you wouldn't mind?"

"I'd be happy to." As she sat down and watched him pour them both cups of coffee, then place two butter cookies on each of their napkins, Landon realized that everything felt right.

It didn't matter to him that she couldn't serve him.

He didn't even care if she had baked the cookies herself or bought them from a store. And that made him think of all the other ways they could make her life easier, but still give her dignity.

He'd been so narrow-minded. For so long, he'd thought that there was only one way to do things—his way. These last few days had taught him the value of being more open-minded about things.

He hadn't even known that Elsie was a bookworm when he picked up those audio books at the library. To think that her family had never considered how they might help Elsie still enjoy the things she loved with her disability . . . well, it made him think maybe she needed him more than she knew. She needed someone who was open enough to look around and see how life might be lived and enjoyed even with her limitations.

After taking a fortifying sip of coffee, he plunged right into the doctor's visit. "So, I saw Roman outside."

Predictably, she tensed up. "And?"

"And he said you have an eye doctor's appointment tomorrow."

"And?"

Her voice was cooler now, disappointment mixed with resignation. Letting him know that she assumed she'd become one of his chores. "And I want to go with you."

"I already have someone to go with me. Amanda volunteered." Her voice sounded a bit bitter. A little sad.

"Elsie, your hearing must be going, too," he teased. "I just said I *want* to go."

"I didn't think you meant it."

"I do. I want to spend time with you, even if it's just a matter of going to a doctor's appointment."

Her gaze warmed. "Hmm."

Taking advantage of her thawing, he said, "I have some news for you, too. I spent a couple of hours at the library yesterday, trying to learn more about your eye disease. If we're going to be seeing a lot of each other, I might want to ask some questions, too."

"You think so?"

"Maybe." Needing to be closer to her, he reached out and pulled her coffee cup from her hands and set it on the table. Then, he did the unthinkable and linked their fingers together. Just as if they were an engaged couple instead of two neighbors who'd only spent a little bit of time together.

Staring at their linked hands, liking how her slim fingers looked against his larger tanned ones, he went on. "I want to know what you're facing, Elsie. I want to know so we both can discover the truth about how you can get help."

But instead of bringing her closer, his words seemed to push her away.

With a look of regret, she removed her hand from his. "My future is no great secret, Landon. One day I won't be able to see."

"I understand that, but I guess I just want the chance to hear it from the doctor myself."

"Why?"

"Because then we'll know what we're facing." When he noticed that her bottom lip was trembling, he pushed his case. "Look what I found at the library," he said, pulling out one of the audio books. "It's a book you can listen to instead of read. I asked your brother to ask the bishop to give you permission to have a CD player to listen to the books."

"Really?"

She looked so dumbfounded that he had to coax himself not

to smile at her. If he did that, she would no doubt misunderstand. He nodded vigorously instead. "If the bishop approves, you can get your own CD player and headphones. Then you can read what you want to read whenever you want to."

"I wouldn't have to do without books. I could read again. I mean, almost."

She looked so grateful, it just about broke his heart. "Elsie, I don't want to shelter you, I want to help you. There's a difference, don't you think?" he asked softly.

Before his eyes, she softened. "Landon, I don't know what to tell you. I put up a strong front, but I think I'm scared to know the truth. I don't want to hear the news about my future. I don't want to be blind and helpless."

"I can understand that."

"If I let you go to the doctor with me, will you let me ask the questions?"

"I'll do my best. But if I have questions, I'm going to ask them, too."

At first she looked irritated because he didn't agree to her wishes right away. But then she chuckled. "Is this how it's going to be between us, Landon?"

"If you mean, am I not going to let you walk over me? *Jah*."

To his pleasure, she laughed. Picking up her coffee cup again, she leaned back against the couch. "In that case, you may go to the doctor with me. My appointment is at eleven. The driver is picking me up at ten."

"Okay. I'll walk over a little before then."

"Now, can we talk about something else? Anything but my eyes?"

There it was again—that rush of adrenaline he felt every time she smiled at him. Letting him know that with prayer and hope and faith, anything in their future was possible.

As long as he didn't lose her, anything was fine with him. "Elsie Keim, we can talk about whatever you want." He'd never been more honest.

Do you hear them, Peter?" Marie asked from their spots on the couch in the living room. "I think Elsie and that Landon are really getting along."

"They might be getting along too well," Peter grumbled, thinking that they'd already heard too much soft murmuring coming from the next room. "She seems to really like this man."

"Of course you feel a bit worried. You're Elsie's father," she teased with a smile. "No father wants to watch his daughter fall in love."

"I didn't do too badly with Viola," he protested.

"Elsie's always seemed younger."

"True. But it's more than that. Elsie has been the one we've all sheltered."

"As much as she's allowed us."

"I don't want her to get hurt, Marie. You know, not all romances end with love and marriage. She could get her heart broken."

"She told me she'd rather get hurt than never have a chance to do everything she wants to do. She said that even though her eyes aren't perfect, she wants to live her life to the fullest."

That was just the kind of thing he didn't understand. Elsie was precious. Special. Pain didn't feel good. How could she want to get hurt? It made no sense.

"She's been living, Marie."

"Don't be thickheaded, Peter. You know what I mean."

She looked as if she was about to add some more when she was seized by a coughing fit.

Instantly, the worry about her health rushed forward all over again. Rubbing her back, he said, "Marie, I fear you are wearing yourself out. You need to rest more."

"I've been resting. Peter, you've practically kept me in bed from the moment I got home from the hospital. I haven't had a chance to get tired."

"Your body says otherwise," he said when she coughed again.

"It's a lingering cough. That's all." Sitting up straighter, she said, "Actually, I think tomorrow morning I'm going to go back to my regular routine. It's high time I got out of bed with the sun, got dressed, and take back control of my *haus*."

"Not so fast. You are supposed to rest."

"I did."

"There's no hurry. For your information, I've been doing pretty good at keeping the house running."

"Oh, I've heard how you've been doing," she said with a wry smile.

Feeling a bit embarrassed, he frowned. "I've discovered that taking care of the house is more difficult than I thought."

"Luckily the girls helped you some."

"They helped a lot." He felt his neck redden. "Yes, Viola and Elsie and Amanda have been doing their fair share, for sure. More than their fair share, as a matter of fact."

"How are you getting along with the *kinner*?"

"For the most part, okay, I guess. I've had a couple of good conversations with each child."

"That's *gut*."

"It's a start." He nodded. "I think it helps that my parents are in Pennsylvania. With Mamm and Daed gone, we all have even more work than usual."

"Work can be a blessing."

"And this might sound unfeeling, but your being in the hospital helped me get back to normal with the *kinner*. We were so worried about you, we didn't have time to bring up all of my faults."

She winced. "Peter, don't say such things. They weren't simply 'faults.' You had a problem. A serious problem. A disease, remember?"

"If I do have an alcohol disease, it's been of my own making, I'm afraid." He wondered if he would ever be able to forgive himself for the trouble he'd put everyone he loved through. His own weakness had forced everyone in the family to pick up the slack—most of all, his lovely wife. "I don't know how to ever tell you how sorry I am, Marie. I feel like I've really let you down."

"You did not let me down. We've been together for many, many years, Peter. These problems only lasted a brief moment of that time."

Thinking about that, about one of his favorite Scripture verses from First Corinthians, "This too shall pass," he agreed. "Though I did have a problem, it's behind me now. My counselors have told me that I'm well on my way to a complete recovery. They reminded me that my treatment program is an ongoing thing. I've had to learn to make some changes in my life. I've had to learn to adopt these new habits even on difficult days."

"And you've been successful, Peter."

"It's still been hard, Marie," he murmured so softly she had to lean closer to hear. "I don't know if I'll ever completely lose the craving I had for alcohol."

"I know."

Her confidence in him was humbling. "Sometimes I don't think I deserve you, Marie."

"You do. Once more, we deserve each other. For better or worse." After gazing at him for a long moment she said, "Peter, it's time we got back to normal."

"Are you sure? You've been able to forgive me?"

"Of course. I love you, Peter. That has never changed."

"Well, maybe things really can get back to normal."

She rolled her eyes. "Well, as normal as things can get around here."

For a moment, he was tempted to reach for her hand.

Years ago when they were first married, he used to kiss her palm. She would then close her fingers around the kiss, saying that she wanted to keep that kiss close to her heart.

But were they that close again? He was afraid to kiss her palm and not see her fold her fingers around it.

Instead, he stood up and forced himself to smile easily.

"Now, I do believe, I'll go check on our Elsie and her suitor. Just to make sure, you know, that things are all right."

Her musical laughter filled his heart as he left the living room and stayed with him right until he noticed just how close that Landon Troyer was sitting next to Elsie on the couch.

Too close, by his estimation.

Feeling almost pleased to have something constructive to do, he strode into the room. "Elsie, is there a problem?"

As he'd hoped, both she and Landon jumped . . . and scooted a bit farther apart.

"Nothing's the matter, Daed."

"*Gut.*" For good measure, he scowled at Landon. "Nothing had better be the matter."

While Landon looked slightly embarrassed, and Elsie sighed, he turned and walked into the kitchen to make a fresh pot of tea for Marie.

He had to smile to himself. Oh, how he remembered the early, tentative days of courting Marie. It was so long ago, but that feeling of anticipation that settled in your stomach—he remembered that as if it were yesterday. Well, if Elsie really was falling for this man, all he could do was pray that God would guide her and protect her precious heart.

chapter nineteen

Sara and her husband, Jay, were waiting at the Old Candle Barn in Intercourse when Lovina and Aaron's bus pulled in at two in the afternoon.

Lovina recognized them immediately. Sara was tall, and Jay had bright red hair and a bright red beard. They were easy to spot in any crowd. But privately, Lovina suspected she would have spotted them anywhere, she was so anxious to see them.

When he noticed them, Aaron faltered a bit as they gathered their items and started down the aisle. "Sara came."

"*Jah*. She did."

"I was afraid to hope that she'd be here," he murmured.

"Me, too," she admitted. Feeling embarrassed, she added, "I've felt so bad about our long separation, I couldn't even bring myself to call her before we left. I wrote her a hasty note instead. I wasn't even sure the letter would get here before we did."

"Perhaps she was as eager to see us as we were to see her."

Well, they could only hope.

Peeking at Sara again, Lovina noticed that their eldest daughter looked as beautiful as ever. And also just as determined and reserved. She always had had that look about her, Lovina thought. By the time Sara was five or six, Lovina had begun to rely on her help.

Sara had never shied away from it. She'd always been by Lovina's side, helping with everything from dishes to watching the little ones to feeding the animals in the barn. But then the teenage years had come. Sara had fallen in love with Jay and eventually moved to Lancaster County, much to her parents' dismay. That was the one place Lovina and Aaron had vowed never to visit. And because Lovina and Aaron had been more determined to stay far from the pain of their pasts instead of keeping a close relationship with their daughter, their bond slowly strained, then finally broke apart.

"I've missed Sara," he murmured. "To my shame, I tried not to think about her, because I missed her so much."

"I did the same thing sometimes," she said as they waited for the driver to pull out one more of their bags from the luggage compartment of the bus.

Lovina peeked at Sara again. She didn't look all that happy to see them, but to be fair, she'd rarely ever showed her emotions. Of all their children, Sara was the most like her father. She rarely spoke her mind and had a habit of standing rather stiffly, watching the world go by with a quiet expression on her face.

It used to drive Aden and Peter crazy when they were younger. Both had been chatty boys with big hearts and had never had much patience for a sister who rarely smiled.

Much of Sara's reserved manner had seemingly changed overnight when she and Jay started courting, though. Jay was as easygoing as Sara was not. Lovina had been relieved to see that he could always manage to coax a grin or a burst of laughter from Sara when no one else was able to.

Finally their bag was retrieved and they were on their way.

When they were within calling distance, Lovina raised a hand and called out a little hello.

After a moment's pause, Sara lifted her hand. Her husband smiled but remained quiet. Lovina knew he was letting Sara take the lead.

Please Got, she prayed silently to herself. *Please help me find the right words to say.* Now, more than ever, Lovina wanted to heal their relationship, not make more fissures.

After a pause, Aaron took the lead and quickened his steps. "Sara and Jay, it's mighty *gut* to see you again!" he called out heartily. "Thank you for coming here to meet us."

Right away, Jay stepped forward. "I'm glad to see you, too, Aaron. We wouldn't have wanted to be anywhere else."

"I am glad to see you, Daed. At long last," Sara said quietly.

"Ah. *Jah,*" Aaron said, then looked over his shoulder at Lovina. Her heart sank. She knew that look. He was disappointed with their daughter's greeting and unsure of what to do next.

Well, she supposed she could do her best to patch things by keeping her voice merry and light. "You two are a sight for sore eyes. And sore backs, too," she joked. "Boy, am I happy to get off that bus," she said as she caught up with them.

Then, without giving Sara a chance to do anything else, Lovina reached out and hugged her daughter. After the briefest of seconds, Sara lifted her arms and hugged her back. Tightly.

And just like that, the years and the distance and the excuses melted away. For a few moments, at least, things were back like they used to be when Sara was a little girl. Her sweet daughter was close at hand, and because of that, Lovina felt better than ever.

"I've missed you, Sara," she said. "I truly have."

"I've . . . I've missed you, too, Mamm."

Oh, those were golden words. Wonderful to hear. Never

would she take such things for granted ever again. Too soon, they broke apart. That's when Lovina realized her eyes were a bit damp.

"My eyes can't seem to stop watering," she muttered as she wiped her cheeks.

"It's all right, Mamm. Mine seem to be doing the same thing." This time, when Sara smiled, it looked far more genuine.

"Sara, do you think you can give me one of those?" Aaron asked, his arms already half open.

"Of course, Daed," she said, walking into her father's arms.

As Lovina shared a quick hug with Jay, she realized that this trip had already accomplished something wonderful. It had brought them to their daughter.

Before it was too late to make things right.

"I can't wait to see the *kinner*," Lovina said. "Aden said when he saw them your boys were mighty rambunctious."

Jay chuckled as he grabbed one of their suitcases. "That's one way of putting it. There's others, far less complimentary."

After getting the other bags, Aaron and Lovina followed Sara to the van and driver who was waiting.

After they all piled into the van, they were on their way to Bird-in-Hand. She and Aaron were in the back row of the van, Jay and Sara in the bench seat in front of them.

As the driver pulled onto the highway, Lovina couldn't help but gaze out the window, anxious to see everything that looked the same but yet so different.

Beside her, she noticed Aaron doing much the same. "It looks so different," he murmured. "I should have realized that it would."

"When was the last time you were here, Aaron?" Jay asked.

"Long before you were born."

Sara turned to look at them. "I wish you would have come out here before now."

"I know. I wish we would have, too." Lovina paused, then dived in. "I know you've talked to Peter and Sam and Lorene about everything . . . "

"Your past wouldn't have made much difference to me, Mamm."

"I know that. I guess I was hoping that might explain a bit more our reluctance to visit. And I just kept hoping you would come back home," Lovina said. She felt bad about their estrangement, but she wasn't willing to take all of the blame. Though she'd never exactly said so, Lovina was fairly sure that Sara had moved far away on purpose.

"Lovina," Aaron whispered. "We will talk. But later. Now is not the time."

"I can't help how I feel." She needed to defend herself. "But you're right. I feel bad about how I handled things."

Sara stared at her again. "Muddah, you are going to tell me everything now, right?"

"I hope so."

"Good, because everyone has a different story about what is going on with the two of you."

Lovina raised a brow. "And who is everyone, child?"

"You know. Sam, Lorene, Aden . . . "

"I suppose everyone has something to say. You could have asked me, you know," Lovina reminded her.

But instead of taking the olive branch, Sara's voice hardened. "Oh, please. For as long as I can remember, you've never talked about things that make you uncomfortable."

Jay laid a calming hand on his wife's arm. "We're almost home, Sara. We can discuss things there."

She shrugged off his touch. "Mamm, when we get home, we're going to be surrounded by the boys. Please, just tell me. . . . Are you both okay? I already know about your English past and Daed's former marriage. Why else did you two travel here? What else do you two possibly have to discover?"

Before Lovina could formulate a reply, Aaron said, "Only the truth, daughter. Your mother and I learned something mighty important over the last few weeks. Sometimes it ain't enough to admit a problem. Sometimes a man must seek forgiveness . . . and the whole complete truth."

Sara's eyes widened. Obviously Aaron had surprised her with his bluntness. "And that's what you intend to do?"

"I'm going to try," Aaron said.

"But . . . what if nothing goes like you hoped?"

This time it was Lovina who answered. Unable to help herself, she chuckled. "Oh, Sara. If nothing goes as we hope, I have a feeling we'll feel right at home. That, my dear, has been the story of our lives!"

Next to her, Aaron grinned. Slowly, Jay did, too. At last, Sara looked at her, really looked at her.

And Lovina saw something in her eyes she'd long given up ever seeing: hope.

Softly, Lovina added, "Besides, your *daed* and I wanted to see you and Jay. And the *kinner*, of course. Now that I've gotten to see you? Now that I've gotten to hug you? Why, it's already made this trip a successful one."

Aaron added, "We should have paid you a visit years ago. I'm sorry, Sara."

Sara's eyes widened, and Lovina knew it was her father's touching words as much as the fact that he even verbalized them that shook her up so much.

Anxious to move the conversation on, she gave Sara's arm

a little pat. "Tell me about the *kinner*, Sara. Tell me about your projects and your gardening and your travel plans. We want to know everything."

"You knew about my garden?"

"*Jah*. And your upcoming trip to Pinecraft." She sniffed. "You are not the only one who asks questions, daughter," Lovina said with a bit of a smile.

And that did the trick. Slowly, Sara began to talk. And as she did, Lovina felt as if a lifetime of broken fences that lay between them slowly started to mend.

The feeling was a glorious one, indeed.

Elsie was nervous, and the man beside her knew it.

"Elsie, just tell me what you want," Landon said as she fidgeted beside him in the waiting room of the ophthalmologists' office. "Do you want me to go into the examining room with you? Or, would you rather me stay here?"

"It might be a while. . . ."

"I'm happy to be wherever you want me to be. Elsie, I want to help you in any way I can."

His selflessness almost took her breath away. For so long, everyone around her told her what they thought she should do . . . as loudly as possible.

But here was Landon, ready to do her bidding.

She was debating what to tell him when the door opened and the receptionist called her name.

"Landon, would you come with me?" she asked.

He stood up and waved a hand, gesturing her forward.

"Got company today, Elsie?" Jennifer, the receptionist, asked.

"*Jah*, I brought a . . . a friend. This is Landon Troyer."

"Hi, Landon," Jennifer said as she led Elsie down the hall. When they got to the examination room, Elsie sat down on one of the plastic chairs instead of the fancy examination chair in the middle of the room.

Jennifer left, then a nurse named Maggie came in armed with a blood pressure cuff and a large folder with her health history.

As Landon sat quietly, Elsie awkwardly told the nurse about all the recent problems she'd been having. Sometime during the drive to the office, she had made the decision to be completely honest with both the doctors and nurses and Landon. She had come to find out that the only person who was getting hurt by withholding information was herself.

As Elsie carefully explained her symptoms, stopping often while Maggie wrote down notes, she took care to keep Landon out of her sight. She didn't want to risk seeing his reaction to her news. If she did, she was sure she'd see pure dismay written all over his face.

If she could even see his true expression, she added dryly to herself. At this point, it was becoming harder and harder to do.

Finally, she stopped for breath.

Maggie's pen hovered over her notepad. "Is that everything, Elsie?"

"That is everything." Inside, her heart sank. What more could she share? It felt as if she had more problems than a dog had fleas.

After Maggie took her blood pressure and pulse, she left the room.

When they were alone, Landon leaned forward. "That was quite a list, Elsie. Are you doing all right? You seemed nervous earlier."

His tone hadn't been as full of shock as she'd feared. Instead, he sounded caring and worried about her.

Figuring that there was nothing more surprising that she could share, she gazed his way in complete honesty. "I'm doing all right. Fine. Actually, I had imagined telling Maggie the truth was going to be harder than it was."

"Isn't that how most things are? It's the worrying that gets us."

She was about to try to come up with something clever to say when the door opened after two brisk raps.

"Elsie Keim. I'm happy to see you, but not for the reasons I heard!" Dr. Palmer said as he gazed at her over the top of his wire-rimmed glasses. "You are having a time of it, aren't you?"

"I suppose I am."

Right away, her doctor shook Landon's hand. "I'm Scott Palmer."

"Landon Troyer."

"Nice to meet you. Glad you came with Elsie. Sometimes I think she tries to do too much on her own."

"I try to be normal. That's what I try to do."

Dr. Palmer set her file on the table before folding his arms across his chest. "And what does 'normal' look like to you?"

"Being able to see."

"Well, you can't see all that well, can you?"

There was his matter-of-fact way of speaking again. It was one of her favorite things about Dr. Palmer, as well as one of the things she dreaded about him. He never sugarcoated things

Well aware of Landon observing and listening, she shook her head. "*Nee*," she said finally. "I'm having a lot of trouble lately."

He turned to Landon. "We're going to need to run some tests. I'm glad you're here, but I think things might go easier if you went on back to the waiting area."

Immediately Landon stood up. "I'll be out there until you come out, Elsie."

After he exited the room, she slumped. Feeling slightly peevish, she said, "I thought it was a good thing that I wasn't alone."

"I am glad about Landon coming with you. But I'm afraid we're going to have to have a difficult conversation, Elsie, and I didn't want you being distracted."

"You think my eyes are mighty bad now, don'tcha?"

"It sounds like it. But you don't need me to tell you that."

"Am I about to be blind?"

He paused. "Now, that I don't know. I'm going to test your eyes, but I think we need to make some decisions today, Elsie. Decisions about what to do next."

She nodded. That had been what she'd been afraid of. But as Dr. Palmer washed his hands, and as she removed her glasses and folded them neatly on her lap, something struck her—

Before that very minute, she'd only thought of her life in terms of seeing and not seeing.

Never before had she really thought about a "next." And for some reason, simply knowing that things weren't "over" gave her reason to have hope—even when Dr. Palmer shined a light in her eyes and she realized that things really were as bad as she'd feared.

chapter twenty

An hour had passed. Then two. By now, Landon had read through both ancient copies of *Sports Illustrated* and most of the headlines of the morning paper.

As the time wore on, he found himself watching the second hand slowly make its way around the white face of the clock on the wall. When he realized that he'd followed the red hand around the clock five times, Landon knew he needed to do something else.

What he ached for was his mother's ear. She had a talent for listening to almost anything without making a comment. When he was younger, it used to irritate him a bit. He had needed her to tell him what she thought, and to direct him, to tell him what he should do.

Now that he was older, he realized that she had been even wiser and stronger than he'd imagined. Staying silent was hard to do. Most folks ached to talk about themselves, to interrupt someone's story with a tale of a similar situation they'd been through.

His father had loved to offer lots of advice. He loved to fix things and people's problems.

Not his mother. No, Faith Troyer had the innate ability to simply listen. Over the years, he'd come to her with all sorts of dilemmas. Because she never pushed, he'd always end up telling her more than he'd anticipated.

Then, before he knew it, he would find himself reaching a decision all by himself, much to his—and his mother's—satisfaction.

Since his mother wasn't by his side, he reached out to the only one who was. To his shame, Landon knew he prayed too rarely these days. Often, he found himself having to remind himself to share his thoughts and feelings with the Lord.

Now, though, he knew no one else could help as much.

Leaning back in his cushioned chair, he prayed as hard as he could, asking for patience and guidance and understanding for Elsie. He asked God to stay by Elsie's side for the next few hours. Landon had a feeling that when she came out of the offices, she was going to need as much support and protection as possible.

After he asked for these things, often asking in a jumbled, ragtag way, he sighed. He could only imagine what the Lord had thought of his clumsy thoughts.

But just as he was about to chastise himself for not speaking to the Lord in a better, more organized manner, Landon realized that the Lord hadn't cared about polished words or fancy phrases.

Instead, He'd lifted Landon's worries from his shoulders and given him a measure of peace that he hadn't felt in quite a while.

He felt better.

At long last, Elsie stepped out into the waiting room. He practically jumped to his feet. "You're done."

Her expression somewhat winsome, she nodded. "Yes."

"Do you need to schedule another appointment?"

"Uh, no." She shook her head. "I mean, I've already done that," she added, as her words came tumbling out, sounding just as confused and jumbled as his prayers had. "Well, I mean, I made plans to do that. If I need to."

He was confused.

"What's going on?" he asked.

Looking at the receptionist standing on the other side of the counter, she shook her head. "I'll tell you after we leave."

Concerned, he followed her out of the office and down the carpeted hall. Next to him, Elsie seemed a bit woozy and in need of a break. "When is your driver returning?"

"If you don't mind, I asked him to give me another hour and a half. I wanted to have lunch over at Buehler's Fresh Foods. It's a short walk from here, and they have a coffee shop, grocery store, and a little restaurant, too. Do you mind if we go there? I'm not ready to go home yet, but now I realize I should have asked you first. Do you have plans? Should I call the driver back?"

"I'm good," he said slowly as they headed toward the front of the office building. "Going to Buehler's sounds fine." As a light breeze fanned their cheeks, he asked, "Elsie, are you ready to tell me about the tests?"

"Ah . . . not yet." She smiled slightly, but the light didn't meet her eyes. Instead, she still seemed preoccupied.

Now he was starting to get worried. Part of him wanted to take her hand and lead her back into one of the sitting areas in the building's lobby. There he would sit her down and make her tell him everything.

But then he remembered his mother's patience and his prayers, asking for strength to be the person Elsie needed him to be. With that in mind, he held his tongue as they continued down the sidewalk, past two office buildings, then approached a quaint shopping center, each building made almost entirely of red brick.

At last she stopped in front of Buehler's. "Here's the cafe. Is this place all right with you? They have sandwiches and soup."

"It's perfect." He hadn't even bothered to look around. All he cared about was her well-being.

He held his tongue as they ordered their meals—Elsie not looking at the menu, choosing to order one of the specials the server mentioned.

Across from him, Elsie looked tense and nervous. A number of times, she looked on the verge of saying something, but then would change her mind.

After they'd gotten their sandwiches, he couldn't take it anymore. "Elsie, did you want to tell me what Dr. Palmer said?"

Finally, finally, she looked his way. "He said two things." She took a breath, then blurted, "I am going blind. But I'm also eligible for eye surgery."

Once again, he felt as if God was at his shoulder, cautioning him to go slowly. "What kind of eye surgery?"

She opened her purse and pulled out two pamphlets. "Corneal replacement surgery."

He picked up the pamphlets and opened them, scanning the pictures, though none of it made much sense to him. "What kind of surgery is that?" he asked, trying his best to keep his tone light and easy.

"I don't really understand it, but I would get my corneas replaced with new ones. If I got this done, there's a chance I'll be able to see."

"Really? Such a thing is possible?"

She nodded. "That's what my *doktah* said."

"What do you think about that?"

"I'm not sure what to think. Ever since I received my diagnosis, I've always assumed that I would be blind one day. I've been pretty much living each day hoping that it wouldn't be for years and years." She waved a hand. "Now, though, Dr. Palmer said that it wouldn't be years and years. It's a matter of months."

"And?"

"And I could be completely blind one year from now," she said with a rush of air.

"But if you got the surgery?"

"If I got the surgery, and it worked? There's a chance that I would be able to see much better than I see right now. Almost like a normal person."

He was floored. "That would be a miracle, wouldn't it?"

She shrugged as she picked up her sandwich.

Landon watched her chew, anxiously waiting for her to explain herself. But instead of doing that, she only took another bite.

"Elsie, what are you concerned about?" Thinking fast, he blurted, "Is it the cost of the surgery?"

"It is expensive." She bit her lip.

"But we can work around that. Families in the community help each other all the time."

"That is true."

"But the money would be well spent, yes? I mean, you'd rather see than not, right?"

"Of course I'd rather see. But this decision isn't easy."

"Are you worried about the surgery itself? Is it dangerous?"

"Dr. Palmer said it wasn't too dangerous, there is just a chance that it won't work."

"If it didn't work, you'd still be blind."

"*Jah.*" Looking more despondent than ever, she took another bite of her sandwich.

Landon didn't understand why she wasn't more excited. This surgery seemed like an answer to his prayers, and surely it was an answer to her prayers, too.

If she could see, he would no longer have any worries about them marrying one day. She'd be able to see their babies and raise their children without any assistance.

If she could see, she'd be normal, just like her sister.

Honestly, he couldn't imagine why she wasn't smiling from ear to ear. "What is the problem, then?"

"I am wondering if it would be wrong to do such a thing."

She pushed her plate to the side and looked at him directly. "Landon, my life is not in danger. My disease isn't spreading to other parts of my brain or body. All that will happen will be that I won't be able to see."

"But that is important."

"Also . . . the only way to have new corneas is for someone to not need theirs." Looking stricken, she said, "They would have to die, Landon."

"And this would bother you?"

"I think it would, yes." She hesitated, then said, "Landon, I've never told anyone this, but perhaps my blindness is God's will. For some reason, He might want me to not be able to see."

Though he practically could hear his mother's voice in his ear, cautioning him to hold his tongue, he rushed forward. "If it was God's will that you have an eye disease, then it was also His will for you to see that physician. And it was God's will for that doctor to learn how to heal you."

She dug in her purse again, this time pulling out her wallet. "How much is our meal, Landon? This is my treat."

"Nonsense. I'll pay for your lunch."

"This was my idea."

"Elsie, please. Put that away." He opened his own wallet and pulled out a twenty-dollar bill. "I've taken care of it. Now, do you want to walk around for a bit?"

"*Nee.* I'd rather we just wait for the driver."

"I think we should talk about things instead."

"Landon, I do believe we've talked enough. At least for now."

Just as he was about to argue that point, he heard his mother's voice in his ear again. Deciding it was time he listened, he nodded, then took her arm. "Let's go, then." He knew his tone was harsh, practically daring her to argue with his attempt to help her navigate her way through the maze of tables.

After a pause, she stepped closer to his side and let him guide her.

But though she was letting him take the lead right now, it was very clear that Elsie was a stubborn woman, and even if Landon wanted her to get this surgery, it was her decision. And he didn't like that feeling of powerlessness.

chapter twenty-one

Lovina didn't know whether she should laugh or cry as she sat on the corner of their bed in the beautiful Harmony View Inn. "I remember when they built this place. I thought this was the prettiest hotel on earth. I would have given anything to spend the night here."

From his spot by the window, Aaron smiled at her. "It seems you've gotten your wish, then. It is a pretty hotel for sure."

She noticed his tone didn't nearly match her forced enthusiasm. And it brought her back to the real reason they had returned to Pennsylvania.

"Aaron, are you terribly sorry that we're staying here instead of staying with one of your relatives?"

"Not at all. It's going to be hard enough to see my family, and Laura Beth's, too. I have no idea how they will greet me, if they're even going to let us share a meal with them. It's best that we're staying in a hotel. At the very least, we're going to need someplace to rest that's peaceful."

"I agree. If we were staying at one of their homes, it might be too much to tackle all at once."

"I'm glad you feel the same way. So, are you ready to call your family?"

Lovina looked at the phone with a grimace. "*Nee*. But that don't count for much, does it? I'm still going to have to make that call."

He smiled. "We knew this trip would be hard. At least we saw Sara."

She couldn't deny how happy that visit had made her. "Sara seems happy."

"She does. Praise God."

Lovina started to say more. To admit how worried she'd been about the reunion. But Aaron already knew her feelings, and they'd already rehashed the meeting more than once.

As she glanced at her husband, she realized that he was patiently waiting for her to make the first move toward their pasts. Though he might never say it, he needed her strength as much as she needed his.

Standing up, she opened her purse, pulled out her address book, and made the decision. It was time to face her parents. Only by visiting them in person and doing her best to apologize for her absence could she begin to feel any sort of peace. It didn't matter that they, too, had been stubborn. It was a child's place to make that first move.

Before she could back out, she picked up the phone and began to punch in the numbers.

Her heart started racing as she heard the line connect, then start to ring. Mentally, she began to practice what she was going to say to her mother or father.

With a clatter and a bit of static, someone finally picked up. "Hello?" a woman asked, her voice thin, almost reedy.

"Hello? This is Lovina Keim. I'm calling for Amy."

"Who?"

"This is Lovina, I mean, Lolly." When she heard no response, she said, "Is this the Johnson residence? I'm calling for my parents."

"I'm afraid you have the wrong number."

"I'm sorry." Feeling dismayed, Lovina rushed ahead, afraid to stop talking. If she stopped she was sure she was going to burst into tears. "I'm from Ohio. This was the only number I had for my parents." Only when she took a breath did she remember that this wasn't the correct way to handle this situation. Strangers didn't want or need to know personal information. She should have simply apologized and hung up.

After a second's pause, the woman said, "Are you talking about Amy and Stan Johnson?"

"Yes. Do you know them? Are you in their old house? Did they move?"

"Hold on, Lolly," she said around a chuckle. "One question at a time."

"Sorry."

"About the Johnsons. I do believe I heard that they moved into a retirement home out in Wisconsin."

"Wisconsin?" She felt dizzy all of a sudden.

"Yep. Saint Clare, or something like that. Gosh, they moved about seven or eight months ago."

"Thank you for letting me know."

"Not a problem," she replied, before hanging up.

When she heard the *click* of the phone, Lovina carefully set the receiver down, too. After she hung up, she looked at her husband, noticed his kind blue eyes. He was staring at her, reflecting surely everything that she was feeling—worry and relief. Confusion and sadness.

"What happened?" he asked.

"It seems we were too late. The woman I talked to thought my parents moved to Wisconsin less than a year ago."

"Wisconsin."

Tears pricked her eyes. But for the first time in ages, instead of willing them away, she relaxed enough to let them float down her cheeks. "I can't believe I'm disappointed. I mean, what did I expect? That everything here would stay the same after all this time?"

"You're not alone in your thinking. I suppose I thought all we'd have to do was find the strength to reach out to our relatives. That they would be here, waiting for us."

"We were so naïve. We should have thought things through." She wanted to say more, but she was afraid she'd already said too much. Berating herself wouldn't do any good. "Aaron, I've been so silly. I let far too many years pass without staying in touch with my folks. Even though they never understood why I became Amish, I should have continued to try to keep in touch."

The lines around Aaron's mouth deepened as he continued to gaze at her. "I am sorry. I know you broke things off with them because of our marriage."

"It's not your fault. I made my choices. My parents did, too."

"But still, Lolly, I know you are disappointed."

The use of her English name surprised a smile from her. "Aaron, you haven't called me that in years! Decades, even."

"I know, but it's still a *gut* name. I've always thought it had a nice ring to it." Looking a bit bashful, he added, "It's the one I fell in love with, you know."

"I know," she whispered, remembering that first time he took her out for a soda and she'd noticed that his blue eyes were peppered with tiny flecks of gray.

Feeling mixed up and remarkably tender, she pointed to the phone. "I guess it's your turn now, Aaron. Do you want to call?"

"I don't want to," he said, echoing her words. "But I guess if you can be brave enough to call, I can, too. Who knows? Maybe my family will have moved away, too."

She knew he only said such a thing because he was nervous. It really was so much easier to push things away instead of facing them.

Matching his tone, she said, "If that's the case, I think we should sightsee. I've always wanted to visit that Amish Experience theater."

"If Laura Beth Swartz's family has moved to Wisconsin, too, I'll buy us two tickets."

"I'll hold you to it," she teased. But inside, she knew they couldn't be that lucky. Everyone in their past couldn't have left.

The tension in the room increased again as she watched him dial the number and listen to the rings. But then, instead of hanging up, he took a deep breath and began speaking.

"Ah . . . this is Aaron Keim. My wife, Lovina, and I are in town and I was hoping to see you. We're staying at the Harmony View Inn in Bird-in-Hand. If you'd like to talk, give me a call when you get this."

He left the phone number, then hung up.

"Well, I did it. If they call me back tonight, we can go over there later or in the morning."

"Yes, that sounds like a *gut* plan."

"Then, ah, I'll talk to them about Laura Beth's family. And seek their advice about what I should do."

"That sounds like a good decision."

He shifted on his feet, looking as uneasy as she felt. "I guess we could walk around the hotel now."

"I would like that."

"Yes. I mean, you've always admired the place."

"You're right. I have."

"I'm, uh, just going to wash my hands," he said as he strode to the bathroom and shut the door firmly behind him.

She didn't blame him needing a moment to himself. She needed it, too.

Do you want me to stay with you when you tell your family about your appointment?" Landon asked Elsie when their driver passed the sign announcing that they'd arrived at the outskirts of Berlin.

As his question hung in the air, Elsie forced herself to remember how kind he'd been to her over the last few hours. Ever since she'd gotten the news about a possible surgery, she'd been short-tempered and on edge.

But it seemed that the more disagreeable Elsie had been, Landon had been even more generous with his patience, and even more eager to help ease her burdens.

She was grateful for his presence, but he also made her uneasy, too. For the first time, she was actually thinking how her blindness—or lack of it—would actually affect other people.

That had been a bit of a shock to her system.

She'd begun to realize that for most of her life, she'd been intent on only how her loss of vision would affect her, and her wants. Not how everyone else would have to deal with the consequences.

Now, here Landon was offering to help her out again. She was almost tempted to take him up on it, simply so she wouldn't have to face her family's questions by herself.

But no matter how much she might have wanted to do that, the timing wasn't right, not for either of them. Though she knew there was a good chance they could eventually have a romantic relationship, at the end of the day, Landon was currently only a new friend. She certainly didn't want to expect more from him than that, not with her uncertain future.

Finally, she shook her head. "Landon, *danke*. I am grateful for your offer, but I can't take you up on it."

"Why not?"

There were many reasons, but she opted to share the main one. "I truly don't know what I'm going to tell them. As far as they're concerned, this was simply a routine eye exam."

"I think you should tell them the truth. You have options now, Elsie. Options that could change your life."

"I know, but I don't know if I'm ready to do that yet."

"That doesn't make sense."

"I know it probably doesn't, but that doesn't change how I feel." Though she wasn't ready to tell Landon, there were other concerns to weigh, too. Her large family had never been shy about sharing their opinions or taking charge. If she didn't have an idea of what she wanted to do next, the situation would turn very bad, indeed.

"Elsie, do you not trust me?"

When she turned to him, he reached for her hand. His touch soothed her, helped her remember that she wasn't alone. But she didn't want to take advantage of him. "I trust you, but we are still getting to know each other."

"This can only make our relationship stronger."

But because he was still holding her hand, still looking so intent on solving her problems, she knew he really didn't understand how wary she was about moving forward. "If what we have is meant to be, I want to be an equal partner to you. I want to be strong, too."

"When you can see, you'll be an equal partner."

Slowly, she pulled her hand from his and clasped it with her other on her lap. This was the problem, she realized. He was already counting on her getting the surgery, while she wasn't sure what the right decision was.

He only saw her as an equal if she could see . . . while she'd lived the last ten years of her life sure that she would be all right even if she was blind.

This was a problem.

chapter twenty-two

Peter supposed the discussion he was having with Roman was long overdue. But that didn't make it feel any less painful. It was difficult for a man to know that he'd disappointed his son—especially when he knew that his son was justified in his disappointment.

As he stood next to the wagon and watched Roman unload the supplies he'd bought early that morning, Peter felt even more at a loss for words than usual. Roman had refused his offers to help, and now seemed to be afraid to give him any responsibilities.

It was tempting to walk away, to give them both some space. The Lord knew that there had been more than one occasion when his father had walked away from him when they were at a standstill.

But he didn't want to be a man like his father. He yearned to be closer to his son.

At the very least, he had to try.

"Roman, I won't be leaving you again," he repeated, not even caring that his voice sounded as strained as he felt. "You don't need to shoulder everything any longer."

"I'm not doing that."

"But you're not letting me do my fair share." He held out a hand to stop Roman's continual unloading. "Son, I would have gone to the supplier with you this morning if you'd told me you were going."

"Daed, there was no need for you to go. I handled it."

"But I could have gone. I used to meet with the supplier by myself."

"Daed, this is my farm, too." Roman's voice was harsh sounding. Clipped.

"I'm aware of that," he soothed. "But you have other responsibilities now. You're preaching, you're attending to our community, plus you've got Amanda and little Regina, too. Trust me, there's no need for you to put in forty or fifty hours a week on the farm, too."

"You're talking like I've been doing a poor job."

"No, I'm saying that you mustn't spread yourself too thin."

A shadow of annoyance crossed his face. "I'm not."

Knowing that his son thought he was being criticized, Peter chose his next words with care. "Sometimes trying to do too much only causes more problems. I found that out the hard way."

"Daed, you're making too much of this."

"I hope I am, but part of me feels like you're doing all this . . . to shut me out. Part of me feels like you don't want to forgive me for having a problem. And that worries me."

"Daed, it ain't my place to offer forgiveness. Only the Lord can do that."

"I know. . . ." He let his voice drift off, hoping Roman would pick up the conversation and share more of what he was feeling.

But all he did was reach for another sack of grain.

Determined to smooth things over, Peter was just about to try another tack when Marie stepped out the back door.

"Peter? Roman?" she called out, her voice bright with tension. "Come inside. We need to talk."

"Can't it wait, Marie?"

"*Nee*, I don't think so."

Roman tossed down the sack in frustration. "Can't anything ever just be fine around here?"

"Go ahead. I'll make sure the horses are watered."

After a moment's pause, Roman nodded, then strode toward the house, impatience dogging every step.

After checking on the horses, Peter followed in his son's steps, his pace much slower.

He, too, was curious about Marie's summons. But to his great relief, he realized he didn't feel that knot that used to be ever present in his stomach. Instead, he felt like he could handle anything now without any help from a bottle of liquor.

Every day he was getting stronger. That was a wonderful sensation, indeed.

Mamm, you should be in bed, not standing in the doorway, calling for Daed and Roman," Elsie said as she watched her mother pace the kitchen floor. "You're going to get sick again and end up back in the hospital."

"I feel much better, Elsie. I'm almost back to normal."

"But you're still recovering. The nurses said it would take days, if not weeks, before you were back to your regular self."

"Elsie, I am fine. Don't start telling me what I can and can't do."

"Oh, for heaven's sake," Elsie grumbled under her breath as she sneaked a look at Viola. Viola shrugged her shoulders, but didn't look all that calm, either.

Already things were going poorly and she hadn't said a word yet! For at least the twelfth time, Elsie wished that Landon would have listened to her and simply let her go inside by herself.

Instead, he'd carefully walked her inside, announced that Elsie had learned some important news at the doctor's office, then left.

Leaving her to answer a flurry of questions, which was exactly what she'd hoped to avoid.

Now the boys were coming in, and Amanda had joined them, too. For once, she wished her grandparents hadn't left for Pennsylvania. Her *mommi* had always been her greatest supporter, and Elsie would have certainly appreciated that support right now.

"Viola, do something," she hissed into her twin's ear. "Mamm is going to make herself ill."

"I'm afraid there's nothing I can do," Viola answered. "I'm just as curious as she is." Lowering her voice, she inflected a tinge of guilt that set Elsie's teeth on edge. "I also happen to be pretty disappointed that you had intended to keep us in the dark. Thank goodness for Landon."

Folding her arms across her chest, Elsie turned away and walked into the living room by herself. If she couldn't prevent what was about to happen, she was determined to at least have a place to sit.

She was sitting there grumbling to herself, silently blaming Landon, when everyone joined her.

As Elsie stared at her family, she noticed that not a one of them was looking at her in a sympathetic way. Instead, each looked wary and a little perturbed.

"Well, Elsie?" Roman said impatiently. "What news did you learn? Tell us and be quick about it. I have things to do."

Amanda squeezed his arm. "Roman, you are being rude."

He tapped a foot. "I'm sorry, but I don't understand why we couldn't have talked about Elsie's appointment at supper."

Elsie wished she was anywhere else. "Don't worry, Roman. This won't take long." She took a deep breath. "Um, first I must admit that I've been lying to you a bit."

Her mother raised her brows. "A bit?"

"*Jah*. Um . . . the truth is that my vision has been blurrier than ever. Sometimes it's been so bad it's made me feel a little queasy. The appointment I had today wasn't the regularly scheduled checkup. I asked to come in."

"But you never said a word," her father said.

"I could tell you that I never said a word because everyone's been so busy." She looked around the room, pausing a second on each person's face. "You all have been getting engaged and married." She smiled slightly. "Or you've been sick and out of town. It's been a rare thing, to have all of us in the same place at the same time."

"That's no reason to keep secrets," Viola chided. "We would have made time for you. We always have."

The gentle reminder of how Viola—and the rest of her family—had seen themselves as her caregivers was all Elsie needed to continue. "Like I was saying, I could tell you that . . . but it wouldn't be the truth. The truth is that I haven't wanted to face what was really happening."

"Which was what?" Roman asked, concern now lacing his tone.

That concern made tears prick her eyes and her bottom lip quiver. It took everything she had to keep her voice calm. "The truth is that my kerataconus disease has gotten mighty bad and it ain't going to get any better. I could be technically blind in a year's time. Unless I have surgery," she added.

"What kind of surgery?" her mother asked.

"It's called a corneal transplant."

"Transplant?" Her mother looked at Elsie's *daed* in concern. Even with her impaired vision, Elsie could tell her *mamm* was on the verge of tears.

Elsie cleared her throat. "It's when they replace my corneas with someone else's corneas."

Stunned silence met her statement.

She understood their disbelief. She felt the same way. The Amish she knew weren't ones to embrace experimental procedures like this. Some didn't even trust modern medicine, preferring to rely on tried-and-true treatments that had been passed down from generation to generation.

Viola was the first to speak. "What will happen if you have this surgery?"

"I might be able to see perfectly well."

"You'd be cured? Forever?" Her mother looked like she was about to cry.

"I think so. The *doktah* gave me some papers to read. I mean, for you all to read. He said I was a *gut* candidate for the surgery, because I am young and healthy."

"Elsie, you could be cured?" Amanda said with a smile. "What a true miracle that would be!"

Elsie bit her lip. "To be honest, the idea of having another person's corneas doesn't set well with me."

Her father sat down. "We're going to have to give this a lot of thought and prayer, Elsie. I'll talk with your mother about this, too."

"But it's my eyes, Daed," she whispered. "It's my decision."

"But it's our values." He shook his head slowly. "I just don't know what to think."

"I'll speak about it to the other preachers and the bishop," Roman said. "Perhaps they could give us some guidance."

All at once, the family started talking and planning. Elsie leaned back in the chair, listening to the chatter. Letting the words *bake sales* and *fund-raisers* and *schedules* float over her.

It would be so easy to let all of them lead the way, to tell her what she should do. After all, she'd done that before. Elsie realized that, to some extent, she'd always let her family take the lead. It was easier to meekly follow instead of fighting or to argue.

But this time? She couldn't do it.

These were her eyes, and her future, and no matter how much her family might think they knew what she was experiencing or thinking or going through, she knew they didn't.

No, this decision was up to her, and her alone. She was the one who would have to deal with the consequences, just like she was the one who had been losing her vision little by little for most of her life.

"*Shtobb*," she said quietly.

But still the conversation continued, no one paying her any mind. Irritated, she repeated herself, only far more loudly. "Stop," she said again, this time in English.

When that didn't get their attention, she gave in to her impatience and practically yelled. "Everyone, hush now! Stop your planning!"

And like a light switch getting flipped, the room fell silent.

As a group, they stared at her. Some wore expressions of shock, others seemed irritated.

At the moment, she didn't care how anyone else felt. She wanted to speak her mind and be heard. Before any of them could chastise her for speaking like she did—or begin to argue yet again—she stood and started talking fast.

"Roman, yes, please do speak to the bishop about this surgery. But I'm not saying I'm going to do it. I may not." Actually, right at this moment, she didn't want to have the surgery.

"But—"

She neatly cut him off. "We don't need to talk about this, Roman."

"You're making a mistake," Viola warned.

"*Nee*. I don't think so." She took a deep breath, feeling braver by the second. "Actually, I think it is time for me to make some decisions, especially since it concerns *my* eyes."

"But, Elsie," her mother said, "I don't think you're thinking through things clearly. You need our help."

Ironically, Elsie felt as if for the first time she was actually thinking with a clear head.

While it was true she couldn't see well, she realized that was really all that was wrong. She was just as capable and strong as the rest of the family. And maybe even more so, too, because she'd been living with a disability while everyone else had not.

Indeed, no matter what happened, she would be the person who had to live with the consequences and repercussions.

Weighing her words carefully, she said, "Mamm, Daed, right now, I can't help but think about Mommi and Dawdi. They both made decisions that none of us knew about for years and years and years."

"But they regret that," her father said.

"Do they? Do you think they would have changed things all that much if they could do it again? Something tells me that Mommi and Dawdi are glad they got married. They are glad that they stayed Amish. I think they're glad they didn't burden their children with their pasts, either." She shrugged.

Viola, ever impatient, scowled. "Twin, what does this have to do with you getting new corneas?"

"They made their choices and, for better or worse, they've lived with them. No matter what I decide to do, it will affect the rest of my life. It sounds like both Mommi and Dawdi did things that their parents and siblings didn't understand, but they did them anyway."

"That doesn't mean you have to act the same way," her mother said.

"I realize that. But I also realize that at the end of each day, when they said their prayers at night, they had to live with their decision. For better or worse, at the very least they knew that the things they decided were what they wanted, not what someone else thought they should do. That is what I need. I need to be able to go to sleep, feeling at peace with myself."

Taking a deep breath, she continued. "I need to know that even if I'm not proud of my decision—or if you aren't proud—that I did it because it was what *I wanted*. *What I needed*. I need to be able to stare in the dark and know I did what I wanted—not because I wanted to make the rest of you happy."

She turned and left them, stumbling a bit on the edge of a chair before she climbed the stairs and slowly made her way to her bedroom.

Finally, she realized. Finally, she'd grown up. It had only taken twenty-two years.

chapter twenty-three

"Nice of you to show up today," Daniel said when Landon entered their office a little after three in the afternoon.

After his adventure with Elsie, Landon had gone home and taken a short twenty-minute walk around his property. He needed some time alone to decompress and think about everything that had just happened. And to give thanks to the Lord for the many blessings He'd given them.

He was still amazed that Elsie could one day be perfectly fine.

And now that he was certain she was going to see one day? That erased the last of his doubts about marriage. Elsie was most definitely going to be the perfect wife for him.

Eager to discuss Elsie and the doctor's news, he'd hitched up his buggy and drove to the office.

But obviously his brother wasn't quite ready to hear his good news. "I'm not that late, Daniel."

"Late enough. Landon, you said you'd only be gone the morning. It's almost closing time."

"We rarely work nine to five. Don't act like I don't put in my time at other hours. What can I help you with?"

Daniel held up a stack of folders. "All of this. I've been trying to settle accounts and schedule jobs. It's making me crazy."

Landon hid a smile. His brother's strengths centered on

working with his hands and organizing teams—not numbers or the hundred details that needed to be double-checked before each job began or was billed.

"Hand it all over. I'll work on it here for a while, and take home the rest."

"Danke." Looking a bit sheepish, Daniel said, "Sorry. You know how much I hate paperwork."

"I know." Taking a seat at their long conference table, Landon began organizing the folders by date. "Sometimes I wonder how you got so much done before I got here."

"Edith helped."

"Your Edith is a good woman." Landon opened the top folder, picked up a pencil, and began carefully reading about the job, what materials had already been ordered, and what still needed to be taken care of. He enjoyed the work, and enjoyed making sense of so much that his brother considered gibberish.

"So, what did the *doktah* say?"

"That her eyes have gotten worse, but there's a chance she could see much better with surgery."

"Truly?"

Daniel's surprise was palpable and he scooted back from his work.

"Jah. God is so *gut!* I was trying to make sense of having Elsie as a wife even though she would always be visually impaired, but now it seems that may not be the case."

Daniel slapped him on the back. "I'm pleased for ya. This is mighty *gut* news, indeed. When is the operation?"

"I don't know." Feeling a bit awkward, he added, "Actually, she hasn't decided to move forward with the operation a hundred percent. She wanted to talk to her family first."

"That makes sense, but surely they would be all for the

operation. I imagine it will be costly, but I bet everyone we know will help pitch in for the bills."

Roman nodded. "We can do a charity auction, too. Maybe even a couple of bake sales."

"We'll all do what we can to make things as easy as possible for her and her family, for sure." Grinning, Daniel slapped him on the back again. "This is truly a blessing for ya, Landon. Why, if Elsie can see, she won't be a burden for you."

Something about his brother's words sounded too harsh. "It's not quite like that. She's not a burden now."

"You know what I mean. I meant that she'll be a normal woman now."

That sounded even worse—partly because Landon realized that he'd thought just about the same thing. "She is normal."

Daniel looked like he was about to argue, then took a long look at him and held up his hands in mock resignation. "Sorry. I can see that you're not going to be happy with anything that I say about this. I'll just say that I hope to meet her soon. Remember that we asked you to bring her over?"

"I remember. How about tomorrow night, if it's okay with Elsie? Will that work for Edith, do ya think?"

"It should be fine. Hey, who would have thought that we'd end up like this? Here we are, having to check with our women to even plan a meal!"

Put that way, Landon had to agree that it was something that would have sounded far-fetched even five years ago. "Mamm and Daed would get a bigger kick out of this than we are."

"I'll say. Mamm spent half her time trying to get us to come inside for supper."

Feeling better and more at ease, Landon went back to his paperwork. Finally, he felt that he was getting everything he'd dreamed about when he'd started to make plans to come to Berlin. He wanted to work beside his brother, have his own little plot of land, and find a woman to have by his side for the next twenty or thirty years.

Now it seemed as if it was all coming together better than he'd ever imagined.

Lovina felt as if they were long-lost celebrities in their own hometown. No matter where they went, once their names were given and their connections recalled, she and Aaron were greeted with hearty handshakes, slaps on the back, and welcoming smiles.

She'd been stunned, as had Aaron. They'd had many talks, imagining how everyone had either forgotten them or still held on to bitter feelings about the way they'd left their community and had chosen to stay out of touch.

Little by little, they'd found themselves sharing more about their lives. Talking about Ohio and their six children. Proudly talking about their many grandchildren.

And reaching out to others, too.

By her side, Aaron seemed to smile more. She'd occasionally glimpse a side of him that she'd first been enchanted with all those years ago.

But now, as they exited the taxicab and walked toward the front walk of Karl's house, Lovina knew it would be difficult to say who was more nervous or uneasy.

"I sure wish we had a way to leave easily," she joked. Since the taxi had left, they were going to have to walk several miles if no one at the Swartz house was willing to give them a ride back to the inn.

"*Jah*, this visit puts a whole new perspective on putting faith in others, don'tcha think?"

"Do . . . Do you wish you would have asked someone to join us?"

"*Nee*. This is between me and Karl. And you, of course."

Aaron would probably never have any idea what his words meant to her. For most of their married life, she'd felt disconnected from Aaron's first life. He kept silent about his first wife and child, but she knew he harbored regrets and feelings that he kept from her. But lately, it seemed like they were growing closer to each other, culminating in this very moment, where they were standing together, ready to meet his worst fears head-on.

With that in mind, she stepped forward and knocked. "Let's get this over with then."

A step behind her, he eyed the door like it might bite him. "It is time."

Before they could say anything more, the door was opened by a man almost as old as them.

She didn't recognize him, of course. But by Aaron's sudden tensing of muscles she knew that the man had to be Laura Beth's brother.

After a few seconds' pause, it was obvious that he knew who Aaron was. A brief intake of air was followed by a look of surprise and disbelief.

And quickly followed by an ugly scowl. "Aaron Keim. I never thought I'd see your face again."

"I wanted to see you, Karl."

"Why?"

"Because we have a lot to talk about."

"I don't think so."

To Lovina's amazement, her husband smiled. "Karl Swartz, you've sent me letters for well on forty years, blaming me for Laura Beth's death. Did you never think we'd meet again?"

Karl didn't say anything. Instead, he gripped the side of the door more tightly, as if he was considering shutting it in their faces.

Lovina felt herself aching to say something, to say anything to ease the tension between them. But for the life of her, she could think of nothing that would make Aaron's job easier to bear.

"I didn't kill Laura Beth and Ben, Karl."

"You were driving the buggy."

"I was."

"And you were arguing. You were yelling at her." He was visibly upset. The skin covering his jaw tightened, turning his haunted expression into something more pained. "That is the last memory I have of my sister, Aaron. And of my nephew. Of her cringing while you yelled at her. Of your boy sitting silently, watching the exchange. That is not how their last moments on earth should have been."

"I agree," Aaron said quietly.

Karl blinked. "What? You're not going to deny what you did? You're not going to deny what happened?"

"I can't. It was a terrible thing. Those last moments will continue to haunt me, just as they always have. But what happened was an accident."

"Are there such things as accidents?"

"I hope and pray so," Aaron replied solemnly. "I couldn't bear the idea that Laura Beth and Ben were meant to die that day."

Lovina noticed something flicker in Karl's eyes, right as the door opened wider behind him.

"What is going on?" a man asked before narrowing his eyes at the two of them. "Aaron Keim, is that you?"

"*Jah.* And this is my wife, Lovina."

"New wife," Karl grumbled.

As the newcomer's eyes widened, Lovina noticed that Aaron looked even more uncomfortable. "Um . . . How are you, John?"

"I'm surprised to see you, that's how I am. But happy, too." After shaking both their hands, he turned to his brother. "Karl, why are Aaron and Lovina standing out here on the front porch?"

"They aren't welcome inside."

"That's nonsense!" Looking confused, John opened the door and shuttled them all inside. "What in the world are you talking about? Aaron is family."

"He is not," Karl snapped.

As they walked into a small, neat living room with several sheets covering the furniture, Lovina bit her lip so she wouldn't say anything, but she ached to tell John the whole story.

Her husband looked completely stunned. "John, do you not share Karl's anger?"

"About what?"

"You . . . You don't still blame me for Laura Beth's and Ben's deaths?"

"What? That was forty years ago. And they were your son and wife! Of course, we don't blame you. I can't imagine that you would think we would hold such a grudge." He rubbed a hand along his graying beard. "Is that why you haven't stayed in touch?"

Now Karl remained silent, but Lovina could tell he disagreed with his brother completely. And, she realized, it was becoming obvious that he'd been writing to Aaron secretly all this time.

Lovina couldn't hold her tongue any longer. "For forty years, Karl here has sent Aaron hateful notes, reminding him about their deaths."

John's eyes widened. "Can this be true, Karl?"

"They weren't hateful. There were merely reminders of what happened."

"As if I could ever forget," Aaron said dryly.

When John stared at her again, Lovina said, "Every year on the anniversary of their deaths, he's sent my husband the news clipping of the accident, along with a note that says it's all his fault."

John visibly paled. "Please sit down. We need to talk this out." When Aaron hesitated he said, "For what it's worth, we haven't kept in contact because you never answered our letters."

"I never got any letters from you. I only received Karl's. I thought all of you felt the same way."

A shadow appeared in John's eyes. "It sounds like Karl has done some things we never knew about. Aaron, I, ah . . . I promise you, we all grieved with you. The whole family did. We knew how happy you were together. We knew how happy you made Laura Beth. And you were a wonderful father to Ben."

Lovina noticed that John was looking very determined to not look at his brother. She hoped that Aaron was noticing it, too. Goodness, could the impossible be true? Had Laura Beth's family really not been aware of Karl's hateful notes?

Had they not been feeling the same way as Karl at all?

When she glanced at her husband, she realized that he was stunned.

Well, perhaps it was time to help a bit. *"Danke.* We'd enjoy visiting with you." She took a seat on a sofa.

After a moment, Aaron followed. He looked like he was in a daze, but she knew what that was like. It was hard for a man to look at his ghosts up close and personal. And this moment was everything he'd looked forward to and dreaded at the same time.

And after such a long time, there was no choice but to feel awkward and hesitant.

But that was why they'd come on this journey together, she decided. After all this time, it was still possible to face the past. Even discovering that everything hadn't been quite the way they'd envisioned it to be was worth everything.

The truth always was.

chapter twenty-four

Still groggy after tossing and turning all night, Elsie stayed in bed when her sister rose at dawn.

She lay with her eyes closed as Viola got dressed, neatly plaited her hair, and pinned on her kapp. She didn't even move when her sister paused at her bedside.

Only when she heard the door close and Viola's footsteps fade away did Elsie dare to open her eyes.

There, in the hazy light of dawn, she met her imperfections head-on. Almost everything in the room was blurry and out of focus. It was uncomfortable and a bit disconcerting to notice that there was a part of her that still hoped her eyesight would somehow miraculously get better.

Sitting up, she pulled the quilt up around her chest and tried to imagine a different life, or at least a different way of viewing it.

Would she be happier if everything she looked at was perfectly clear?

She wasn't sure. Did one need perfection for happiness? Or was she simply thinking about things the wrong way? Maybe she should concentrate on the operation itself.

Should she take advantage of science and the doctor's medical knowledge? God had given scientists and doctors the ability to heal the problem with her eyes. Was it wrong to not want to take advantage of it?

But what if she was afraid to have a transplant surgery? Was that a bad thing? She just didn't know.

She was still weighing the pros and cons of it all when her door opened and her mother poked her head in. "Elsie?"

"I'm here, Mamm. Just being lazy."

"I was hoping you'd still be in bed," she said as she closed the door behind her. "I wanted the chance to talk to you, just the two of us."

"Oh?"

She sat on the side of Elsie's bed. "Are you still upset with everyone?"

"I wasn't upset. I simply wanted to be heard."

"That seems to be our downfall, ain't so?" her mother mused. "We are a family of talkers."

"Some of us are," Elsie said dryly.

Her mother smiled. "Perhaps. Elsie, there's no sense in me beating around the bush. I wanted to talk to you about the transplant surgery."

"Yes?"

"What have you decided to do?"

Surprised to be asked instead of told what to do, Elsie said slowly, "I haven't made a decision yet."

"You haven't?"

She didn't want to ask her mother for her opinion. After all, she'd just told everyone that she needed to decide this for herself.

But this was her mother, and now that they were sitting alone together, Elsie realized that she needed to hear her mother's thoughts. "Mamm, what do you think?"

"You know what? I think you were right to say what you did yesterday. In the end, it doesn't really matter what I want or what I think."

"I'm sorry I was rude yesterday."

Her mother laughed softly. "Perhaps you were. But we weren't listening, you know. Sometimes even the best of us has to lose patience every now and then."

"I'm ready to listen to you now."

Fingering the diamond pattern stitched neatly in Elsie's quilt, her mother murmured, "Well, I will tell you that I have a whole new appreciation for people who struggle with a part of their body that doesn't work like it should. Having pneumonia made me realize that none of us are as strong as we think we are. I tried to do too much, even when I knew I didn't feel good."

She crossed her legs. "And even when I knew I should rest or at least try to get some medicine . . . Instead of doing those things, I pretended I was okay."

"I've done that," Elsie blurted.

Her mother stilled. "You've done what?"

"I've pretended that I could see better than I could. I've also pretended that I don't mind not being able to see," she confessed.

"Here's the million-dollar question: Does your failing eyesight bother you?"

"Of course it does. And it scares me, too. I get sad when I think about living the rest of my life in the dark."

"Anyone would feel that way," her mother soothed. "That is nothing to be ashamed about."

"I don't want to live being sad or depressed, Mamm. I want to be the type of person who shows the rest of the world her best. Even if my best is being visually impaired, I don't want to hide behind my insecurities. I want to shine through in spite of them."

"It sounds like you'd rather live at peace with your disability than constantly wish for things to be different. "

Slowly, Elsie nodded. "I've spent almost ten years preparing for Dr. Palmer's diagnosis, Mamm. I had pretty much made peace with it. I mean, I thought I had."

"Until this very moment, I don't think I ever truly realized how strong you are, Elsie. You make me so proud."

The praise was gratifying. But it didn't change the fact that she had so much to overcome, both inside herself and with her disability.

But perhaps God was showing her yet again that there was no need to be so impatient for everything to be "right." Here, her mother was patiently listening to her discuss the pros and cons of her future—not pressing her to make a choice right away.

"Elsie, no matter what you decide to do, please don't forget that you have a whole family who is eager to lend a hand. Not to *do* things for you, but to *help you do them*. There's a difference, you know."

"I hear you, Mamm."

She got off the bed and stretched a bit. "Goodness, but I can't wait until I get my full strength back. I seem to always be so tired."

"Perhaps you, too, shouldn't forget to let us help you."

She chuckled at that. "It seems I need to learn to listen to my advice!"

When Elsie was alone again, she crawled out of bed, then looked around the room, straining her eyes to see through the blurriness. Then, she closed her eyes and turned in a circle, trying to determine how much she would one day miss what little sight she had. For the first time, she relaxed and quit fighting her fear.

As she became more aware of what she could hear, of the air brushing against her bare ankles, she realized that she wasn't as flustered or upset as she imagined she would be. It was as if her body had already accepted that her eyes didn't work well and had begun to make up for it in other ways.

She was going to be okay.

With that knowledge came a curious sense of relief. Instead of concentrating on the pressure around her eyes, instead of feeling frustrated and disappointed that she couldn't do something most others could, she felt curiously free.

Liberated.

As if she'd finally delivered herself into God's hands.

After they'd left the Swartzes' house, Lovina and Aaron had gone back to their hotel. For most of the evening, Aaron had stayed particularly quiet, and Lovina let him have his peace.

She imagined it was difficult for him to match the reality of their visit to Karl with what he'd dreaded all this time.

In the morning, over a breakfast of hot biscuits and sausage, eggs and cinnamon rolls, they discussed it some more. "I still can't believe Laura Beth's whole family doesn't hate me," Aaron confided with a shake of his head. "On our way there, I was prepared to have the door slammed in our faces."

Lovina thought about that. "You know, Aaron, when you first told me about Laura Beth and Ben, I don't remember you saying that her whole family blamed you. Was that really the case?"

Looking surprised, he shook his head. "I don't remember any of them blaming me. Of course, I was so grief-stricken that it was all a blur. But, Lovina, I truly didn't feel like I had caused the accident." He paused to sip his orange juice. "You know, it was only after I had received Karl's letters for years that I began to feel that all of Laura Beth's family blamed me."

"Folks say time heals all wounds, but that ain't always the case, is it?"

"*Nee.* Sometimes it seems to make those problems even more pronounced and difficult to handle."

Lovina thought about that. Then she thought about Jack. About how much that boy had meant to her for a brief amount of time . . . and how she'd made his memory into something much different from the way he'd really been.

She knew why she'd exaggerated his good points and minimized his faults over the years, too. She'd needed him to be a better person than he was in order for her to feel better about herself, too.

If she had faced her own faults—that she'd made foolish choices with a boy she hadn't really known all that well, she'd have to come to terms with the fact that she couldn't blame anyone other than herself for her pain.

When her husband finished his eggs, he pushed his plate aside. "Are you ready to visit your old neighborhood now?"

"Not especially. I don't think it will serve any purpose since my parents are in Wisconsin. Plus, the friends I did have drifted off long ago when they discovered the lifestyle I chose."

"I still think we need to stop by, if for no other reason than you should see your old house."

"I suppose I would like that," she mused. "It was a nice home for me."

Aaron's gaze softened. "You know, Lovina, I don't think I ever truly realized the sacrifices you made to leave everything behind. Leaving Pennsylvania and your family was difficult."

"Leaving it all wasn't a sacrifice. At least it didn't feel that way at the time. I wanted to be with you, Aaron."

"Did you love me back then?"

"I think I did."

When his eyebrows rose in surprise, she chuckled. "It was a long time ago, Aaron. And, to be truthful, we didn't know each other all that well. Did you love me when we first married?"

"I wanted to."

Almost as soon as he said the words, his cheeks started to pinken. He looked embarrassed about his honesty.

But she thought that was probably one of the kindest things he'd ever told her. "This probably won't make sense, but I feel better about our past now."

"Really?"

"*Jah*. Before, I was always sure that I could have done things better, that I could have been a better wife and mother. That I could have made my parents learn to accept me and my decision. But now? I am starting to believe in myself. I'm starting to realize that I really did do the best I could all those years ago. I did my best, and that is all anyone can ever ask for."

"You were asking for more of yourself than you were able to give," Aaron said.

"Yes. I was asking for too much from myself . . . and not enough from others." It was a surprising comment for her to make. But it felt right, too.

"Let's go see my old *haus*, Aaron. I'm ready to see it . . . and then to go home to Ohio."

chapter twenty-five

"Landon, I'm mighty excited to meet your *bruder* and his wife. Her name's Edith, didn't you say?"

Before he could answer, Elsie continued in a rush—the same way she'd been chattering ever since he'd helped her into the buggy. "Oh! And their *kinner*, of course. They're twin boys, *jah?*"

"*Jah.*" Landon couldn't help but steal another glance at Elsie as his horse clip-clopped down the nearly empty streets between her family's home and his brother's house. Though it was dark outside, the lantern on the back of the buggy cast a glow around them, illuminating Elsie's smile. She looked so happy—the way he felt inside.

"I think you're going to like Daniel and his family," he said easily. "I know they'll like you."

"I hope so."

"I know so," he countered, just to see her smile again. "We're almost there. Five minutes at the most."

When Elsie relaxed against him, he gave in to temptation and glanced at her again.

He was so proud of her. Though she hadn't mentioned her doctor's visit or her eye problems once since he'd picked her up, he knew it had to be weighing on her mind. He knew if a doctor had recommended such a surgery to him, it would be all he could think about or want to talk about.

However, Elsie was made from a different cut of cloth, he thought as he guided the horse up Daniel's driveway. She obviously wasn't going to let her worries about the upcoming operation dim her mood.

After pulling the buggy to a stop, Landon walked around to help Elsie out.

"Danke," she said when he reached her side. "Usually I try to climb down on my own, but I don't want to risk falling right in front of your brother and sister-in-law."

"I don't mind helping you at all," he said, realizing how much he meant his words. He liked reaching up and resting one of his hands around her waist while taking her hand with the other. Most of all, he liked how she trusted him to help her. It made him feel strong and sure, like he could do most anything.

As he swung her down, he felt her tremble. Was she nervous about meeting his brother? Or, was it for a far different reason? Was she feeling the same tension between them that he was?

When her feet were steady on the ground, he touched her cheek lightly with the pad of his thumb. "Are you okay?"

She looked up at him, her eyes wide. *"Jah."*

"Daniel and Edith are easy to get along with. Please don't be nervous."

"I won't be," she murmured before reaching to pick up her basket filled with rolls from the buggy's bench seat.

Just as they started toward the door, it opened wide. Then out poured Daniel, Edith, and their twin boys. The boys were barely three and seemed to constantly waver between sticking by their parents' sides and coaxing each other into mischief.

"Hi, everyone!" Landon called out. "This is Elsie."

Edith trotted out in front of her boys. "Nice to meet you,

Elsie. I'm Edith," she said with a smile. "Here, let me help you with your basket."

Before Landon could say another word, the two women were walking into the house together, Edith's hand curved around Elsie's elbow. The boys scampered next to them, already asking a dozen questions.

Daniel chuckled as they watched the procession. "And here we thought our women might not get along."

It felt good to hear Elsie referred to as his. Lately he'd begun to think of her that way, too. She'd become his in his heart before his mind had even made peace with the change. "I guess I was foolish to worry about this dinner," he said softly. "I just didn't want her to feel uncomfortable."

"She's pretty, Landon. You never mentioned that. All you ever talked about were her vision problems."

That caught him off guard. Was that really how he'd been thinking of Elsie? By her disability first? "I'm sure I told you she was attractive."

As they started forward, Daniel gestured to the front steps. "She seems to get around okay even though she can't really see."

"She's not completely blind."

"Oh, I know you said that. But I have to be honest with ya, I was half expectin' to see a woman with a cane, stumbling around."

Landon paused. Had that been how he'd described her? As someone who was helpless?

Feeling his cheeks heat, he rushed to her defense. "Elsie doesn't stumble."

"Settle down. I was only sharing my opinion."

"Let's go inside. I bet the women are wondering where we are."

"I doubt that. They seem as happy together as two old friends," Daniel said, but he led the way inside anyway.

Right away, Landon walked to the kitchen to check on Elsie. When he saw Edith handing her dishes to place on the table, he rushed to her side. "Do you need help carrying those plates?" he murmured quietly enough so that only she could hear.

Elsie shook her head. "I'm fine. As long as Edith doesn't hand me any sharp knives, I shouldn't be a danger to anyone," she joked.

He appreciated that she could make jokes about her vision problem, but he didn't want her to feel too embarrassed to ask for help if she needed it. "You're the guest, Elsie. Why don't you have a seat? I can help Edith take things out to the table."

"Landon, I don't want to sit."

"Elsie's already told me about her eyesight, and about what she feels comfortable doing," Edith informed him with a small smile. "I'll help her if she needs it. But I feel like I should point out that she's already carried over the glasses and napkins to the table."

"Truly?"

Elsie grinned. "Truly. Bo here helped me."

Looking down, the little boy nodded. "I walked with Elsie. I'm her helper."

Daniel must have noticed his hovering and Edith's exasperation. "Come over here, Landon, and help me with Benjamin. He needs a clean shirt."

Once they were in the boys' room, Daniel playfully slapped him on the back. "You sure are smitten! I've never seen a man be so attentive. You certainly were never like that with Tricia."

"Tricia was different. Elsie sometimes needs an extra hand. I just don't want her to—"

"I know, Landon," Daniel interrupted while Ben squirmed as he pulled off the stained shirt and slipped another one on. Lowering his voice, he said, "So when will she have her operation?"

"I haven't asked her that yet."

"No? Well, I hope she mentions it tonight because Edith already told me that she's hoping she can help with the meals at her house."

"I'm sure they will appreciate that when the time comes."

He was about to add more, to talk about how worried he was about the operation, how he intended to go back to the library soon to read about corneal transplants, when Edith called them to the table.

"We'll talk about this later," Daniel said as they walked to the dining room.

As Elsie sat down next to Landon, it took almost everything she had to keep from grinning broadly. Finally, she was doing the living she'd wanted to do for so long. No one had kept her home or had warned her to be extra careful.

No one had cautioned her about Landon or reminded her that she shouldn't really be entering into a relationship. Instead, the rest of the family had merely said goodbye when Landon had come to the door to get her.

At long last, she was living the way she'd always dreamed of living—simply as another woman in the world.

She didn't want to do anything special or be anyone special; she just wanted to be herself and be accepted for that.

After they were all seated, Ben and Bo in booster seats on the chairs on either side of Edith, they all bowed their heads in silent prayer. Elsie was so thankful, she found herself silently praising Jesus for her many blessings, Landon and his acceptance of her foremost in her thoughts.

Then, it was time to dive into the feast that Edith had prepared.

"Fried chicken, mashed potatoes, and two vegetable casseroles," she exclaimed. "It looks *wunderbaar*!"

"Indeed," Landon said with a grin. "My brother is a lucky man to have married such a good cook."

Edith laughed off the praise. "Landon only thinks it's so good because he's a bachelor. Men don't learn to cook much besides sandwiches and cans of soup."

"That's true," Landon said. "Growing up, Daniel and I didn't learn how to do much more than work the can opener. Only now am I learning how to make eggs."

Elsie smiled at that but said nothing.

"Maybe your bachelor days won't last forever," Daniel hinted not so subtly.

"Daniel, stop," Edith said. "You're going to embarrass our guest."

"Sorry," Daniel said.

Luckily, the boys started demanding more attention, and so the rest of the meal was centered on their needs instead of her and Landon's relationship.

After dinner, Elsie and Edith cleaned up the kitchen while the men helped the boys wash up and put on pajamas for bed.

Then, all too soon, it was time for them to leave. Elsie was disappointed that their evening had flown by so fast, but was secretly reminded that now she and Landon would have the chance to spend a few precious moments together alone.

After they said their goodbyes, Landon was once again at her side, helping her back into the buggy.

"Tonight was fun," he said. "Daniel and Edith liked you a lot. I could tell."

"I liked them, too. Edith and I might see each other soon. I told her I'd like to come over and help her with the boys one afternoon."

"She would love that. Edith is mighty capable, but still . . ."

"Twin three-year-olds are twin three-year-olds! Believe me, my parents could tell you stories about the mischief Viola and I caused when we were children."

"You were mischievous? I can't imagine."

"Though it's hard to believe, I wasn't always perfect," she joked.

They were now alone on the road. Happy from the good conversation, relieved that the visit had gone well, hopeful about her future, Elsie felt herself relax. Little by little, she scooted closer to him, letting her muscles ease and lean against him.

Landon wrapped one arm around her as his left loosely held on to his horse's reins. "This is nice," he murmured.

"Jah." She loved the feel of his hand on her shoulder, the way she could feel the warmth from his body, the way he smelled so clean and masculine.

Most of all, she loved feeling like she was finally experiencing something that she'd feared she'd only dream about. At last, she had a boyfriend. She felt so blessed, too, because it seemed that he was accepting her as she was, with her disability and all. That was truly a gift.

As she looked out the buggy's front window, she noticed that the only thing they could see were what was illuminated by the light at the front of the buggy. Otherwise, it was completely dark.

And the darkness wasn't scary because she had someone to travel the road with.

It was as if God had just given her a sign that her dark future was going to be all right. All she'd had to do was stop fearing it.

Landon slowed Mike. "It sure is dark out," he murmured.

"I was just thinking that."

"Are you worried about traveling in the dark?"

"*Nee.*"

"*Gut.*"

Then, to her amazement, she felt him brush his lips on her temple. She felt that whisper-quick brush all the way to her toes . . . and started wondering if he was going to kiss her good night.

Wouldn't it be something to finally have her first kiss? Though Viola never talked about such things, Elsie knew her sister had kissed other boys a time or two—even before she met Edward.

All her life Elsie had ached to know what it would feel like, to be held in a man's arms, but of course she never asked anyone. Viola would feel sorry for her. Or it would be too awkward.

Worse, Elsie had figured such a conversation would make her sad, because it would be so terribly obvious that she wasn't going to be kissed anytime soon.

But now, this night, there was a mighty good chance that her prospects were about to change.

Too soon, he removed his arm from around hers in order to guide Mike onto her driveway.

Already, she felt chilled. "We're home already?"

"*Jah.*" He cleared his throat. "We got back fast."

"We did," she agreed, then winced inwardly. She sounded inane.

When he set the parking brake, he turned to her. Took her hand. "Elsie, I'm glad we did this. The more time we spend together, the more I'm anxious to see you again. I hope my eagerness doesn't scare you."

"I'm not scared." She wasn't scared about anything anymore. Not her future. Not about the darkness. Not about him leaning just a little bit closer and pressing his lips against hers . . .

He straightened. Leaned closer. "*Gut,*" he murmured. "I'm glad."

She sat as still as a statue, half forgetting to breathe. Waiting for him to lean closer still . . .

But all he did was hop out of the buggy and walk around to help her down.

Ah. It was now obvious that tonight wasn't going to be their first kiss.

"Let me help you down," he said as he reached for her hand.

She leaned forward, rested a hand on one of his strong shoulders. Then was taken completely by surprise when her chin bumped his. "Sorry!" he whispered around a chuckle. Just before he brushed his lips against hers. And then kissed her again.

Then, just as if she'd imagined it, their kiss was over. He lifted her down. Stepped away.

"*Gut nacht,* Elsie," he said formally.

"Good night," she replied. Just as formally.

Then she turned around and started for the door. She took care to walk carefully, to grip the handrail as she went up the two steps to the front porch. But inside? Oh, but she was far from feeling staid or stiff.

Inside, she felt as if she were floating on air.

And since no one was standing in front of her to see, she was also wearing the biggest smile ever. She had a tremendous secret that was hers alone.

Well, hers and Landon's.

The very best kind.

chapter twenty-six

"Are you sure you don't want to knock on anyone's door?" Aaron asked as they took a turn around the park where Lovina played as a child. "Now's your chance."

"To be honest, I had thought I would want to talk to Jack's parents, but now I realize that isn't something I want to do."

"And why is that?"

"All this time, I've been thinking that Jack had meant more to me than he did. But once you and I started talking, I realized that he was but a moment in a very long life that I've been blessed to enjoy. Only that!"

Aaron looked skeptical, and she didn't blame him for it. But what she'd begun to realize over the last few weeks was that she had no regrets about becoming Amish. She'd had a nice life with Aaron. Together, they'd built a strong and solid legacy that their children and grandchildren would enjoy.

None of that would have been possible if she hadn't been forced to grow up and reexamine herself that summer after high school. If she'd still been clinging to childish dreams, she never would have looked twice at Aaron.

She certainly wouldn't have fallen in love with him and been willing to give up everything for a life with him.

"Aaron, I think I kept all those mementos in the attic because I didn't want to completely forget my childhood. I had a nice one, you know."

"I do know." Smiling at her old house, he said, "You had a childhood filled with camping trips and neighborhood barbecues. With slumber parties and dances and Ed Sullivan on TV."

She looked at him in surprise, touched by the soft tone she heard in his voice. "I haven't talked about any of that in ages!" Probably not since they'd married and she'd tried so hard to be Amish.

"But I still remember, Lovina."

With a burst of awareness, she realized that she still remembered, too. "I've never regretted becoming Amish," she said. "I had a happy childhood, filled with love and many friendships. But I've never regretted my choice to become Amish."

His gaze continued to search hers. Looking for signs that she was concealing her true feelings.

But she wasn't.

"Lovina, you told me that before," he said, "but I don't think I ever really believed you."

She wasn't shocked by his revelation. "I don't know if I ever really believed it myself," she joked. "Now, being back, it makes me smile, remembering the girl I used to be . . . but not nostalgic."

As they continued to walk along the neatly manicured walkways, Lovina smiled at a few curious children who couldn't seem to help but stare at her kapp and at Aaron's beard. She pointed out several lovely roses and a thicket of bright yellow daffodils and lilies. "I do love spring, Aaron."

"I know you do." He cleared his throat. "I bet your garden at home is starting to bloom."

Imagining the pretty garden that they'd both designed and nurtured over the years, she nodded. "I think it must be. When do you want to head back?"

"Is tomorrow too soon? I want to see Sara and her family one more time, but then I'll be ready to go home. I'm anxious to sleep in our bed."

That was how things were, wasn't it? All of the things that used to seem so familiar now felt vaguely uncomfortable. Like they'd put on someone else's clothes that were the same size and the fit was right, but they didn't feel as comfortable as the clothes hanging in their closet.

"That suits me fine." She smiled at him then, and was surprised to see him gazing at her with an expression filled with affection. "I love you, Aaron," she whispered.

"I love you, too, Lolly," he murmured right back, giving her a little tremor of delight up her spine.

Here she was, in her sixties, and her man could still make a shiver run down her spine!

She was embarrassed and delighted, all at the same time. God was so good. God was so very, very good indeed.

Landon couldn't quite get over how much he enjoyed sitting in the Keim kitchen. At the moment, Elsie was holding Regina on her lap and sharing a few chocolate chip cookies. Across the kitchen, Regina's mother, Amanda, was making taco soup, and Viola and her mother were putting together a layered salad. Goldie was sitting near Viola, looking hopeful for scraps.

Next to him, Roman was studying house plans. He and Amanda had decided to build their own cottage on the other side of the barn. It was to be a small house . . . a cozy place for the newlyweds to spend a few years before moving into the main house.

Landon was interested in the house plans, but he couldn't

help but let his gaze stray to Elsie's every few minutes. She looked so content and peaceful, sitting with a little girl on her lap. He could only imagine how she would look when she held a child of their own.

Roman must have thought the same thing, because he said, "Elsie, when are you going back to the eye doctor?"

"I don't know. In a few months, I suppose."

Before he thought better of it, Landon blurted, "How come he doesn't want to see you any sooner?"

Gently, she helped Regina hop off her lap. When Regina went into the other room, Goldie at her heels, her voice turned sharp. "Landon, why would you ask that?"

Landon was stunned. "Well, I mean . . ." he sputtered.

Little by little, all the action in the kitchen came to a standstill. Anyone could see that they were all on pins and needles, waiting for Elsie to tell them what was going to happen next.

But she was obviously waiting for him to complete his thought. Feeling vaguely apprehensive, he finally continued. "Well, you've got to set up your next appointments, right?"

"For what?" Elsie's eyes narrowed. She looked more than a little confused. And, perhaps, defensive?

He felt that way, too. "Don't you need to get ready for your transplant surgery?" he blurted before he reminded himself to merely listen like his mother had.

Obviously as at sea as he was, Roman chimed in. "You didn't forget that I talked to the bishop about it and he gave his blessing, did you, Elsie?"

"Of course I didn't forget what the bishop said."

But Landon also noticed that she didn't seem as if she cared about the blessing, either.

"Elsie?" her mother asked, turning slowly toward her. "You made your decision?"

"*Jah.*"

"I see," her mother said, then turned back to the stove.

Feeling confused, Landon glanced at Viola and Roman. They were obviously as uninformed as he was because they were staring at him with the same expression.

"I don't see," he finally said.

"I, uh, decided not to have the corneal transplant surgery after all."

Viola spun toward her sister, her expression incredulous. "Why?" she asked.

As Elsie took her time answering them, Landon felt his heart beating faster than normal. He was disappointed and confused. He even felt a little angry. He wanted her to be able to see.

Even more than that, he wanted *her* to want to be able to see.

As he waited, Elsie seemed to measure her words. He hoped she would offer some kind of reason that he could understand.

If he could understand her thinking, he knew he would support her.

But to his dismay, Elsie simply shrugged. "I just decided that I didn't want to do it. That's all."

His heartbeat slowed. There was his answer.

"That's no answer," Roman blurted. "Mamm, do something."

"It's not my place, Roman. Nor yours."

Elsie lifted her chin. "After a lot of thought and prayer, I decided that it would not be the best decision."

"Because?" Roman prodded.

"Well, for one, a surgery like that is expensive. Thousands of dollars."

Viola shook her head in dismay. "Elsie, we're talking about your eyesight!"

"There's more to it than just that," Elsie said softly. "I didn't want to have a part of someone else's eyes in mine. It didn't seem right. And, well, I also realized that I'm at peace with going blind."

Roman looked incredulous. "But, Elsie, the bishop said—"

"I respect Bishop Coblentz," she interrupted. "I do. But these are my eyes, not his, and I think that means my opinion weighs more than his."

Her brother scowled. "It's not a matter of who is right and wrong."

"It doesn't matter now, anyway. I made my choice, and my decision is that I don't want to have the surgery. I already called Dr. Palmer and told him."

"What did Dr. Palmer say?" Viola asked.

"He thought I should get the surgery, but he also admitted that lots of things could go wrong in a transplant surgery. Lots of things."

"And you're scared of that?" Landon asked softly.

"*Jah.* It could make things worse," Elsie said. "There's a chance that I could find myself seeing nothing at all—not even shadows or light. That I would just be in complete and utter darkness." She winced.

Though his mind was still reeling, he tried to offer her some support. "I wouldn't want to live like that, either."

"I know you wouldn't," she said.

Then, to Landon's dismay, Elsie smiled sweetly. "But that's why it's so *gut* that we've found each other, Landon. You made me realize that I don't have to be perfect to have a perfect life."

Roman turned to him with a scowl. "What did you tell her?"

"Nothing."

"You must have told her something." Roman glared.

Landon knew Elsie was waiting for him to respond to her statement.

But he didn't think he had any words in his head. Not any that were coherent, at any rate.

He was so stunned, it took everything he had to keep his expression blank. To keep his mouth shut.

Because inside, he was yelling and cajoling. And wanting to say that he'd only been so forward because he'd thought she was going to have the surgery.

He'd thought they'd actually be able to do everything he'd wanted to do in life; that he could make good on his plans. If she could see, he could still have his job with Daniel. He would still be able to devote fifty to sixty hours a week on their business because Elsie would be home taking care of things, raising their children.

If she couldn't see, none of that could happen. He'd have to give up some of his dreams for success. He'd have to tell his brother that he couldn't do his part in their company. Afraid to make a scene or to make the situation worse, he stood. "I need to go."

"But, Landon, don't you want to stay and talk about things?" Elsie asked.

"Not right now. I can't. I, ah, just remembered some forms I told my brother I'd take care of."

"I'll walk you out then."

He didn't want her to. He didn't want to have a private conversation with her until he had time to get his emotions better under control.

She walked to his side, seemingly oblivious to the rest of her family's stunned expressions.

Once outside, she turned to him and rested a hand on his arm. "I'm so glad you were here when I told my family the news, Landon," she said, her voice light. "You don't know how I've been dreading the moment when I had to tell everyone that I wasn't going to have the surgery. I needed there to be at least one person in the room who agreed with me. Who understood my feelings."

He hated what he was about to say. But this time, he knew he couldn't hold back his thoughts. It would be cruel if he led her to believe he supported her decision. "Elsie, your news was a big surprise to me, too."

She wrinkled her nose. "Really? At your brother's house you didn't seem to mind my disability. Actually, you acted like it didn't bother you at all."

"Elsie, I thought you were going to get your operation." As she stood there staring at him, he forced himself to continue. "I thought you were going to be able to see one day. I thought you were going to be normal."

The moment he said the words, he ached to take them back. *Normal* wasn't the right word, and it wasn't what he meant.

But it was too late.

She took a step back from him. "And right now, you do not think I'm 'normal.' "

"That wasn't exactly what I meant," he said, scrambling. "Elsie, I only meant that if you could see, it would be much easier for you. Everything would be much easier. And better."

"And for you, too, *jah?*" Her voice turned accusing. "You don't want to have a wife who can't see, do you?"

Though he felt guilty about it, he couldn't lie. Not about something so important. Not about this.

His mouth went dry. He ached to tell her something different. He ached to be the type of person who could look at problems in his life and shrug them off instead of dwelling on them.

But he wasn't that type of man.

While he'd thought that he was getting used to courting a woman who was going blind, as soon as the possibility of surgery came up, he realized how much hope it had given him. How happy it had made him.

So it was with regret but not surprise that he answered. "I don't. I need a *frau* who can *see*. Who will be there for me, and for our *kinner*. Who can take care of a *bopli*. I need a woman who I can depend on."

Before she could interrupt, he held up a hand. He needed to tell her what he thought, even if it was painful to hear. And hard for him to say. "This . . . This is nothing personal, Elsie. It's just that I have plans. I've worked a long time to prepare for them, worked a long time to put everything into place. It's too late to change, you see. . . ."

"Too late?"

"I know I sound rigid. Maybe I am. But if I am, that's even a better reason why we shouldn't see each other anymore. I wouldn't be the right man for you." He felt almost justified. Perhaps that was the way to look at things—not that she was lacking, but that they weren't suited. Feeling a bit better, he added smoothly, "I wouldn't be able to be the husband you needed, and that would be wrong."

"Funny, even though I can't see all that well, I had plans, too."

Her voice was bitter. He swallowed his shame and forced himself to think about the future, about the future he'd planned so hard to prepare for. "I realize that, Elsie."

"*Nee.* You realize nothing." She turned her back on him. "Landon, I know you are friends with my *bruder,* but please, don't come back here again. I don't want to see you ever again."

"Elsie, I'd like us to still be friends."

"I don't think that will be possible. I have no interest in being your 'friend.'"

"If you change your mind, you know where I am."

"I won't."

Still staring at her back, he scrambled for something better to say. For some way to make himself feel better, and to make her understand. "With my job, I'm gone for hours at a time. Sometimes over twelve hours. How would you get along like that? Elsie, you could get hurt!" He yearned to mention what could happen to a baby, but stopped himself, knowing that reminder would be cruel.

"I guess we'll never know how I could get on, will we?" she said as she started forward. "And heaven forbid I get hurt," she added, her voice thick with sarcasm.

He flinched, hating that he was hurting her. But he knew his worries were justified. If he didn't stand firm now, things would only get worse in the future.

What he was doing was for the best for both of them. The last thing either of them needed was false hope. To hope for something that they couldn't count on.

With mixed feelings, Landon forced himself to stand still as she walked to the door. As she stumbled on the stairs. When he watched her struggle with the door handle that seemed to stick.

He stood in the cool night air, watching through the window as she walked through the kitchen and bump into a chair before moving out of sight.

Then he was alone, standing alone, in the dark. Exactly how he wanted to be.

And that is when he knew he'd never felt lower or more alone. For a brief moment, he'd been so sure he was going to have everything he'd ever wanted.

Giving up that dream was as hard as telling her the truth about how she wasn't ever going to be the woman he needed.

Elsie Keim was a lovely woman who possessed a very kind, very loving heart. She would make some man a wonderful wife, too.

Just not him.

Only later, when he was sitting in his empty house that needed too much work, did he realize what else he was feeling . . . a pinch of jealousy for the new man in her life.

That new man was going to be a blessed man, indeed. Landon sincerely hoped he realized that.

chapter twenty-seven

After the difficult conversation with Landon, Elsie told her family that she was skipping dinner and had run upstairs to come to terms with what had just happened in private.

She was hurt and weepy. For a few moments, she gave in to temptation, took off her glasses, and cried, but mostly she just lay on her bed and stared into nothing.

She simply had no idea what to do next. She felt suspended, adrift. More alone than ever.

She'd just fallen into an uneasy doze when their door creaked open and Viola joined her.

"Elsie, you have to tell me what happened when you and Landon went outside to talk."

Knowing that it would do no good to ignore her, Elsie replied. "We talked."

"Come on. Please tell me what happened. All I could do during dinner was wonder what the two of you said. Don't leave me in suspense!"

"There's not much to say." She slipped back on her glasses and blinked.

"Well, you got everything ironed out, right?"

Viola's voice was so eager, so happy for her, it only made Elsie feel worse. "Not exactly."

In the dark, Viola slipped off her apron and dress, then

opened her top drawer and pulled out a nightgown. "Elsie, you can't leave me like this." She paused. "Oh my gosh . . . Did it not go well?"

"It was more than that."

"What do you mean?"

"I mean . . ." Her voice cracked. Unable to continue without bursting into tears, she said, "I need to go brush my teeth." Quickly she padded down the hall, turned on the flashlight that they kept on a shelf, and quickly washed her face and brushed her teeth.

And then stood in front of the mirror and wished for once that she could see herself as others saw her. Naïvely, she'd assumed that if she was able to handle her disability, then others would be able to as well.

But now she realized that for Landon, at least, it hardly mattered how she felt about her body. It was his perception that counted.

And unfortunately, that was something that she couldn't change. No matter how upbeat or purposeful she tried to be, she would never be able to change Landon's negative view of her.

Perhaps he was right. Perhaps it was best that they'd ended things now. Before she'd grown to depend on him, or before she'd imagined that he could love her.

When she returned to their room, Elsie could sense Viola watching her from her twin bed. She was tempted to merely crawl into her own bed and pretend to go to sleep, but she now knew she wasn't going to be able to sleep for hours.

Instead, she walked to Viola's bed and scooted in beside her. With a grunt, Viola moved over. It was a tight fit, but being next to her twin felt right.

"We haven't shared a bed in ages," Viola whispered.

"Soon, it will be impossible. You'll be in Belize with Edward."

"And maybe one day you'll be with Landon?"

That was the tipping point. Realizing that no matter how much she might have wanted it, that wasn't going to happen.

Her eyes began to water, and at last she let the tears fall. "That's not going to happen, I'm afraid."

"What do you mean?"

"I . . . Landon told me that I'm not good enough for him. He . . . He wants a normal woman. One who can see."

"He wanted you to have the transplant operation. That doesn't mean he didn't think you were good enough. I felt sure that as soon as you two were alone he'd come to his senses."

"He has come to his senses, they just don't include me. Viola, he—he said he couldn't bear to have a wife who he couldn't depend on," she said, sputtering. "He didn't want to be stuck with a woman who he would have to worry about while he was working."

"Oh, Elsie," Viola murmured. "I am sorry."

She was sorry, too. Rolling over, Elsie turned her back to Viola. Only that way, lying on her side, could she share the worst.

As the tears fell, sliding down her cheeks and staining the collar of her nightgown, she confessed all of it. "He didn't even want to talk about how I could still do lots of things, or how I've realized I hear better than I used to. He wanted that operation. The operation and for me to be 'normal.' Otherwise, he doesn't want me, Viola."

"You must be mistaken. I saw how he looked at you. I thought he was falling in love."

"He didn't." Elsie hadn't misunderstood one thing. "And

while I know I shouldn't have gotten my hopes up, I'm so sad. I really thought he was the right man for me."

Worse, she'd truly thought she had been the right woman for him.

She'd thought she'd mattered enough to him for him to make some sacrifices.

Viola wrapped her arms around Elsie's back. "Do you want to change your mind about the surgery?"

"*Nee.*"

"Sure? You maybe could have Landon then."

"Viola, I've wished I could see, I've wished that Landon saw more of me than my poor vision. But I haven't once thought about getting that operation so he'd have me."

"You sound mighty sure."

"I am. It's . . . It's a tricky procedure. Sometimes the transplant doesn't take. What would happen then? I don't want to change myself to make him want me. What if something else happens to my body one day and I'm not 'normal'? What if I have the operation, have someone else's corneas, but I still can't see? Will Landon push me away then?"

"You're not being entirely fair to Landon," Viola protested. "He's a good man, Elsie."

"I agree. Landon is a good man. But he's not being entirely fair to me, either. After all, isn't love supposed to be blind? Isn't love supposed to be stronger than our weaknesses? Or, at the very least, isn't love supposed to mean that you love someone in spite of their faults?"

After a moment's pause, Viola nodded. "Yes, I'm afraid you are right. Edward loves me even though I'm far from being an ideal missionary wife. He loves me in spite of my imperfections."

"Exactly," Elsie said, glad her twin understood. "I mean,

aren't we all more than our worst parts? Shouldn't we be? I know that I can't see too well, and that one day I'll hardly be able to see at all. But to be perfectly honest, I really thought I was more than just a pair of bad eyes." Lowering her voice to a whisper, she added, "I mean, at least, I wanted to be."

"You are. You are far more than that. You've always been more than that. It's Landon's loss if he doesn't understand that. If he doesn't want a relationship because of this, it proves that this problem isn't only about you, Elsie. It's about his problems, too."

"What do I do now? Should I try to forget about him?"

"I don't know."

"I feel like I shouldn't be as sad as I am. I mean, I hardly knew him. But the idea that we could be more made me so happy."

"What you do now is what we all do. We pray for guidance. And we pray for strength so that we may make some good decisions and choices. And then we're going to give thanks for the blessings we already have."

"And after that?" Elsie had no idea. At the moment, she couldn't imagine meeting another man who would make her feel that way.

"And then?" Viola shrugged. "And then we pray again and try to open our hearts to a hopeful future."

"And after that?" Elsie teased.

"And after that?" Her eyes widened, as if she was finally stumped. "And then? Well, tomorrow morning, I think we'll need to make a cake," Viola said with a smile.

"Cake? Does that make things better?"

"Definitely, if it's chocolate."

Elsie considered the benefits of consuming half of a deliciously dark chocolate cake. "I think cake might help."

Viola giggled. "We're going to need chocolate frosting, too. It's not easy getting a heart broken, you know."

Until that moment, Elsie didn't know that it was possible to laugh and cry at the same time. "*Danke*, twin."

Viola patted her back. "You're welcome. I'm glad I could help. I'll be happy to help you anytime you need it, of course. Anytime at all."

Elsie closed her eyes, finally feeling like she could rest at last. No, her heart wasn't happy. And yes, she was feeling mighty blue. But things weren't without hope.

Viola had showed her that there was always hope. And when that was in low supply?

Chocolate would work. In a pinch.

We liked Elsie a lot, Landon," Daniel began the moment Landon walked into the front door of the office the next morning. "A whole lot."

"Is that a fact?"

Daniel nodded, completely missing the dry humor in his tone. "As a matter of fact, Edith and I can hardly stop talking about her. She was perfect for you. Kind, friendly, and easy to get along with." He paused, then blurted, "And she's so pretty, too."

"Looks aren't everything, you know."

"I know that. But still . . ." He smiled. "Just think, you're going to be a lucky man, starting each day with her smile."

Though his brother was teasing, Landon felt like he'd been kicked in the gut. Elsie really would be a beautiful sight to wake up to. More important, she was so even-tempered, he was sure that each day would begin in a positive way.

To his embarrassment, he knew he'd entertained a daydream or two about sharing breakfast with her in the mornings. Sipping coffee while chatting with her across the table. Instinctively, he knew that she would be the type of woman to raise him up . . . not bring him down.

But now, that dream was gone, and it would be for someone else to appreciate. Someone who had more time to care for her. Someone who wasn't trying to make a go of his business.

"I broke things off with her last night," he said baldly.

Daniel scowled. "Why in the world did you do that? She's practically perfect, Landon."

But that was the point, wasn't it? He reminded himself. She wasn't perfect.

Though now, this morning, perfection didn't seem as important as happiness did.

Steeling himself, he said, "Elsie told me that she elected to not have her eye surgery."

His brother looked dumbfounded. "If she doesn't have surgery, what is she going to do about her eyesight?"

"Nothing. She is simply going to let her vision deteriorate."

"She said that?"

"She did. Elsie told me that she's made peace with losing her vision."

"Wow."

"Yeah. That's what I thought." But funny enough, now Landon wasn't so sure that Elsie had made the wrong decision.

Daniel crossed the room, his expression matching his hard stride. "And that's why you broke up with her?"

"I had to do it. At least, I thought I did." Feeling more confused by the second, he said, "Daniel, Elsie won't be able to do anything."

"She seemed pretty capable when she was at our house. Edith said she was a lot of help in the kitchen. And the boys loved being with her."

"I can't believe you're saying all this. You told me yourself that you didn't want anything to interfere with our business. I thought you would understand where I'm coming from."

"Well, I know I did say those things. But, ah, that was before I met her. She's pretty great, Landon. You're not likely to find any better. Actually, I think Elsie is better than you deserve."

"Is that a fact?"

"Yes," he muttered, not sounding the least bit apologetic. "Landon, I can't believe you broke things off. I don't know what Edith is going to say."

Great. Now he not only was going to be facing his own fears and demons . . . he was going to have to answer to his sister-in-law, too.

This was most definitely not turning out like he'd imagined it would. He'd come to Daniel for support, not guilt.

Somewhat weakly, he said, "Elsie is not going to be able to see, Daniel. That's a mighty big problem. I need a wife to help me."

"*Nee, bruder.* You need a wife to *love* you. That's what's important. Everything else can be managed. You can hire help. You can live close to her family, so they can help her when you can't. She can spend some days with Edith and the boys when we're out of town." After glaring at him another moment in exasperation, he picked up the cell phone that had just started chirping.

As he watched his brother walk to his calendar and start flipping the pages, the words he'd said seemed to taunt him.

Love. His brother was exactly right. Somewhere along the

way of reaching his goals, he'd forgotten what was important.

He'd started concentrating on goals and to-do lists instead
of things like family and caring and love.

He'd started thinking that "home" meant a comfortable
house on a piece of land of his very own. But it wasn't that at
all. No, it was living day to day with people you cared about.
It was laughing when milk spilled and mud was tracked
through the house and when dishes broke.

It was being around each other when things weren't perfect as well as when they were.

And the funny thing was, he had a feeling that Elsie could
deal much better with life's little crises far better than he
could. She would be the one to make bad days not seem so
terrible, and good days even brighter.

She would have been the reason for him to get up in the
morning. And more important, she would have been his
whole reason to come home at night.

But now that wasn't going to happen, because he'd just
completely ruined everything.

Thinking about how easy it had been for him to be around
her, how easily he'd talked to her, how open and giving she'd
been . . . he finally understood the truth.

Elsie Keim was special.

There was a reason that he'd never felt a connection with
any other woman. It wasn't because he hadn't had the chance
to meet other women—it was because the other women
weren't Elsie. She was the one. She was the woman for him.

Daniel had actually made it all sound so simple, and
maybe it was. All that really mattered was that there was
love between a couple. Love and friendship and a willingness
to work hard on a relationship.

If they had those things, other things could be worked out.

What was going to be a lot harder, of course, was finding a way to rectify the complete mess he'd made of everything.

He needed to find a way to talk to her again. And then, once she agreed to see him face-to-face, he was going to need to find a way for her to trust him again.

And then?

Then he was going to have to find a way to get her to fall in love with him.

Just thinking about all the ifs made his head spin. It was obviously going to take a lot of backpedaling. And a lot of understanding from Elsie. And a lot of luck. And a lot of prayer.

Luckily, he believed that with God and prayer, all things were possible.

chapter twenty-eight

To Lovina's surprise, Lorene and her husband, John, were waiting for them at the house when the English driver dropped them off from the German Village.

"Why are you here?" Lovina asked, already worried that another crisis had occurred.

Their daughter rolled her eyes. "Mamm, it's *gut* to see you, too."

"We're tired and worried about everyone, daughter," Aaron said sharply as he stepped forward and gave Lorene a gentle hug.

Lorene looked surprised by the spontaneous affection, but after a moment's hesitation, she returned her father's hug. John stood off to the side, looking concerned, but just as relieved as Lovina felt. It was past time for all of them to have a warm and loving relationship.

Looking bemused, Lorene stepped away, then turned to Lovina. "Mamm?"

Lovina opened her arms, too, and felt tears prick her eyes as she hugged her daughter tight. "I missed you, Lorene," she said.

"We missed you, too."

"Lorene talked about you quite a bit," John said with a wry expression. "It seems she was used to having her parents around to tell her what to do."

"Is that true, daughter?"

"A little," Lorene said with a smile. "John is right, though. You were missed. Both you and Daed."

"We missed being here."

John walked them around to the *dawdi haus* entrance, carrying their two heavy bags like they were small sacks of flour.

When they got inside, Aaron walked right over to the stove and set to brewing a pot of coffee.

After she washed her hands and added cream to her cup, they sat down at the kitchen table.

"Perhaps you can now tell us where everyone is?" Aaron said.

"Roman took Amanda and Regina out to lunch and shopping. He wasn't going to go because you were coming in, but we persuaded him to take some time off for his family," John explained.

"I agree. Amanda and Regina need to see him when they can. Preaching and working the farm gives a man little spare time," Aaron murmured.

"Where are Peter and Marie?" Lovina asked.

"Marie had a doctor's appointment today."

She exchanged a glance with Aaron. "Oh?"

"It was just a follow-up," Lorene hastily explained. "To make sure she is still improving."

"That is *gut*. And the girls?"

"Viola is working, and Elsie asked to go with her to Daybreak. She said she wanted to visit with Atle, Edward's father, and the rest of the folks there."

"I am glad she is doing that." But she also thought it a bit strange. She had to admit that her feelings were a bit hurt. Of everyone in the family, she was closest to Elsie. She would have hoped Elsie would have been as eager to see her as she was to see her precious granddaughter. "I'm a bit surprised, though. When I called here yesterday, she said she was going to be here waiting for us."

"I think she was wanting to keep busy," Lorene said. "To keep her mind off her troubles."

"Troubles?" Aaron set his coffee cup on the table. "What kind of troubles?"

Lorene and John exchanged glances. "Elsie's been having a time of it," Lorene hedged.

Finally, they'd discovered the root of the tension in the air. "What is wrong with Elsie?" Lovina prodded as she did her best to keep her patience. Honestly, it was like pulling teeth to get a bit of information from these two.

After sharing a look with Lorene, John answered. "Quite a bit. First, Elsie went to Dr. Palmer, who said she was a *gut* candidate for a corneal replacement surgery. If she did that, there is a chance she could see."

Lovina reached for Aaron's hand. "I didn't know such things were possible. When will this take place?"

"It won't," Lorene said quietly. "She has decided to not have the surgery."

"No surgery?"

"No. Even though the bishop gave his approval," Lorene said.

"Perhaps she'll change her mind," Aaron said.

"I think not," Lorene said. "See, she already told Landon about this."

"And?" Lovina prodded.

"It seems that when she told him about her choice, he made a choice, too. He said he didn't want to court her no more. Now she's terribly upset."

"I didn't know they'd gotten so close." Lovina exchanged a confused glance with her husband.

"Perhaps you could back up a bit," he said.

John explained everything in a shorthand, no-nonsense way. Through it all, Lovina felt her heart race for Elsie's decisions, and her disappointments, too.

When John finished, she sighed. She hated to hear all what Elsie was going through, but what else could they do?

"I think we should say something to Landon," Aaron said. "He's obviously too dumb to realize how special Elsie is."

Lorene shook her head. "That is not a *gut* idea. We can't do that."

"But we should do something," Lovina said reasonably. "She needs us to get involved."

John stood behind Lorene and placed both of his hands on her shoulders. Then he shook his head. "Forgive me for saying this, but I think all of us here know that interfering in another couple's romance isn't always the best thing to do."

Lovina felt her cheeks heat. But this wasn't the same thing at all. This time, she had legitimate reasons to get involved. She was sure of it! Plus, it was to make Elsie happy. "But—"

"You're exactly right, Lorene," Aaron interrupted quickly. "I don't intend to interfere in romances ever again."

Lorene raised a brow. "Mamm?"

"I won't interfere, either," she said grudgingly. "But for the record, I want to say that Landon Troyer is being a hard-headed mule."

Slowly, John smiled. "Though I was thinking of a bit different descriptor, I have to say that your words are true. That is something we can all agree on."

chapter twenty-nine

Peter paused outside the barn. Elsie was holding three new-born kittens on her lap, smiling softly as the little furballs climbed over her apron, mewing and meowing, their little ears twitching and turning.

When one batted at the string of her kapp, like it was a new ball of yarn, she laughed.

Peter found himself smiling, too. He tried to hold times like these when she was doing something so Elsie-like forever in his heart. She'd always been special to him, had always looked at the bright side of things, even in the toughest situations.

Now, she was managing to smile and find joy in a litter of newborn kittens even though he was very sure she was hurting inside.

Funny, he'd been so certain that letting her become independent was a big mistake . . . until he realized someone else was thinking that!

Now, he wanted to argue with Landon and tell him that there was nothing Elsie couldn't do as well as, if not better than, any other Amish woman.

More than even that, he wanted to give Landon a piece of his mind. He'd just tossed away the opportunity to have wonderful relationship with a very special girl. They all had their faults—he knew that for sure.

And while it was true that her poor vision was going to

create a few problems, he realized that there were so, so many other things that she could be afflicted with—such as Landon's obstinate nature!

Peter was torn between wanting to yell at the man and giving thanks that his sweet daughter hadn't wasted any more of her time on him.

"Daed, are you ever going to come in and join me?" she asked, her voice light and infused with a fair touch of humor.

He stepped in. As his eyes adjusted to the barn's dim interior, he murmured, "You caught me, huh?"

"*Jah.*" She set one of the kittens on the ground, and it carefully started walking toward him. "I may not be able to see all that well, but I sense things better than most. What have you been doing? You were standing there so still."

"Oh, nothing. I was just thinking about something."

After scooping up the tiny orange-striped kitten in one hand, he sat beside her. "The kittens seem like they're doing *gut.*"

"I think so. Now that their eyes have opened, they are learning their way around and giving their mother a little break." As another jumped at a sister or brother, misjudged the distance, and tripped, they both chuckled.

Elsie scooped it up again and set it carefully in the middle of her apron. "There are few things more precious than tiny kittens."

Only children, he thought to himself. His mother had said once that she hadn't completely understood God's infinite love until she'd had children. As soon as Roman was born, he'd understood what she meant. His love for his three children was limitless. He held out his hands and took one of the squirming fur balls, chuckling when it meowed, then snuggled closer.

"So, Daed, are you doing all right now?"

She'd managed to catch him off guard. "Me?"

"*Jah*. Do you feel better, now that you went to the clinic?"

Ah, yes. "I do." He exhaled. "Elsie, I tell ya, I'll always be full of regret for what I did. I'm sure I'll also always be filled with regrets for what my addiction drove me to do. But I have to also admit that some good things came out of it."

She gazed at him. "What did?"

"Well, for one thing, I feel easier inside."

A brow lifted. "Inside?"

"*Jah*. It's as if I can finally breathe deeply now. Like before I always had so much other stuff in my lungs and body that there wasn't enough room for fresh, clean air. Now, though, each breath I take is fresh and new."

"I never thought about it like that."

"I didn't, either. It's amazing how I didn't know how far gone my addiction was until I got better. It's like I had to see myself at my worst, through other people's eyes before I could make changes." It hurt to talk about his faults, especially to the one person he wanted to always think well of him.

But perhaps she was the person who he needed to be the most honest with?

"Elsie, all I can say is that I am sorry for what I put you through. For what I put all of you through."

"You don't need to apologize."

"I may not need to, but I want to."

"I am glad you're better, Daed."

Another kitten, this one almost pure white, scampered toward him. He carefully picked it up and smiled when it licked his finger with a scratchy tongue. "Elsie, I came out here because I was worried about you. We're all worried about you. And sad about what happened with Landon."

"I thought my news would make its way through the family rather quickly. Did Viola talk to you?"

"A little. But perhaps things aren't completely over between the two of you. Maybe Landon will change his mind."

"I doubt he will. And once more, I don't think he should. If he is truly worried about whether I can even be home alone, then he hasn't really gotten to know me."

"That is true. But, ah, I hope you won't be too terribly hard on him if he comes back and apologizes."

"Why is that?"

"Because sometimes men aren't as smart as they need to be. We're all mighty imperfect, you know. Your mother's said she's been tempted to hit me on the head a time or two, just to knock some sense into me."

Elsie chuckled. "Maybe not too many times, Daed. You're a wonderful-*gut* man."

His heart melted—just like that. "Only because of my family. You all have made me a better man."

They sat for a while longer, leaving off the serious discussions in favor of watching the kittens' antics instead. Little by little, Elsie scooted closer. And soon they were joking like they used to, when it was so easy to make her happy.

"I'll be all right, Daed. I'm just sad."

"I know you'll be all right. But I'm still going to keep my eye on you," he said lightly. "It's a father's job to worry, you know."

She simply smiled. A melancholy one.

Which made his resolve to go calling on their neighbor even stronger.

When Landon saw Elsie's father walking up his front walk, he mentally groaned. He knew he had a lot to make up for. But he didn't want to talk to Peter Keim before he talked to Elsie.

But when her father knocked on the door, then entered, his entire body looking ready to go into battle with him, he resigned himself to the inevitable.

They were going to have a discussion about his behavior right now. Whether he was ready for it or not.

"Good evening, Peter," Landon said. "What brings you here?"

He raised a brow. "I can't imagine my being here would be much of a surprise, Landon. Over the past few weeks, you've single-handedly managed to make my daughter the happiest I've ever seen her in years . . . and the most depressed."

He felt his cheeks heat. Suddenly, it was as if he were six years old instead of twenty-six. "I'm sorry to hear that. It wasn't my intention to make her feel that way."

"It doesn't matter. You still did."

"Does Elsie know you're here?"

"*Nee.* She wouldn't be too happy about it, neither. She would tell me that her relationships are none of my business."

Landon knew that Elsie was a smart woman. "But you decided to pay a call anyway?"

"I did. Because, Landon, I've found over time that some things canna be put off. Sometimes if you do, it doesn't make them better, they only fester and get worse." He eyed him knowingly.

And as the man had probably expected, Landon squirmed under his direct gaze.

"I am sorry I've made her upset." After a second, he added, "However, I don't think our relationship is over yet."

Peter scratched his head. "I must be getting old, because I don't know what you mean."

"I, uh, have been rethinking some things."

"Such as?"

"Such as how I might have been a bit shortsighted, as far as Elsie's vision was concerned."

"Might?"

"Was. I realized I was wrong about Elsie." He paused, wanting to keep the rest of his thoughts what they were—private. To himself. But Peter's gaze was unwavering and it was easy to see that he wasn't going to let Landon off with a few vague words.

As he thought about it, it made all the sense in the world, too. Elsie was a special woman. Special and a bit delicate. And not just because of her vision problems, either. No, she had a way about her that was more vulnerable than most women. She wore her heart on her sleeve. There, ready for anyone to do damage to it if they weren't careful.

And he hadn't been.

"I spoke to my brother earlier today and he reminded me of how love isn't something to be taken for granted," he finally said. "Love is hard to come by, and even harder to recognize. I should have realized that my feelings for Elsie were stronger than anything that could keep us apart."

A look of new understanding appeared in Peter's eyes. "So you have strong feelings for her?"

"I love her." Of course, the moment he said the words, he felt guilty. No woman wanted her father to hear those words before she did.

"You look pained, son."

The "son" reference was an encouraging one. "I need to tell Elsie that instead of you."

To Landon's further amazement, Peter grinned broadly. "Well, of course you do. Elsie won't want you saying those sweet words to me."

Peter was now joking with him? The quick change of emotions was incredible. "Peter, I need you to keep what I just said a secret, just between you and me."

"Well, now, that depends on something."

"On what?"

"On when you decide to pay her a visit and tell her yourself."

"Now?"

Elsie's father looked shocked. "I think not. You look like something that's been dragged behind a horse and left to rot."

"That good, huh?"

"I suggest you come over tomorrow afternoon. After you talk to Elsie, you may stay and have supper with us."

Landon was tempted to point out that supper with the Keim family still wasn't quite the romantic gesture he'd hoped for. He had a feeling he was going to have to do a lot of apologizing and coaxing even to get her to agree to see him. He certainly didn't want to do that with witnesses!

"I suppose there is no other way to see Elsie?"

"Nope. You may come when it is convenient for us or you may stay home. All by yourself."

Landon stood up and held out his hand. "I'll see you tomorrow, then."

"And you'll come prepared?"

Landon wasn't sure what that meant, but he figured he would by tomorrow night. "Of course."

"*Gut*," Peter said. Then he turned around and walked out the door.

Landon could have sworn he heard something under the other man's breath that sounded a lot like "young pups" but he couldn't be sure.

That was probably best, anyway. He had enough trouble, he didn't need Peter Keim adding to the pot.

chapter thirty

Pandemonium.

To Elsie, it felt like the whole household had gone bananas, and she was stuck in the middle of it with nowhere to go. Everyone was talking at once, talking too loud, in an overly happy way.

In an overly suspiciously happy way.

It was like they all knew some special joke but hadn't seen fit to fill her in on it.

It had been like this ever since her father had come home from his errands yesterday afternoon. And today had not been any better—for some reason, most of the family had decided to congregate in the kitchen and had forced her to join them. Viola and Roman were there, as well as Amanda and Regina. And her parents and grandparents. All chatting merrily. Just like they had all kinds of wonderful-*gut* things to celebrate.

In fact, it had seemed like she was the only person in the family who wasn't talking merrily or laughing at a new joke. As the minutes passed, Elsie became more and more uncomfortable.

She knew her sour mood hadn't gone unnoticed. Every so often, someone in the family would cast a worried glance her way, then try to include her in the conversation.

She'd had no desire to talk to anyone, and had tried to leave the room more than once.

But each person seemed intent on keeping her with them, Viola most of all. "Come on, Elsie," she coaxed with what looked like a terrible, pasted-on smile. "How about trying out some of the applesauce Amanda and I made this morning?"

"*Nee.*"

"You should try it. It's *gut.*"

"Viola, I'm not hungry."

"It doesn't matter if you're hungry, you can still give it a try, don't you think?"

Elsie wanted to snap that it did, indeed, make all the difference in the world. But she knew such comments would only make her seem surlier than she was already acting. "Viola, I'm sure your applesauce is *gut*, it always is. But I don't want any."

Her mother walked over and peered at her closer. "Are you feeling poorly?"

Her heart was. "I'm fine."

"You don't look fine." Reaching out, she looked determined to pat her face all over to see if she had a fever. It was a habit of her mother's that Elsie had always found rather annoying.

"Mamm, there's no need to put your hands all over my face."

Her mother lowered her hand. "Elsie, I was only trying to help you."

"I know you were, but I am old enough to know if I have a fever."

"Elsie," her grandmother admonished with a heavy frown. "Watch your tongue. There's no need to snap at your mother like that."

The small furor that had been brewing in her belly seemed determined to reach its pinnacle, her true breaking point.

Looking out the kitchen window, Elsie ached to jump to her feet, run out the door, and keep on running until her feet could no longer carry her. Anywhere had to be better than where she was.

Anything had to be easier than the situation she was in.

But since that didn't seem possible, she bit her lip hard. She was now determined to hold her tongue, while hoping and praying she would be allowed to leave sooner than later.

Another ten minutes passed.

It felt like four hours.

She was debating whether to ask again what was going on or to simply leave when her father clasped his hands together. "Everyone, he is here! And it's about time, too."

The tension in the room suddenly dissipated. Which was funny, because Elsie now realized that she hadn't even noticed the tension. She'd thought it was merely her bad mood infecting her gregarious, happy family.

As she looked around, it slowly dawned on her that she was the only person who didn't seem to understand the significance of her father's words.

Even little Regina seemed to be delighted about her *dawdi* Peter's announcement.

The suspense was starting to drive her crazy. "Exactly who is here?" she asked.

Her mother grinned. "It's a surprise."

Exasperation warred with her curiosity. Maybe it was Viola's Edward? She couldn't think of any other reason for the family to be so excited.

"Viola, tell me," she whispered. "Is Edward here?"

"Nope," Viola said as she turned away and started walking to the door. "You sit tight. I'm going to go let him in."

She wanted to stomp her feet like a child. Or complain. Or scream. She wanted—no, needed—to do something!

Not caring anymore if she sounded disrespectful or shrewish, Elsie fairly yelled at her father. "Daed, who is here?"

"Dear, it's Landon, of course," her mother said as the mudroom door opened and Viola's voice floated into the kitchen.

"Landon?" she whispered. This was not good news.

Then, as she waited for someone—anyone—to fill her in, in walked Landon Troyer himself. He looked bashful and handsome and determined.

Without even a quick greeting to the crowd of people standing in the kitchen, he walked directly to her. "Hi, Elsie."

Hi? He came over to say hello?

Still confused and miffed, she eyed him coolly. "Landon, why are you here?"

"I wanted to apologize. And to explain myself, too."

Elsie sat up straight, slowly realizing that everyone in the family intended to be a part of the conversation. "Now?"

"*Jah.* It's as good a time as any, don'tcha think?"

"*Nee.*" It was too much. "I don't believe we have anything to say to each other."

There. She'd done it. She'd just pushed away the best man who'd ever come into her life. She steeled herself to watch him turn and walk away from her for good.

In front of her whole family.

But instead of heeding her words, he knelt down and rested his hands on the edge of her chair. "Your father told me you'd probably tell me something like that."

"My father?"

Landon gestured behind him. "*Jah*. He paid me a visit yesterday."

Now she was really mortified. "Daed, did you tell Landon to come over here and apologize to me in front of the whole family?"

He shifted on his feet in a guilty way. "Not exactly . . ."

"What, *exactly*, did you say to Landon?" When he merely looked at his feet, she felt her temper rise again. "Daed, I wish you wouldn't have done this."

"It's not like you're thinking," he said quickly.

She was so angry, she got to her feet. "Landon, I'm sorry my father made you feel obligated to do this . . . this public apology. I promise, I had no idea he had such a thing planned."

But instead of accepting her apology, Landon shook his head as he got to his feet, too. "Don't be hard on him, Elsie. When your father came over, I had already planned to come over here to see you. I was ah, just trying to gather my courage."

"Gather your courage?"

"*Jah*. Shortly after we parted the other night, I began to have my doubts about all those plans I'd been so proud of. Once more, I began to realize just how stupid I'd been."

"You did?" she asked again. Slowly, she began to be aware of just how much the rest of the family was concentrating on Landon's words. It was so still in the room one could hear a pin drop.

But she was just as aware that she no longer cared about who was listening, or what anyone else thought. All she cared about was Landon and the words she was hearing from his lips.

Landon, too, seemed to be oblivious to all her relatives' ears. He reached out and gently took her hand. "My brother reminded me of something that I'd recently forgotten. That plans are good and all, but they're meant to be only that . . . *plans*. Not something carved in stone that can never be changed."

He paused, and then continued, his voice huskier than before. "Daniel also reminded me of how much harder it is to find a person that you want to spend the rest of your life with. To fall in love with. That is what needs to be sheltered and protected and guarded, no matter what."

Her hand felt secure in his hand. "Is that what has happened to you?" she whispered.

"*Jah.* I've fallen in love with you, Elsie. I'm in love," he said with a sheepish-looking smile. "Completely, definitely, without-a-doubt in love!"

As she looked at him in wonder, he continued. "Elsie, I want to keep you close to me always. That's what is important. That's all that matters. Everything else? It pales by comparison."

These were words out of her daydreams. Words she'd begun to believe she'd never hear. They were so sweet, so kind, she found herself simply staring at him. Speechless.

Landon continued with a smile. "Elsie, I asked Peter to have your family here on purpose. I wanted everyone who is important to you to know how important you are to me. And more important, I want them to be my witnesses."

After looking around the room, he said, "Elsie, I promise you now, in front of everyone present who is important to you, that from this day forward I will do everything I can to make you happy. I want to marry you, Elsie."

"Even if I can't see?"

"Especially if you can't see. No matter how you come to me, I want you, Elsie."

"But what if I can't give you anything in return? I don't want to be your burden."

"Elsie, you already make my burdens lighter. Your happy spirit makes any load feel lighter. Your willingness to accept everyone around you for what they are—not for what you wish them to be—humbles me. Makes me yearn to see other people that way, too. I've already discovered that every day is better with you in it."

She didn't know what to say. How could she? How did one respond to such sweet, heartfelt words? Her mouth went dry as Landon stared at her, looking for a response.

She glanced at Viola. Though she couldn't really make out Viola's expression, she did see what her sister wanted her to . . . a slow, decisive nod.

"Well," she said. Then paused, trying to form words when her mind seemed to have gone blank. Warily, she looked at Landon. Prepared herself to see his impatience with her.

But all she noticed was that he was still there. And her hand was still clasped between his own.

She tried again. "Landon, I've done a lot of thinking about the two of us . . . and about what you thought life might be like if we were married. And, ah, I have to say that you weren't all wrong. It might be a mighty difficult thing, to be married to a woman who can't see all that well. Or at all," she forced herself to say.

"We can make it work."

His words matched his tone. Both sounded certain. Confident.

But how could she be sure what was the right direction to go? Whatever she said was going to affect the rest of her life.

From the back of the kitchen, her grandmother cleared

her throat. "If I may," she began. "I would like to share some-thing that I've learned most recently."

Elsie turned to her, as did Landon.

"What did you learn, Mommi?" Viola asked.

Her grandmother glanced at her grandfather, then drew a breath. "I've learned that nothing is impossible, as long as you have support from people who love you. And you have many people who love you, Elsie. I, for one, think Got ar-ranged your relationship with Landon here mighty nicely."

"Because?" Landon asked.

"Because we're all here, of course, young man," she replied in a huffy voice. "We can help as needed."

That did sound wonderful, but did she want to enter a marriage, knowing that she was going to have to rely on all of them? Maybe it was too much.

Maybe he hadn't really thought about what he was getting into.

"Landon, perhaps you should think this through some more."

"I have thought it through. That's why I called over here earlier and asked for your family to be here. I want us to be married, Elsie. But I want more than just a marriage, I want a future that we can feel good about."

"And you'd feel good with my family here?"

"I'd feel good knowing that you have everything you need. Maybe you won't need them all that much. But just in case you do, I don't want you to be afraid to ask."

She turned, looked at her family. "What do you all think of this?"

To her surprise, Roman laughed. "What do we think? Elsie, why else would we all be here? We want to be here. And we don't want you to ever be afraid to ask for help if you need it."

Viola walked toward her. "And if you don't need our help, I want you to be able to tell us that, too."

"Could it be as easy as that, Landon?"

He held out both hands to her. "Only if you want it to be."

It could be easy . . . but only if she wanted it to be.

That was what life was like, wasn't it? You could grasp the future with two hands, or hold yourself apart and be afraid.

You could live independently by yourself, and not do things because they were too hard.

Or you could depend on others . . . and let them carry you through when you needed it. Her wonderful, noisy, complicated family was right there for her.

As was a man who was willing to have everything . . . if he could have her, too.

And so there was only one choice. One beautiful, awe-inspiring, blessed, wonderful choice.

Reaching out, she clasped Landon's hands.

Then right there, in front of everyone, she looked him in the eye as best she could and said what was in her heart.

"Yes."

As the room exploded in cheers and Landon wrapped his arms around her and held her close, Elsie felt as if for the first time in a long time, she saw the world clearly. She was loved.

And because of that, all was well with the world.

It was perfect.

epilogue

Oh, what a day! Dear Viola's wedding day! She was as tired as she'd ever been, Lovina decided, as she stepped out onto the narrow front stoop of the *dawdi haus*.

Looking out into the yard, she recalled the faint impressions left from the dozens of buggies parked on the lawn. The flower beds that she and Marie and Lorene had so carefully tended and nurtured were a bit trampled now. No matter what the occasion, children had a way of forgetting to watch where they were going!

Taking care to shut the door quietly behind her, she sat down on the step, letting her bare feet graze the soft spring grass that was already turning damp with dew. Viola and her Edward had been quite the happy couple.

Actually, everyone in the family had been happy. Happier than they'd been since she could remember. Lovina let herself smile as she recalled how merry the wedding luncheon had been, and how pleased Peter and Marie had looked as they watched Viola flit about.

Roman and his wife, Amanda, and Elsie with her fiancé, Landon, had been just as exuberant. But that was to be expected, she mused. Newlyweds and soon-to-be newlyweds were supposed to be all smiles.

It was only recently that she'd realized that older married couples could enjoy the same bliss.

It was late. Very late. Aaron had gone to bed hours ago. She had a feeling the rest of the family was asleep, too.

But for some reason, she wasn't quite ready to say goodbye to the day.

But of course, the day had already passed.

As far as she could see, the only lights to be found were in the form of twinkling stars overhead. Leaning back slightly, Lovina gave into a childish impulse and attempted to count them.

When she got to thirty, she giggled softly. Many years ago, her own father had told her that he'd sometimes felt decades younger than his age. At the time, she hadn't believed him—but probably because she had been at the stage in her life when she yearned to be older.

It had been too hard to imagine wanting to be younger.

But here it had happened. Here, she was doing something she'd done back when she was eleven or twelve. . . . And counting those faraway stars still felt as exhilarating as it had when she was small.

Yes, time really did move on. Day became night and then day again. Before she knew it, another week had gone by, then a month, and then yet another year.

Life had a way of doing that, she supposed. People fell in love, got sick, had babies, simply *lived*. Time kept passing whether a person was ready or not.

And what a year her beloved family had been through!

At last, all of their carefully hidden secrets had come to light, and one by one, each of them had been forced to deal with the revelations.

To her surprise, they'd all become better people because of the disclosures. She and Aaron had finally dared to return to Pennsylvania and confront the people they'd tried so hard to leave behind. And in doing so, they'd reconnected with Sara and her family.

They'd even learned that forgiveness is always possible, even after forty years.

Peter, after finally seeking treatment for his alcohol problem, seemed to be happier. He and Marie had reached a better place in their marriage, too.

Each of Lovina and Aaron's *kinner* were calling and writing often now. And Lorene had finally found love with a man she'd first been infatuated with ten years ago.

They'd all done a lot of growing up, too. Roman was now preaching to the community, Viola was now married, and would be moving to Belize in just a few days.

And Elsie? Her sweet Elsie was engaged and bravely facing a future she knew she'd never see.

Since she was alone, Lovina allowed the tears to come. Elsie's blindness, and her eventual decision to not have surgery had been quite a blow. For a family who ached to fix everything, it had been hard for them to accept Elsie's decision to keep things the same.

But of course, Elsie had also taught them so much about acceptance and perspective. Elsie had taught them about patience and perseverance. About inner strength.

That was when they'd all realized that Elsie wasn't broken at all. Instead, she was as she was meant to be—sightless but full of insightfulness about the world around her.

Now, as Lovina sat alone on the stoop, fighting the urge to go to sleep in order to eke out the last minute of the day, she realized that Elsie was the smartest one of them all.

At the end of the day, when darkness fell and the light of others dimmed, believing in yourself was really all that mattered, wasn't it?

Everyone was blind to what lay ahead of them. It didn't really matter how much a person planned or struggled or fought. . . . What was in one's future depended on God's will.

And a person's acceptance of that will, of course.

Here in the dark, where she saw nothing but the stars . . . where she felt only the cool spring grass and warm air caressing her skin, Lovina smiled.

And finally, she understood.

At the end of the day, when only her thoughts lay between herself and sleep's oblivion, God gifted her with eventide.

Eventide . . . those blissful few moments when day turned to evening, that precious time that hovered between action and sleep.

That time when she could embrace the future and all of its surprises and beauty and fears and its unknowns.

The moments when she could cling to the silence and hold it to her heart, knowing that in a few, brief hours the light would come again and carry with it the dawn of a brand-new day.

Gripping the door frame for support, Lovina Keim got to her feet. It was time to finally bid the day farewell and give her problems to the Lord.

Time to finally let the beauty of sleep claim her, and let the mystery of her future be what it always had been . . . just out of her reach.

She opened the door, stepped inside, and let the door close behind her.

The day was over, night had come, and she was at long last able to receive it with open arms. Just as the Lord had intended.

"I am blessed," she murmured as she walked through the

house on bare feet. "I am blessed. I am happy. I am at peace," she whispered as she climbed into her bed and carefully pulled the smooth cotton sheet up to her chin.

And when she closed her eyes, felt her body relax and her mind drift . . . she knew that God was very, very good.

Insights,
Interviews
& More . . .

Meet
Shelley Shepard Gray

I GREW UP IN HOUSTON, TEXAS, went to
Colorado for college, and after living in
Arizona, Dallas, and Denver, we moved
to southern Ohio about ten years ago.

I've always thought of myself as a
very hard worker, but not "great" at
anything. I've obtained a bachelor's
and master's degree . . . but I never was
a gifted student. I took years of ballet
and dance, but I never was anywhere
near the star of any recital. I love to
cook, but I'm definitely not close to
being gourmet . . . and, finally, I love
to write books, but I've certainly read
far better authors.

Maybe you are a little bit like me. I've been married for almost twenty years and have raised two kids. I try to exercise but really should put on my tennis shoes a whole lot more. I'm not a great housekeeper, I hate to drive in the snow, and I don't think I've ever won a Monopoly game. However, I am the best wife and mother I know how to be.

Isn't it wonderful to know that in God's eyes that is okay? That from His point of view, we are all exceptional? I treasure that knowledge and am always so thankful for my faith. His faith in me makes me stand a little straighter, smile a little bit more, and be so very grateful for every gift He's given me.

I started writing about the Amish because their way of life appealed to me. I wanted to write stories about regular, likeable people in extraordinary situations—and who just happened to be Amish.

Getting the opportunity to write inspirational novels is truly gratifying. With every book, I feel my faith grows stronger. And that makes me feel very special indeed. ᝄ

Letter to Readers

Dear Reader,

I have a secret. Lovina turned out to be my favorite character. I had been sure it would be Amanda. Maybe Elsie. Maybe Atle (I really liked Atle!). I almost always write about people I would like to know.

But when I first started *Daybreak,* I was thankful I did not have a Lovina Keim in my life.

There were many times I was tempted to highlight her scenes and press delete, and make up a different grandmother. You know, someone cozy. Pleasant. Happy.

But something kept me from doing that. As I wrote *Daybreak,* continued on to *Ray of Light,* and then finally began *Eventide,* I started to see her flaws, her hurts, and her attributes, too. By the time this series closed, I was very fond of her. I liked how fragile she was inside, and how she'd developed a somewhat hard shell to make up for that. Most of all, I loved how she slowly let the Lord's light shine inside her.

It turns out I would have enjoyed a Lovina of my own after all! I hope you, too, connected with one or two of the characters in this series.

Yet again, I find myself getting ready to close a thick spiral notebook. The one for the Days of Redemption series was bright blue. Now that I'm at the end of the series, it's in pretty sad shape. It's filled with notes and pictures and poems—everything in the made-up world of the Keim family.

Soon, I'll head back to the grocery store and pick up a new notebook, this one for my return to Sugarcreek. I, for one, can't wait to begin to write the new series. It will begin with *Hopeful*, followed by *Thankful* and *Joyful*.

This letter would not be complete without conveying my thanks to you for reading my novel. Someone the other day asked what I'd rather be doing instead of writing, and I drew a complete blank. I love to write, and I'm grateful that you've given me the chance to do so every day.

God bless you all, and I hope, like the Keims, you will get the chance to celebrate today.

With blessings and my sincere thanks,
Shelley Shepard Gray ～

Shelley Shepard Gray
10663 Loveland, Madeira Rd. #167,
Loveland, OH 45140

5

Questions for Discussion

1. What do you think about Elsie's role in her family? Would that have changed if she hadn't been afflicted by a vision problem? What is your role in your family? Has it evolved over the years?

2. What problems, if any, do you think Peter will have now that he's back? How did Marie's time in the hospital affect the reunion with his family?

3. Roman's new wife, Amanda, comes alongside Elsie in several key moments. How do you think her perspective helps Elsie?

4. Aaron and Lovina have grown closer together throughout the series. How have they grown and changed? What do you think would have happened to their marriage and their relationship with their children if they'd divulged their secrets ten years earlier?

5. Did you sympathize with Landon's worries about getting involved with a wife who was going blind? Were you surprised he changed his mind?

6. Elsie grows stronger and more independent as her vision weakens. How can this be?

7. Did you understand Elsie's refusal to have surgery? What would you have done? What would you have said to a loved one faced with the same decision?

8. How do you envision the Keim family growing and changing in the future? Which character appealed to you the most? ∿

A Sneak Peek of Shelley Shepard Gray's Next Book, *Peace*

Head back to Crittenden County for an exciting preview of *Peace: A Crittenden County Christmas Novella,* coming in fall 2013 from Avon Inspire

BLOOD WAS DRIPPING onto the pristine doormat under his feet. As he watched one drop, then another, and another fall to the ground, then glow eerily in the reflection of the thousand white lights adorning the rooflines of the Yellow Bird Inn, Chris Ellis felt his resolve slip.

He should never have come back, and certainly not in the condition he was in. But he'd come anyway.

He peeked into the long rectangular window next to the door, and his fingertip hovered like a nervous hummingbird over the doorbell. Over and over again, he would almost push the button, but then a bizarre sense of conscience would surface and he'd stand motionless a little bit longer. Trying to persuade himself to do what was right.

What he should do was turn around. Walk away. Never return.

But at the moment, he wasn't sure he could take even one more step forward, never mind make a complete U-turn. He was dizzy, he was weak, and he was sweaty and hot—even though it was barely thirty degrees out. Chances were slim to none that he'd even be able to remain in an upright position for much longer.

Besides, where would he go? Back to his beat-up SUV to spend the night in a vacant parking lot again? Somehow drive back to St. Louis? Lexington?

Where did a man who was beaten up and bleeding go when he'd been working deep undercover for so long that even his family thought he was a person to avoid?

The only place that had come to mind was Frannie Eicher's Yellow Bird Inn. Frannie had a brisk, efficient way about her that he appreciated. She was the type of proprietor who would treat him with kindness . . . but give him his distance, too.

And he was desperate for a little bit of kindness.

But of course, even the nicest people weren't always understanding when it came to near strangers bleeding on their front porch three days before Christmas.

Before he could talk himself out of it again, he knocked. Well, he let his hand slip and fall against the smooth planes of the door. Just once. If no one answered, he'd go back to where he'd hid his truck and drive away.

Almost immediately, the front porch lights turned on. Then a face peered through the window just to the right of the door. ▶

9

But it wasn't Frannie. It was the one person he'd hoped to never see again.

He was still standing there, stunned, when he heard a deadbolt click, followed by a high-pitched squeak as the door opened.

And there was Beth Byler. His mouth went dry as his gaze ached to take in every single inch of her.

It didn't help that she was looking as perfect and beautiful with her crisp white kapp as she'd been when he'd last seen her. Looking just the way she did when she appeared in his dreams.

Chris fought to keep his expression neutral. Which was crazy, of course. Like she'd care about his look of shock when he was bleeding all over the front porch.

Sure that she was about to slam the door in his face, he anxiously continued to look his fill. A man needed as many sweet pictures to store for times when nothing he was seeing was good.

Dim candlelight cast a mellow glow behind her. The scents of pine and cinnamon and everything clean and pure wafted toward him, teasing his senses. He reached out, gripped the doorframe in order to keep from falling.

Blue eyes scanned his form. Paused at the cuts on his hands. At the new scar near his lip. At the way his right eye was swollen shut.

He waited for the look of revulsion that was sure to come. What kind of man let himself get in such a state?

"Chris?" she whispered.

"Yeah. It's me."

"Wh-what are you doing here?"

He needed someplace quiet to stay. He needed an out-of-the-way place to hide out, to recover. To heal his body and his soul. To try to remember who he was.

He was just attempting to say that. To come up with a way to convince her to let him in without making a big fool of himself, or scaring her. When he looked down at his boots.

Noticed the blood again ruining the doormat.

"I guess I'm bleeding on your front porch," he muttered.

"Bleeding?" Her gaze darted away from his swollen face. Traipsed down his body. Down his legs to his thick black boots. Then her eyes widened as she, too, noticed the blood.

"You must come inside!" And then she snaked an arm out, tugged at the hand against the doorframe. The one that had been holding him upright and had stopped him from doing something foolish, like swaying toward her.

She pulled him in.

But even she wasn't strong enough to keep him on his feet. Those three little steps took the rest of his strength, while the relief he felt at finding comfort sapped the rest of his energy. "Beth. Sorry," he muttered. Then the pain and his clumsy apology got the best of him. He collapsed at her feet.

No doubt staining her freshly scrubbed floor, too.

"Chris!" Beth cried as he slipped through her hands and fell to the floor. "Chris?"

Heart beating so hard she felt like she'd run a mile, she knelt at his side. Looked at his swollen cheek, the cut near his lip. The blood on his shirt. "Oh my goodness. Oh my goodness! Chris? Chris, what happened to you?"

Of course he didn't answer. But when the cold wind blew against her cheek and threatened to douse the flame on the kerosene lantern behind her, she focused on the present once again. Quickly, she slammed the door shut, then carefully bolted the deadlock. Just in case someone was after him.

Like the last time he'd been there.

Now, satisfied that he was safe—from the elements at the very least—she knelt back down by his side. His eyes were closed now, making his whole appearance shift. Until that very moment, she'd never realized just how much his piercing gaze affected her. Now, he seemed almost approachable, which was laughable, considering how damaged his body was.

"Oh, Chris. What in the world has happened to you? What have you been doing since we last met?" she murmured as ▶

she reached out and gently smoothed back a chunk of wayward brown hair from his forehead.

She'd last seen him nine months ago. She'd offered to help watch the inn when Frannie had a kitchen accident and had to be hospitalized. During that time, the whole area had been under a lot of stress, what with the body of Perry Borntrager being found on the Millers' farm. At first, she'd feared Chris. She'd been half afraid he was one of Perry Borntrager's drug-dealing friends.

Then she'd learned that Ellis wasn't even his real last name. And that he had no intention of telling her what it was. Her suspicion of him had grown and warred with her attraction to him.

Only later did she discover that Chris was a good man after all. He'd only looked dangerous because he'd been working undercover for some kind of alphabet agency.

But to her shame, even before she'd known he could be trusted, there had been something about him that appealed to her. She'd been drawn to him like a fly to butter or a moth to a light or a bee to honey.

And, that, of course, had been a bad thing. She was Amish; he was not. She lived a quiet existence, spent most of her days either caring for her mother or babysitting other people's children.

His life was the opposite of that.

And he'd been stronger than her, too. With little more than the slightest hint of regret, he informed her that she should forget about him. That no good would ever come from a relationship between the two of them.

But yet, he'd come back.

Now he looked to be in worse shape. Taking inventory again, she noticed how more than just his cheek was swollen, how there were cuts and scabs along his fingers and the knuckles of his hands.

And that there was even more blood staining his clothes.

After getting the lamp, she knelt and examined him more

closely. Pushed herself to ignore everything she'd ever found attractive about him and focus solely on his injuries.

Remembering the pool of blood under his feet, she hastily untied his boots and yanked them off. He groaned as she gently pushed up his dark jeans, one leg at a time.

When she shoved the fabric up his left calf, she saw nothing out of the ordinary—just a man's finely muscled leg.

But the right brought a cry from him . . . and the uncovering of a bleeding hole in his leg.

He'd been cut badly.

Leaning close, she pulled his arms out from the sleeves of his jacket. Tossed it on the ground.

Then saw the other source of the bleeding. He had a deep gash at the top of his chest. So deep, the area around the cut was saturated with blood, and little drops of the excess pooled, then dripped to freedom.

Desperately she tried to keep her cool. *You take care of babies, Beth,* she told herself sternly. *You've nursed children through all sorts of illnesses. Even helped a boy recover from an emergency tonsillectomy when his father had been out of town.*

Surely she could help one man seek medical help?

Carefully, she laid his leg back on the ground. Then, getting to her feet once again, she went to find the phone Luke insisted Frannie keep at hand for emergencies.

She'd just picked up the receiver when Chris called out her name.

"Don't, Beth. Don't call."

"I must. You're injured. And . . . and you're bleeding, Chris. Something awful." When he merely raised a brow, she said, "Chris, this . . . this is mighty bad."

"No, Beth. You can't contact the police. Or an ambulance."

"But you need help. You need stitches."

"Then you're going to have to stitch me up. You know how to sew, right?"

"*Jah* . . . but—" ▸

"But nothing."

But everything! She couldn't sew *him*. "Chris—"

Looking weary, he propped himself on his elbows. Stared at her again with those unusual pale eyes. "Beth, no one can know I'm here."

The agitation that had been teasing her conscience switched to fear in the span of a heartbeat. "Why are you here? Are you in trouble?"

"I don't know why I came. I was driving and so tired. And then I saw the signs for Marion and I remembered the inn. I couldn't go home. I . . . I had thought Frannie could help me."

"You wanted Frannie's help?" Oh, she hoped he wouldn't hear the pain in her voice.

"Yeah. Where is she?"

"She went to Cincinnati with her husband. With Luke. For Christmas," she added, somewhat lamely.

"So they did get married." His voice turned soft.

She cleared her throat. In order to hide her nervousness. In order to hide the hurt feelings she was trying to conceal.

"I need to hide, Beth. Or, at the very least, I need to lay low for a day or two, until I'm healed enough to get away. Can I stay?"

"I . . . I just don't know."

He met her gaze again. Seemed to come to terms with whatever he saw in her expression. Then came to a decision.

"All right. I'll go. Just give me a few minutes, and I'll get out of your way."

The right thing to do would be to stand firm. To agree with that plan of action. She was only living at the Yellow Bird Inn in the evenings, as a way to keep an eye on things for Frannie. Never had Frannie imagined that there would be a visitor.

So, yes, it would be best for Chris and his blood and injuries and mysterious life to leave.

But yet . . .

"Chris, it's almost Christmas."

"I know."

"Do you have somewhere to go for the holiday? Do you have plans?"

The look he sent her spoke volumes. "Not everyone remembers it's almost Christmas, Beth." His voice was gentle, almost as if he'd hated to be the one to tell her that for some people Christmas was only another day to get through.

It broke her heart. "No?"

"No." The skin was white around his mouth as he struggled to his feet, obviously favoring his right leg. "I'll be fine. Don't worry."

He was going to be alone. She knew it as surely as she knew that even after all this time, she still dreamed about him.

Still thought about him. Thought about what would never be. Except for this moment?

Before she could change her mind, she said the word. "Stay."

He stilled. "You sure?"

Her gaze met his. And in that instant, she knew he saw the tears in her eyes. Saw how vulnerable she was . . . at least when it came to him.

"I'm sure. Stay here until after Christmas. I'll help you get better. I'll sew up your wound."

"No one can know I'm here, Beth."

"Then I won't tell anyone you are." There. The decision had been made.

"Thank you," he said simply. "Now, if you could, please tell me where to go. Because I'm afraid I've only got about another two minutes in me before I pass out again."

Taking a deep breath, she wrapped an arm around his waist and guided him to the one bedroom on the first floor. Their progress was halting and painful. But finally they made it.

When she helped him lie down, he looked up at her. "Beth?"

"Yes?"

"Don't forget about the blood. I . . . I parked in the back, near the woods. But you've got to check for blood. No one can see it. Do you understand?"

Then he closed his eyes and fulfilled his earlier promise. ▶

A Sneak Peek of Shelley Shepard Gray's next book, *Peace* (continued)

    He'd passed out.

    And left her with a terrible load of problems as well a miserable trail of blood to remove. Why did the worst things always happen when Frannie was gone? ❧

Don't miss the next book by your favorite author. Sign up now for AuthorTracker by visiting www.AuthorTracker.com.